Munshi Premchand's

Nirmala

Another story inside

Shatranj ke Khiladi

Cedar books

Published by:
Cedar books

An Imprint of
Pustak Mahal®, Delhi

Administrative office and sales centre
J-3/16, Daryaganj, New Delhi-110002
☎ 011-23276539, 23272783, 23272784, 23260518
E-mail: info@pustakmahal.com • *Website:* www.pustakmahal.com

Branches
Bengaluru: ☎ 080-22234025, 40912845
E-mail: pustakmahalblr@gmail.com
Mumbai: ☎ 022-22010941, 22053387
E-mail: unicornbooksmumbai@gmail.com

ISBN 978-81-223-1249-2

Edition 2019

Printed at : Param Offsetters, Okhla, New Delhi-110020

1

Although Babu Udaybhanulal had a large number of people in his family, maternal and paternal, brothers and nephews, and so on, but they are of no concern to us here. Udaybhanulal was a competent lawyer, blessed by Goddess Lakshmi and he felt it was his duty to support the more needy members of his large family. Here, our concern lies with his two daughters – the elder one called Nirmala and the younger, Krishna. Till quite recently, these girls played together with their dolls. Nirmala was fifteen and Krishna, ten; still there was not much difference in their behaviour. Both were active and restless, and loved to indulge in playful antics and much wandering around – indeed, their very lives depended on it. Both would play with their dolls with great gusto, getting them married and always trying to escape from work. Their mother would keep calling them, but they both would run and hide on the roof terrace, wondering what work their mother might be possibly calling them for. Both girls would fight with their brothers, scold the servants and instantly rush to the entrance door on hearing the sound of instruments playing in the street. Suddenly, something has happened today, which has clearly identified the older sister as the 'elder' one, and the other, the 'younger' one. Krishna is the same as before, but Nirmala has turned serious, solitary and timorous. For the past few months, Babu Udaybhanu had been discussing Nirmala's marriage. Today, all his endeavours have borne results. Nirmala's marriage has been officially arranged with Babu Bhalchandra Sinha's elder son, Bhuvan Mohan Sinha. Babu Bhalchandra said that he was not bothered about dowry and left it on Babu Udaybhanu's whim. The groom's father was only concerned that his wedding guests be attended to with respect and due hospitality so that there be no public mockery of either the bride's or the groom's father. Though Babu Udaybhanu was a lawyer, he did not know how to save money. The entire issue of dowry itself was a thorny problem for him. That is why when the groom's father himself had said that he did not care about it, then, Babu Udaybhanu knew himself to be of equal stature with the groom's family. He had been afraid and wondered who all he would have to beg for financial assistance or how many money lenders' would he have to visit. According to his estimate, even if he spent economically, the expenses would not amount to less than twenty thousand rupees. This assurance made him feel light with happiness.

The same information had sent Nirmala to one corner of the house, where she sat hiding her face from everyone else. A strange suspicion had seeped into her heart, an unknown fear was circulating in her entire being: 'Who knows what will happen?'

She did not have the excitement usually seen in young girls that found its way into their twinkling eyes, the honeyed smiles on full lips and the sweet, pleasant lethargy in their bodies. No, there were no hopes or expectations – there were just doubts, worries and fearful imaginations. Her youthful beauty did not shine forth in its full splendour till now.

Krishna knew a little of what was happening, but there were some aspects that she did not know about. She knew that her sister would get beautiful jewellery; music would be played at the doorstep; guests would arrive; and there would be dancing. She was happy about all this and she also knew that her sister would embrace everyone and cry. She would weep and weep, and be given a loving farewell and then, she, Krishna, would be left alone. She became sad when she thought about this last part, but what she did not know was why it was all happening. She could not understand why her parents were so eager to send her sister away from home. Her sister had not said anything to anybody; she had not fought with anyone. She wondered whether they would send her away, too, one fine day. Would she also sit, crying in a corner with no one to pity her? So, that was the reason why Nirmala was so frightened!

It was dusk and Nirmala was sitting alone on the terrace, gazing at the sky with desperation in her eyes. She thought if she had wings she would fly away and free herself from all the troubles. Usually, at this time, both the sisters went for a walk. If the horse carriage was not available, then they would walk in the orchard. That is why Krishna was looking for her. When she could not find her anywhere else, she came to the terrace and laughed on seeing her, "I have looked for you everywhere and you are hiding here. Come on, I have kept the carriage waiting for us."

Nirmala said sadly, "I won't go!"

Krishna said, "No, my dearest sweetest *Didi,* you must come with me today. See, what a lovely cool breeze is blowing."

Nirmala repeated, "I don't feel like going. You go."

Krishna's eyes filled with tears. In a quavering voice, she said, "Why won't you come along today? Why won't you talk to me? Why are you hiding in one place or another? I am feeling scared, sitting all alone. If you won't go, then I won't go, too. I will keep sitting right here with you."

Nirmala said, "And when I leave what will you do then? Tell me, then who will you play and roam around with?"

"I will also go with you. I won't be able to stay here alone."

Nirmala smiled and said, "*Amma* won't let you go."

"Then, I also won't let you go, too. Why don't you tell *Amma* that you will not leave?"

Nirmala said, "I did, but does anybody listen?"

"So, is this not your home?"

"No, if it was so, then would anyone have forcefully turned me out?"

Krishna said, "Then, in this same way, I shall also be made to leave one day?"

Nirmala said, "Of course, what else? Will you keep sitting here? We are girls. Girls do not have a home anywhere."

Krishna said, "Will Chander also be turned out?"

Nirmala explained, "Chander is a boy. Who will send him away?"

"So, are girls very bad?"

"If they weren't, why would they be chased out of the house?"

Krishna said, "Chander is so wicked, but nobody chases him out. You and I are not up to any mischief at all."

All of a sudden, Chander came thumping up the stairs to the terrace. He saw Nirmala and said humorously, "Very well! You are sitting here! Oh ho! Soon, there will be music and *Didi* will become a bride and sit in a *palki*! Oh ho! Oh ho!"

Chander's full name was Chanderbhanu Sinha. He was three years younger than Nirmala and two years older than Krishna.

Nirmala said, "Chander, if you tease me, I will tell *Amma* about it right now."

Chander said, "Why are you getting annoyed? You also listen to the band. O ho! Now you'll be a bride! Kishni, you will listen to the musicians play, won't you? You must not have ever heard such music."

Krishna said, "Will it be better than a band?

Chander replied, "Yes, yes, better than a band, a thousand times better, a million times better! What do you know? You have just listened to one band and started thinking that better musicians don't exist. The musicians will be wearing red-coloured dresses and black caps. They will look so grand! What more can I tell you? Fireworks will rise high up in the sky and when they strike the stars, they will break into red, yellow, green and blue-coloured glitters and fall. It will be great fun."

Krishna said, "What else will happen, Chander? Please tell me, *Bhaiya*!"

Chander said, "If you come with me for a stroll, I will tell you everything on the way. There will be such shows and events that you will be left wide-eyed. There will be fairies floating in the air . . . real fairies."

Krishna said, "All right, let's go. But if you won't tell me, I will beat you."

Chanderbhanu and Krishna went away and Nirmala kept sitting there alone. She felt quite agitated when Krishna left. Today, Krishna, whom she loved more than her life, had become so heartless and had left her alone. There was nothing the matter really, but an aching heart is like an aching eye that feels the stinging pain of the slightest breeze. Nirmala sat and cried for a long time, thinking, 'Brother, sister, mother, father – they will turn their eyes away from me, then probably I'll always be longing to get just a glimpse of them.'

In the garden, flowers bloomed and the air was scented with sweet fragrance. The cool breeze of spring was blowing. The scattered stars twinkled in the sky. Nirmala went to sleep having dreadful, sorrowful thoughts and the moment her eyes closed, her mind took her wandering in the land of dreams. She dreamt of a river with lapping, surging waves and of waiting on the bank, watching for a boat to come her way. It was evening. The darkness kept advancing, like some fearsome creature. She stood there deeply worried about how she would cross the river, how she would reach home? She cried thinking that if it became dark, then how would she stay there alone? Suddenly she saw a beautiful boat approaching the bank. She jumped with joy and as the boat came close enough to the bank, she tried to board it. As she tried to place her foot on the boarding plank, the boatman said, "There is no place for you here!" She tried to persuade the boatman, fell at his feet, cried, but he kept repeating, "There is no place for you here." In another moment, the boat loosened its anchor. She screamed and shouted in desperation and started crying. She wondered how she would spend the entire night on this lonely river bank Then, she jumped into the river trying to catch up with the boat, when suddenly she heard a voice: "Wait, wait, the river is deep, you will drown. That boat is not for you, I will come. Sit in my boat I'll take you to the other side." She was afraid and looked hither and thither to trace where the voice was coming from. A few moments later, she saw a small canoe-like boat coming towards the bank. It neither had a sail nor oars nor a mast. The bottom had holes, the planks were broken; the boat was full of water and a man was bailing out the water. She told him, "This is broken. How will it take me across?"

The boatman said, "This has been sent for you, come and sit down. She thinks for a fleeting second, 'Should I sit in it or not?' She ultimately decided to board the boat, thinking it was far better to sit in the boat than to be left alone, onshore. Drowning in the river was still preferable to being eaten up by some dangerous creature. Who knows, maybe the boat may reach, after all. Thinking thus, she sat in the boat with her life tightly clenched in her hands. For some time, the boat moved ahead unsteadily, rocking; but with every passing minute, water seeped into it. She also started throwing out water with both her cupped hands, along with the boatman. Even though her hands were tired, the water level kept rising. Ultimately, the boat floundered and spun in circles; she felt it drowning every minute. Then she threw open her arms for some unseen support; the boat slipped from beneath and her feet lost their balance. She shouted loudly and as she screamed in her dream, her eyes opened and she awoke. She saw her mother standing beside her, shaking her shoulder.

2

Babu Udaybhanu's house looked like a market place. The goldsmith's hammer tapped away in the verandah and tailor's needles scurried inside the room. Out front, under the *neem* tree, a carpenter was making cots. In a tiled section of the house compound, a furnace had been erected for the confectioner. A separate house had been arranged for the expected wedding guests. It was being seen to that each guest had a cot, a chair and a table to himself. It was being mulled over whether the ratio of one servant to serve three guests was appropriate. There was a month left for the arrival of the groom's wedding party, but preparations had already begun. All efforts were focussed on treating the wedding guests to such memorable hospitality that nobody would find the occasion to say anything to the contrary. The brides' family wanted the guests to always remember this wedding reception as one worth having been a part of. An entire house was full of utensils – there were tea sets, plates for breakfast, platter, *lotas* and glasses. People, who usually lay on the cots, idly smoking hookahs, were working with great eagerness. They knew they would not get such a good occasion to prove their worth for a long time after this. Where one person was required, five would jump forward to take up the task. Naturally, there was less work and more uproar. Small matters of consideration attracted lengthy arguments for and against, until ultimately, *Vakil Sahib* would have to take the final decision. One would say: "This ghee is bad," while another would say: "If you get better stuff than this in the market, I will crawl out from between your legs, in defeat." A third would say: "This has a funny stink to it," while a fourth would reply: "Your nose has rotted, how would you know what good ghee is like! Only because you are here, do you get ghee, otherwise you didn't even get to see it!" Upon this, the quarrel would reach a crescendo and again, *Vakil Sahib* would have to make peace.

It was nine at night. Udaybhanulal was sitting in his room and calculating the estimate of the expenditure. He reviewed the estimate everyday, and each time, he would have to increase the allotted amounts. Kalyani was standing before him, frowning. Babu Sahib raised his head after a long time and said, "It is not less than ten thousand, instead it might increase."

Kalyani said, "In ten days it has gone from five to ten thousand. In a month's time it might eventually reach a lakh."

Udaybhanu said, "What shall I do? Public mockery is not good. If there is any complaint, then people will say that although we are a renowned family, our hospitality is ungenerous. Then, when the groom's family is not taking a single *paisa* as dowry, it's my duty that the guests be treated with the utmost care and they have no reason for a single complaint.

Kalyani said, "Since Brahmaji's inception of the Universe, nobody has ever been successful in making the wedding guests happy. There is bound to be some reason to find fault or condemn something. Those who are so poor that they cannot even afford a roti at home will behave like lords as wedding guest. 'The hair oil is not scented . . . the cheap soap has been brought from an unknown place . . . the servants do not listen . . . the chairs are full of bedbugs . . . the cots are loose . . . the lanterns give off too much smoke . . . the residence is not airy enough . . . there will be thousands of complaints like this.' To what extent can you stop them? If they do not get this opportunity, they will root out some other fault. If they get scented oil their complaint would be, 'Oh, this oil is more appropriate for prostitutes to use, we need some simple, unscented oil.' 'You have not sent this particular soap,' he will remark, as if his esteemed self is displaying his own richness, and as if we have never ever seen soap! 'These are not servants, but messenger of Yama, whenever you see them, they are sitting on your head!' 'You have sent such lanterns that our eyes are blazing, if we sit here for five-ten days more, we'll lose our eyesight!' Is all this only housing arrangement for wedding guests or something destined for the unfortunate, like us, receiving continual gusts from all sides? I will again stress . . . leave aside all considerations of the fuss that wedding guests might make."

Udaybhanulal said, "So ultimately, what will you have me to do?"

Kalyani said, "This is what I'm saying. Be determined that you will not spend more than five thousand. There isn't a *paisa* at home, and we are totally relying on loans. Then, why borrow so much that we cannot repay in a lifetime? And, I do have other children and we need some for them also."

Udaybhanu quipped, "So, will I die today?"

Kalyani replied, "Nobody knows about life and death."

Udaybhanu said, "So you sit and keep praying for this only?"

Kalyani said, "There is no need to be annoyed at what I said. Everyone has to die one day. Nobody is an immortal here. Something that has to happen can't be avoided if one simply closes one's eyes to it. I see it daily with my own eyes – a father dies and his children are forced to wander in the streets, facing terrible hardships. Why should a man work in such a way, that this might happen?"

Udaybhanu was angry and he said, "So, now I should understand that my days are numbered, and death is close at hand. This is what you foretell! I had not heard of a married lady getting bored of his husband, but today I came to know something new. There must be some happiness in widowhood!"

Kalyani said, "If I tell you anything commonplace, you start speaking venomously. It is because you know that she doesn't have any other place to go to, she is dependent on what I give her or is it something else? The moment I say anything, that's it, you pounce on me, as if I'm your bonded labour, and the link between us is merely one bread and cloth. The more I bend, the more you suppress me. Freeloaders may waste things, but no one should open their mouths; money be thrown away on meats and wines, but no one should dare utter a word. All these thorns are being sown for the future of my children only."

Udaybhanu, "So, then am I your slave?"

Kalyani retorted, "So, am I your bonded labour?

Udaybhanu said, "I am not one of those men who dance to their wives' tunes!"

Kalyani said, "I am also not a wife who bears the brunt of her husband's shoes!"

Udaybhanulal said, "I am the one earning for my home, so, I will spend it the way I want. No one has the authority to say anything about it."

Kalyani said, "Then, you manage your own house. I salute such a house from a great distance, one where I am of no importance. I have as much authority as you have in the house. Not a grain less! If you are the master of your mind, then, I am also mistress of mine. We can do as we please. Congratulations on your fine house, it is all yours! There is no scarcity of bread for me. They are your children, kill them or burn them. If I don't look upon them, I won't feel the pain. 'My eyes are gone, I feel no pain'."

Udaybhanu said, "Do you think that if you are not there to manage the house, my house will not be taken care of? I can alone manage ten such houses!"

Kalyani said, "I am certain that in a month's time this house will be reduced to dust. Then you can say, someone had already predicted this."

Saying this, Kalyani's face flamed with anger; she leapt up and went towards the door leading out of the room. *Vakil Sahib* was adept in finding faults whilst fighting court cases, but he had only the slightest knowledge of the female temperament. This is one field of study in which a man draws a complete blank even when he otherwise grows old with experience. Even now if he had behaved tenderly and held Kalyani's hand and made her sit beside him, she might have stopped. However, he could not do this, instead, to the contrary, he made another stinging remark. "You must be full of the pride of your paternal home!".

Kalyani stopped at the door, looked at her husband with fiery eyes and said unhappily, "My parents are not the companions of my destiny. Neither will I stoop so low as to foist myself on them and eat their rotis."

Udaybhanu said, "Then, where are you going?"

Kalyani said, "Who are you to ask this? God's creation has place for innumerable creatures. I will find a place for myself."

Saying this, Kalyani left the room. After stepping into the courtyard, she looked up at the sky as though she were making the clustered stars witness to the cruel manner in which she was being turned out of the house. It was eleven o'clock at night. There was complete silence in the house. Her boys used to sleep in her room. She came to her room and saw that Chanderbhanu was asleep. The youngest one, Suryabhanu, woke up and sat up in bed. Seeing his mother, he lisped, "Where had you gone, *Amma*?"

Kalyani, standing at a distance, replied, "Nowhere, my son. I had gone to your *Babuji*."

Suryabhanu said, "When you had gone I felt alone and frightened. Tell me, why had you gone?"

Saying this, the child opened his arms in order that he might clamber into her lap. Now, Kalyani could no longer stop herself from picking up her child. The nectar of motherly love flowed as her distressed heart melted. The heart, like a tender sapling, which had wilted with the heat of her anger, turned green once again and her eyes filled with tears. She took the child in her arms and embraced him. She said, "Why didn't you call me, son?"

Suryabhanu answered, "I did call you but you did not listen. Tell me, you will never go away now?"

Kalyani said, "No, my dear, I will not go now."

Saying this, she lay on her cot with Suryabhanu. The child slept without a care in his mother's embrace, close to her heart. She started mulling over what she had said and what she could do and other such doubts in her mind. When she recalled what her husband had said, she felt like sacrificing her children's care and leaving the house. Then she would see her childrens' faces and her heart overflow with love for them. 'Under whose care would she leave the children if she went? Who will bring up my dear ones? Whose children will they be finally? Who will give them milk and *halwa* in the morning? Who will sleep with them and wake up with them? The poor babies, they will be there of little value, then. No dears, I will not leave you and go away. I will tolerate everything for you – disrespect, insult, brutal frankness, rudeness, rebuke and scolding,' she promised them silently.

Kalyani lay down to sleep with the child, but the Babu Sahib could not sleep at all. The earlier conversation still rankled – he found it difficult to forget hurtful conversations. There was a spate of thoughts. 'Ooh! That temperament! Behaving as if I am her wife! It's difficult to speak to her any longer without getting an answer. Now, I should stay on as her slave. She will stay alone in the house and the rest, who belong and those who don't, will be thrown out. She is envious. She wants that somehow I die and that she will live alone, comfortably. Deepest feelings do slip out, no matter how much one tries to hide them. I have been observing for some time now, she has been speaking harshly to me. Her arrogance stems from her paternal house; but nobody will even ask after her with time, though right now everyone might be welcoming her. When all responsibility will fall heavily on her shoulders, then she will know the worth of everything. She will come crying then. Oh, this pride! She thinks that she runs the house! If I go away for four days, then she will realise; all her pride will fall flat. Just once, I should shatter her pride. Let her get a taste of widowhood. I don't know from where she gets the courage to berate me the way she does. It seems she knows no love and thinks 'he is so attached to the house that no matter how much I berate him, he will not stir.' This is the case, but I am not one to cling to the world! To hell with such a house, where one's lot is shared with such people! Is it a house or hell? A man comes from outside to his home feeling sick and tired, then he finds rest in his house. But here, one is berated instead of being comforted. Fasts are kept with my demise in mind. This is the end of twenty-five years of married life! Now, I should leave. When I'm certain that all her pride has turned to dust, and she is calm again, only then will I return. Four to five days will be ample. You will also remember just who you were dealing with, Kalyani,' he thought smugly.

Thinking over this, Babu Sahib got up and wrapped the silken sheet around his neck. He took some money, placed his card in the pocket of another kurta; picked up this kurta and his walking stick and quietly stole out of the house. All the servants were in deep sleep. The dog startled with the footsteps awoke and trotted behind him.

However, who knew that this entire, illusory play was being crafted by the Creator? The impartial manager of life's theatre was sitting in some inaccessible, secret place and demonstrating his intricately, realistic play. Who knew that what was merely to be faked was going to turn real; that the simple acting would take on the form of truthful reality.

It was night; even the moon was covered and this darkness had firmly spread all over, much like an invader establishing its supremacy. Its infernal, monstrous army had terrorised and driven away all the goodness of nature. She lay hidden, while darkness triumphantly walked around. Wild animals were wandering in search of prey. In the town, evil-minded humans were loitering in the by lanes.

Babu Udaybhanu was walking swiftly towards the Ganga. He had decided to leave his kurta near the riverbank and go to Mirzapur for five days. Seeing his clothes, people would believe him to be drowned; the card was inside the kurta pocket. There would be no difficulty in the investigation. The news would spread rapidly in a few moments throughout the town. 'By the time it would be eight o'clock, the whole town would have gathered at my door. Then let's see, what will *Deviji* do?' he thought gleefully.

Babu Sahib pondered this as he walked through the lanes. Suddenly, he heard footsteps behind him and realised someone was there. He proceeded, but the person followed him everywhere. Then Babu Sahib suspected this person was following him. His instincts told him this person did not have good intentions. He immediately took out his pocket flashlight and shone the light on him. A strong, well-built man was approaching with a big stick on his shoulder Babu sahib was shocked to see him. He was a well-known criminalof the town. Three years ago, a case of theft was lodged against him. Udaybhanu Lal had fought the case on behalf of the government, and had sent him to prison for three years. Since then, he had been after his life. He had been set free just the previous day. Today by pure coincidence, he had seen Babu Sahib alone at night and grasped this good opportunity to take revenge. He knew he may never get a better chance, again. Immediately, he started following at his heels, and was in the process of attacking him, when Babu Sahib switched on the pocket flashlight. Taken by surprise, the fellow stammered slightly and said, "Why *Babuji,* do you recognise me? It's me, Matai."

Babu sahib shouted, "Why are you following me?"

Matai said, "Why? Is it forbidden for someone to walk on the road? Does this lane belong to your father?"

Babu Sahib had wrestled in his youth; till date he was fit and healthy. He was also not weak at heart. He brandished his walking stick and said, "It seems you are not fully satisfied. This time you will go in for seven years."

Matai said, "Whether I go in for seven years or fourteen years, I will not leave you alive. Yes, if you fall at my feet and promise not to punish anyone, then, I will leave you. Tell me, do you accept?"

Udaybhanu said, "Your bad fortune isn't close by, is it?"

Matai said, "It is not my bad fortune, but yours. Tell me, do you agree to take a vow at the count of three? One!"

Udaybhanu said, "Are you moving or shall I call a policeman?"

Matai counted, "Two!"

Udaybhanu shouted loudly, "You wicked fellow! Move out of my way!"

Matai said, "Three!"

As soon as the last count left Matai's lips, he gave a well-balanced and severe blow on Babu Sahib's head. As he fell unconscious, he was only able to utter, "Ahh! He killed me!"

Matai came closer to see his handiwork. Babu Sahib's head had split open and blood was flowing out. There was no pulse. He understood that it was all over – this man had died. He unstrapped the gold wristwatch, removed the gold buttons from the kurta and pulled off the ring from the finger, and walked on as if nothing had happened. Yes, he took this much pity – he dragged the body from the lane onto the side. Alas! What had the poor man thought when he had left home, and what had happened? Life! Is there nothing more meaningless than you in this world? Is it not even momentary like a lamp that stays lit only to be extinguished by a slight breeze? You see a bubble of water, but it takes some time to burst; life does not even have that much meaning. What trust can we repose in breath, but on this destructible foundation, we build huge mansions of our desires? We do not know whether the indrawn breath will come out or not – but we think of things so far-off, as though we are immortal.

* * *

3

We will not make the readers' hearts ache by describing the widow's bitter sobbing, laments and the orphan's cries. Whoever goes through this ordeal cries, wails and laments, mourns and falls senseless on the ground. This is nothing new. Yes, if you want, you can guess the profound mental agony coursing through Kalyani because she thought she was responsible for her husband's murder. The unrestrained sentences uttered by her in anger were now piercing her heart like arrows. She would have been satisfied if the husband had died groaning, in her lap; at least she would feel she had fulfilled her duty towards him. A mournful heart gets the best consolation from knowing this. She would have been greatly satisfied by the thought that her husband was happy with her; until the last, he had loved her. Kalyani did not have this satisfaction. She thought, 'Yes! Twenty-five years of penance was unsuccessful. I was deprived of my husband's love at the very end of his life.'

Kalyani's head swam with thoughts. 'Had I not used such harsh words, he would never have left the house. God knows what thoughts must have occurred to him.' She reproached herself endlessly, thinking of his state of mind and emotions, and simultaneously exaggerating her own crime, making it enormous by contrast. The children whom she would have given her life for, she grew irritated at their sight. 'Just because of them, I fought with my husband. They are my enemies,' she concluded. 'The place which always used to be full of people, like at the court, was empty and only dust devils whirled there. That hustle-bustle, that fair is over!' When the bread-earner was gone, then how would the dependants remain? Gradually, within a month, all the relatives bid farewell and left. Those who had claimed they would fight for him, spill their blood for him, left as soon as possible, without a backward glance. Life changed in such a way that it became another world altogether. The children whose faces were so adorable and attractive that one felt like embracing them, had flies on them now. It was hard to tell where the radiance had gone.

As the intensity of the shock reduced, the problem of Nirmala's marriage presented itself. Some suggested that it would be better to wait for a year. Kalyani disagreed and said, "After so many arrangements have already been made, to stop the wedding would mean that all this would be wasted. The next year, the same preparations will be required, which we cannot hope to fulfil. It is better to have the wedding. There is nothing to give and take. Enough material has been collected for the guests' stay; there is just loss after loss in waiting." Thus, along with the tragic news, this message was also sent to Mr. Bhalchandra. Kalyani wrote in her letter: 'Have mercy on this orphan and be kind enough to help this sinking boat across. Swamiji had big desires for her, but God wished it otherwise. Now my reputation lies in your hands. The girl is promised to you. I consider it my good fortune to serve others, but if there is something lacking, some mistake committed; forgive me, keeping in mind my situation. I have full faith that you will not let her be condemned in any way...,' the letter ran on in this vein.

Kalyani did not send the letter through the post; but told the Punditji, "You will be definitely bothered, but you must personally take this letter. And with the utmost politeness request on my behalf, that the fewer the invitees, the better. There is nobody here to look after the arrangements."

Pundit Moteram took the letter and reached Lucknow after three days.

It was evening. Babu Bhalchandra was lying stark naked in an easy chair in front of the *diwankhana,* smoking a hookah. He was a fat and tall man.

It seemed as if he was some black God or a coal-black African. He had a single colour from head to toe – black. His face was so inky-black that it was difficult to guess where his face ended and his head started. He was a live statue of coal. He was tortured by the heat. Two men stood fanning him; even then he was dripping with sweat. He was in a reputed position in the Excise Department. He drew a salary of five hundred rupees. He took a lot of bribes from contractors.

The contractors could sell water in the name of liquor, keep their shops open for twenty-four hours; all it required was that he be kept happy. The entire law was the source of his happiness. He was such a fearsome figure that if people suddenly saw him on a moonlit night, they would be startled. Not only children and women, even men got scared. A moonlit night has been mentioned because he merged so completely with the dark night that he could not be seen. Only his eyes were red in colour. Just as a staunch Muslim who sits for *namaaz* five times a day, he consumed liquor five times a day. It could also be said that he was an officer in the department of liquor. He could drink as much as he wanted to – there was no one to stop him. Whenever he felt thirsty, he drank liquor. Like a few colours are complimentary to each other, similarly there are colours antagonistic to each other also. The combination of the red colour of his easy and the black colour of his body became a truly terrifying sight.

Seeing the Punditji, Babu Sahib, at once, got up from the chair and said, "Oh! It's you! Come. Please come. We are fortunate! Oh, is anyone there?

Where has everyone gone? Jhagdu, Gurdin, Chakauri, Bhawani, Ramgulam! Is there anyone? Is everyone dead? Come on, Ramgulam, Bhawani, Chakauri, Gurdin, Jhagdu. Nobody speaks. Has everybody died! There are a dozen men, but not even one can be seen when required. God knows where they disappear to. Get a chair for Punditji."

Babu Sahib repeated these five names a number of times, but did not take the pains to send one of the men fanning him to get a chair. After three to four minutes, a man who was blind in one eye came in coughing and said, "Master, what will happen to me with such a low paying job? How long can I feed myself on credit? I have asked so often that no one listens or gives anymore."

Bhalchandra shouted, "Stop your nonsense! Go get a chair. Whenever he is asked to do any work, he starts complaining. Tell me, Punditji, is everything fine there?"

Moteram said, "What good news can I give, *Babuji*? Now things are not fine there. Everything is ruined."

In the meantime, a servant got a broken box made of pine and said, "I am unable to pick up the table and chair – they are too heavy."

A little embarrassed and nervous, Punditji sat on the box, fearing it might break and placed Kalyani's letter in Babu Sahib's hand.

Bhalchandra said, "Now, how else will they be further ruined? What can be a bigger catastrophe than this? I was an old friend of Udaybhanu's. He was not an ordinary man but as precious as a diamond! What a heart he had and what courage," and wiping his eyes, continued, "it is as if my right hand has been cut off! Believe me since I have heard the news, there is only darkness in front of me. When I sit to eat, food refuses to go inside my mouth. I see his face before me. Having hardly tasted the food, I get up. I do not have the heart to do anything. The grief of losing a brother would be less than this. He wasn't an ordinary man, he was a rare gem."

Pundit Moteram said, "Sir, the town doesn't have such a noble man anymore."

Bhalchandra said, "I understand very well, Punditji, you don't need to tell me that. You can find one such man among one or two million people. I knew him so well. No one else could have known him the way I did. I became devoted to him after meeting him twice or thrice, and will remain so, till my last breath. Please convey the message to Kalyaniji that my heart is grieving."

Moteram said, "This is what we had expected! The sight of a gentleman like you is rare otherwise, who gets his son married without dowry these days?"

Bhalchandra said, "*Maharaj,* one does not talk about dowry with such idealistic, honest men. To have a relationship with them is in itself equal to millions. I consider this my good fortune. Yes, what a generous soul he was. He did not give any importance to money, did not care in the slightest about it. It is a bad custom, very bad. If it was in my hands, I would shoot both kinds of people – those who take a dowry and those who offer it. Yes, Sir! I would unhesitatingly shoot them, even if after that, I were to be hanged. Ask, do you get your son married or do you sell him? If you desire to spend lavishly on your son's wedding, then do so with pleasure, but whatever you do, do it on your own strength. Why do you have to strangle the daughter's father? It's meanness. Meanness of the lowest order! If I had my way, I would shoot these wicked fellows."

Moteram said, "Sir, you are blessed! God has gifted you with wisdom. This is the light of virtue! My mistress wishes that the time of marriage remain the same, and the rest, she has written in this letter. Now, only if you pull us out, can we escape from this situation. Whatever be the number of guests attending the wedding, we will take care of them. But, Sir, now the circumstances have changed considerably and there is no one to assist. I humbly request you to do whatever keeps the late *Vakil Sahib's* name unblemished."

Bhalchandra sat with closed eyes for a minute deliberating; then drew in a long breath and said, "It wasn't God's will that the Lakshmi should enter my house, otherwise would he have let this calamity befall us? All the plans have been reduced to ashes. I used to be so pleased thinking that the auspicious moment was nearing, but was unaware that some conspiracy was being hatched in God's court. Just the memory of the dead is enough to make me cry. This wound would be further aggravated on seeing her. I don't know what I will do in that condition. You may consider it a virtue or vice that once I develop a deep friendship with someone, then his memories reside in my mind at all times. I can never forget him. Anyway, till now just his face keeps appearing in front of me, but if that girl comes home, then it will become very difficult for me to live. Believe me, I have been crying so incessantly that my eyes might burst. I know my grieving is in vain. The one who has died cannot return. There is no other alternative to being patient, but my heart is helpless. My heart will burst upon seeing the orphaned girl."

Moteram was alarmed and said, "Do not say this, Sir! If *Vakil Sahib* is no longer here, then at least you are. Now you are her father's equivalent. Now, she is no more *Vakil Sahib's* daughter – she is yours now. Nobody knows what you feel inside, but most people are bound to think that *Vakil Sahib* died and you turned back on your word. You stand to lose your good name. Strengthen your mind and happily and gladly get her married and release her from mourning. Nothing has changed. The family is still valuable, just like a dead elephant is still of high value. They may face a million difficulties, but my mistress will not leave anything undone in your service."

Babu Sahib understood that Pundit Moteram was not only a learned priest, but also well-versed in social etiquette and clever in such dealings. He said, "Punditji, I swear upon this. I love this girl more than I love my own daughter, but when God wills it otherwise, then what can I do? That death is a kind of inauspicious notice that God has sent us. This is an oracle which indicates an imminent misfortune. God is clearly saying the wedding will not be auspicious. In such a state, just think, how far is this match suitable? You are a learned person. Just think, what has begun inauspiciously, can its end be good? No, knowing a fly is present in a drink, I cannot swallow it. You may explain it to Kalyaniji, and make her understand. I am ready to obey her, but the consequences will not be good. Influenced by self interest, I cannot do injustice to my best friend's child."

This argument rendered Punditji speechless. The speaker had shot a sharp arrow, one for which he had no response. The enemy had attacked him with his own arms and he found himself unable to retaliate. He was still in the process of dredging up a suitable answer, when Babu Sahib started calling the servants again. "Oh! You have all disappeared again? Jhagadu, Chakauri, Bhawani, Gurdin, Ramgulam! Not even one speaks. Everyone is dead. Is anybody concerned about water or something for the Punditji? I don't know how long anyone will have to explain things to them. Senseless fools, it doesn't even enter their heads. They can see that a gentleman has come from far, is tired, but no one cares in the least. Go get water and something to eat. Punditji, should I get a sherbet made for you or have some fruits and sweets brought?"

Moteram did not accept any kind of limitation where sweets were concerned. He believed firmly in the principle that clarified butter purified everything. He cherished *rasgulla* and *besan ke laddu*, but did not like beverages. It was against his rule to fill his stomach with water. He hesitantly said, "I am not in a habit of drinking beverages. I will eat sweets."

Bhalchandra asked, "No fruits?"

Moteram said, "I was not thinking about eating fruits."

Bhalchandra said, "Fine, then this is it. All this untouchability is hypocrisy. I, myself, don't believe in it. Oh, nobody has come till now? Chakauri, Bhawani, Gurdin, Ramgulam, somebody speak up!"

This time, the same servant came along coughing, and stood and said, "Master, have my wages given to me. I cannot do this job. Where all can I run? My feet ache with all this running around."

Bhalchandra said, "Whether you do any work or not, but the first thing you need are your wages. Lie around the whole day coughing! Your wages are being recorded. Go to the market and get some fresh sweets for one *anna*. Go quickly!"

After giving the servant this order, Babu Sahib went inside the house and said to his wife, "A Punditji has come from there. He has brought this letter. Just read it."

Bhalchandra's wife's name was Rangilibai. She was a fair-complexioned lady with a pleasing countenance. Her youth and fine figure were slowly fading, but like a lover, who excitedly embraces another, Bhalchandra had clung to her for thirty years, and couldn't bring itself to part from her.

Rangilibai was sitting and making paan. She said, "You've said that we are not willing to marry there?"

Bhalchandra said, "Yes, I have said so, but I couldn't utter those words due to hesitation. I spoke of other things needlessly, instead."

Rangilibai said, "Why do you hesitate in speaking clearly? It is our wish, we will not do it. We haven't taken anything from anybody, have we? When we are getting ten thousand in cash from somewhere else, then why won't we fix it there? Their daughter isn't made of gold. If *Vakil Sahib* would have been alive, then with the greatest embarrassment, he would have given us fifteen to twenty thousand at least, in modesty. What is left there now?"

Bhalchandra replied, "It is not good to go back on your word after promising, even if no one says anything clearly but ill-repute will get attached to one's name. But I am helpless in the face of your stubbornness."

Rangilibai ate the paan and started reading the letter. Babu Sahib could not read Hindi and although Rangilibai might have hardly brought herself to read a book, she would read letters. The first sentence made her eyes wet and by the time she finished reading the letter, tears were rolling down her face. Each word was full of tender, pitiable emotions, depicting great distress. Rangilibai's sternness was that of pliable lac, not hard stone, so she melted with the first flame that touched her. The touching words of Kalyani had melted her selfish heart. With a choked throat, she said, "The Brahmin is still sitting there, isn't he?"

Seeing his wife's tears, Balchandra was increasingly frightened. He was irritated with himself for having needlessly shown her the letter. Had it been necessary? He had never committed such a terrible mistake before. He spoke doubtfully, "Perhaps, he might be. I had told him to go."

Rangilibai peeped from the window. Pundit Moteram was watching the road leading to the market place with complete concentration, like a crane. Absorbed in his desire for sweets, he shifted his body – once this way, then, that way. The command, 'Sweets for one *anna*,' had already shattered his hopes; then on top of that, this delay – it was a difficult situation. Seeing him seated there, Rangilibai said, "Yes. Yes. He's still there. Go and tell him, we will go ahead. We will definitely go ahead with the marriage. The poor thing is in deep trouble."

Bhalchandra said, "Sometimes you start talking like a child. I've just told him that I am unwilling to have this marriage performed. For that, I had to weave the most long-winded context. Now, if I give him this message, then what will he think in his heart? Just think about it. This is a matter of matrimony, not child's play, that once we say one thing, and the next moment, the opposite. This is not the word of a gentleman, but a joke."

Rangilibai said, "All right, don't say it yourself. Send the Brahmin to me. I will explain things to him in such a manner that your word will be kept and mine, too. I hope you don't have any objection to this."

Bhalchandra said, "You consider the whole world innocent, except yourself. Whether you say so or I do, it is just the same. If something has been agreed upon, it is done. Now, I do not want to raise the matter again. You used to say repeatedly that you do not wish for an alliance with that house. Because of you, I had to go back on my word. Now you are changing your mind. You are doing this to pain me. At least, you should think a little about my respect and dignity."

Rangilibai said, "Did I know that the widow's condition had become so pitiable? You had said that she has hidden her husband's entire property, and wanted to get her work done by donning the garb of pretended poverty. You said she is crafty. Whatever you said, I believed. Shame and hesitation lie in doing a wicked deed after a good one. But, there should be no hesitation in doing a good deed after a bad one. If you would have said 'yes' and I would've refused, then your hesitation was justified. We will be the nobler for having said 'yes' after 'no'."

Bhalchandra said, "You consider it to be greatness, and I think it to be low and mean. Then how could you believe that whatever I said about the *Vakil's* wife was a lie? By seeing the letter? The way you are simple, you consider others are also that simple?"

Rangilibai said, "The letter doesn't seem to be false. Anything fabricated doesn't touch the heart. It would definitely stink of falsity."

Bhalchandra said, "Fabricated stories pierce in such a way that truth seems pale before it. These writers of stories and incidents, whose books you read for hours and cry over, do they write the truth? It is out and out lies tied together. This is also an art."

Rangilibai said, "Why are you trying to make a fool of me? You can't conceal the truth from me anymore than a pregnant lady can hide her condition from the midwife! I always agree with whatever you say and you think that 'I deceived her.' But I know you inside out. By squarely planting all your faults on my head, you want to be safe, spotless and innocent. Tell me, am I lying? When *Vakil Sahib* was alive, you thought there was no need for a pre-marriage settlement – he would give whatever was appropriate. Instead, you had hoped we would get more because there was no settlement, but greater obligation on his head. Now when *Vakil Sahib* is no more, then you've started making excuses of all kinds. This is not gentlemanly behaviour, but meanness, and this is also laid on my head. Now I shall not talk about weddings and marriage. Do whatever you wish. I hate hypocrites. Whatever you say, say it clearly – good or bad. 'The elephant eats with another set of teeth and shows another' – following this double-faced policy doesn't grace you. Tell me, now do you still wish to fix the marriage there or not?"

Bhalchandra said, "When I am considered dishonest, deceitful and a liar, then why do you ask me? But I must say that you know men so well. What can I say, about this understanding and intelligence of yours? Take on the responsibility of the entire dilemma as well."

Rangilibai said, "You are so concerned with your own dignity that you are not ashamed. Tell me sincerely, if I have judged correctly or not?"

Bhalchandra said, "Oh, leave it alone. The women who know men are of a different kind. Till now, I used to think that a woman has keen insight into matters, but today this belief has gone. Now I will have to believe what the great men have said about the essence of a woman."

Rangilibai said, "Just go and take a look at your face in the mirror, upon my word. Just take a look – see how ashamed you look?"

Bhalchandra said, "Tell me the truth, how ashamed am I?"

Rangilibai said, "As much as a good man is when his thieving is revealed to all."

Bhalchandra said, "Very well, I may well be ashamed, but still the marriage will not take place there."

Rangilibai said, "Not that I'm troubled, wherever you wish, get it performed there. Listen, why don't you ask Bhuvan once?"

Bhalchandra said, "All right, the decision rests with him."

Rangilibai warned, "Do not give him the slightest hint."

Bhalchandra said, "Oh ho, I will not look at him also."

Coincidently, Bhuvan Mohan entered the room at that moment. Such a good-looking, well-built, strong youth was rarely seen in the college. He had inherited features from his mother – the same fair, smooth complexion, thin lips like rose petals, the same broad forehead, those big almond-shaped eyes and his physique was like his father's. He wore a short coat, breeches, tie, boots, hat and these suited him beautifully. He held a hockey stick in his hand. His gait spoke of youthful pride; his eyes sparkled with self-esteem.

Rangilibai said, "You are very late today. Look at this; it is a letter from your in-laws. It is written by your mother-in-law. Tell me clearly, it's still early enough for that. Are you willing to be married there or not?"

Bhuvan Mohan said, "*Amma*, I should get married there, but I will not."

Rangilibai said, "Why?"

Bhuvan Mohan said, "Get me married somewhere where I will get a lot of money. If not more, then at least it should be a round figure of a lakh. Now, what is there? *Vakil Sahib* is no more, what will the old lady have now?"

Slightly shocked, Rangilibai said, "You don't feel ashamed saying these things?"

Bhuvan Mohan replied nonchalantly, "What is there to be ashamed of? Who is troubled by money? I will not be able to accumulate one lakh rupees if I live one lakh lives. Even if I pass this year, I will not be able to see substantial amounts of money for at least the next five years. Then I will start earning hundred to two hundred rupees per month. By the time I start earning five or six hundred, three-fourths of my life will be over. The situation where I can save money won't arise at all. I won't be able to enjoy my life. If I get married to a rich man's daughter, then life could be spent so peacefully. I don't want much, just one lakh in cash or a widow with her own property who just has one child – a daughter."

Rangilibai said, "No matter what kind of a woman she is?"

Bhuvan Mohan said, "Wealth hides all faults. Even if she abuses me, I will not utter a squeak. Who objects to the kick of a milking cow?"

Babu Sahib said in a pleased tone, "We have sympathy for those people and feel sad that God had put them in great difficulty, but decisions must be taken intelligently and wisely. No matter how poorly we may be, still, there will be a considerable wedding party. Then, there is no certainty about the food arrangements. What will happen if that people will mock us and that will be the only result of all the efforts."

Rangilibai said, "You father and son belong to the same category. Both are ready to run a knife across the poor girl's throat."

Bhalchandra said, "Poor people should seek alliances with the poor. Rising above one's station…"

Rangilibai cautioned, "Be quiet. Do you think you arrived here bringing your status with you? Who do you think you are – a rich man? If a person comes to this door, he will die, thirsting for a *lota* of water. Behaving like a man of status!"

Saying this, Rangilibai got up and went to the kitchen to prepare the next meal.

Bhuvan Mohan went to his room, smiling. Babu Sahib came outside twisting his moustache to convey the final decision to Moteram, but there was no sign of him.

Moteram had waited for the servant for some time. When he did not return after a long time, he was unable to remain seated any longer. Thinking that it was of no use to just sit there, he decided that he should do some work on his own. He thought, 'If I keep sitting here, relying on luck, then I will die of hunger. Nothing is going to happen here.' He quietly picked up his stick and went along the same way the servant had taken. The bazaar was not very far from there, so he reached in a minute. He saw that the old man was sitting in the confectionary shop, smoking a *chillum*. Seeing him, he said with complete informality, "Is anything ready till now, servant? Your master is getting annoyed wondering whether you've gone to sleep or to drink toddy. I defended you, saying, 'Sir, this is not the case. The man is old; he will walk slowly and will reach late.' He is quite a strange person. I don't know how long any servant stays with him."

The servant said, "Except for me, nobody else has stayed on till now, and neither can they. I haven't been paid my wages for a year. He doesn't pay anybody. The minute anyone asks him for their salary, he starts scolding them. The poor chap runs away leaving his job. The two men fanning him are government employees. He has been given two orderlies by the government. He gets his work done by them. I also think that I will also do only whatever I can. Ten years have gone by, a year and two will also go like this."

Moteram said, "So you are the only servant? he was calling out many names."

The servant spoke, "They came in the past two-three months and left. He chants their names so that he can impress others with his clout. Get me a job somewhere, shall I come with you?"

Moteram said, "Oh, there are many jobs. It is difficult to find a good servant even after searching. You are an experienced man. Why should there be a dearth of jobs for you? Is there anything fresh here? Your master said to me, 'Shall we make *khichdi* or *bati*?' I told him, 'Sir, the man is old. He will find it troublesome to cook for me at night. I will go to the bazaar and eat something there. Do not worry about this.' He said, 'all right, you'll meet the servant at our shop. Tell me, Shahji, is any fresh sweet ready? The *laddu* seem to be fresh. Weigh one *ser* worth! Shall I come up there?'"

Saying this, Moteram went and sat in the confectionery shop and started tasting the freshly prepared sweets. He ate to his heart's content. He finished two and a half to three *ser* of sweets. He kept eating and praising the confectioner, "Shahji, I had heard good things about your shop and find the sweets to be as good. The confectioners in Banaras cannot make such *rasgullas*, though they make good *kalakand*. But yours is equally good. Delicious food is not made by using good ingredients only; you need to have the knowledge."

The confectioner said, "Take something else as well, sir. Eat a little bit of *rabri* – I recommend it."

Moteram replied, "I do not feel like eating. Still, give me a quarter."

The confectioner said, "Why will you take only a quarter's worth? It is good, take at least half a *ser*."

Punditji ate a meal fashioned after his own desire. Then he roamed around the market for some time and came back to the house at around nine o'clock. There was pin drop silence. A lone lantern shed some light. He prepared his bed on the platform and went off to sleep.

According to his routine, he woke up at eight o'clock, and saw that Babu Sahib was taking a walk. Seeing the Punditji awake, he touched his feet and said reverentially, "*Maharaj*, where had you gone at night? I waited till late in the night for you. Your food was also prepared and kept covered for some time. When you did not come, we kept it inside. Did you eat anything or not?"

Moteram said, "I had eaten something at the confectioner's shop."

Bhalchandra said, "*Puri* and sweets don't have the taste that *dal* and *bati* have. You must have gone and spent ten to twelve *anna*s and still it would have not been enough. You are my guest. Please take from me whatever you have paid."

Moteram said, "I ate at your confectionary's shop, from the one who sits in the corner."

Bhalchandra said, "How much did you have to pay?"

Moteram said, "I got it noted in your account."

Bhalchandra said, "Please tell me the amount of sweets taken, otherwise, later the man might try cheating me. He is a real thug."

Moteram said, "About two and half *ser* of sweets and half a *ser* of *rabri*."

Babu Sahib looked at the Punditji with shocked, staring eyes as though he had heard something astonishing. The total amount of sweets eaten in a month never amounted to three *ser*, and this man had gobbled stuff worth four rupees in one go! If he stayed for half a day more, then he would be eaten out of house and his savings. Did he possess a stomach or was it the devil's bottomless grave? Three *sers*! Was there no limit! In great distress, he ran inside and told Rangilibai, "Do you hear, this man polished off three *ser* of sweets yesterday! Three *ser* – the exact weight."

Rangilibai, struck by surprise, said, "Oh come on, who can eat three *ser* worth? Is he a man or an ox?"

Bhalchandra said, "He says so himself. It won't be less than four *ser* in exact measure!"

Rangilibai said, "Is Saturn sitting in his stomach?"

Bhalchandra said, "If he stays on today, then he will tuck away six *ser*!"

Rangilibai said, "So, then why should he stay on today? Send whatever reply you want to her letter, and bid him farewell. If he stays, then clarify that we do not give sweets for free. If he wants *kichdi*, he can get it made, otherwise, he can go his way. The ones who are liberated by feeding such gluttons, they should do so. We do not want such liberation."

However, the Pundit was ready to take his leave, so Babu Sahib was not required to use his skills.

Bhalchandra said, "What? Are you prepared to leave, *Maharaj*?"

Moteram said, "Yes, Sir, now I shall take your leave. I'll get the nine o'clock train, won't I?"

Bhalchandra said, "At least stay on today..."

Whilst saying this, *Babuji* was fearful that the Pundit would really stay on, therefore, he completed the sentence by saying, "... Yes, people must be waiting for you there, also."

Moteram said, "It is not a matter of a day or two, and I had thought of taking a holy dip at the Triveni, but don't mind my saying so. You people do not have the slightest respect for Brahmins. Our hosts keep looking at our faces, waiting eagerly for us to order them, so that they may obey and fulfil them. When I reach their doorstep, they feel honoured by my presence and everyone – young to old, are absorbed in serving me. I cannot bear to stay for a minute where I do not get respect. There will be no prosperity wherever a Brahmin is not respected!"

Bhalchandra said, "*Maharaj*, we did not commit such a crime."

Moteram cried, "Did not commit a crime! And what is called a 'crime'? Just now, you went into the house and said that *Maharajji* polished off three *ser* of sweets, to the actual measure! You haven't yet seen people eat! Feed them once and you will be left wide-eyed. There are such great men who can eat five *ser* of sweets at one time, without burping. People insistently request that I eat one sweet, and then another, and another, and money is also given. I am not a Brahmin who will lie around and beg at your doorstep. I had come after hearing of your good name, but I did not know there would be such lack of food for me. Go! God bless you."

Babu Sahib was so ashamed that he could not speak. In his whole life, he had never been scolded thus. He then made many excuses: "You were not being discussed; we were talking about some other person!"

The Punditji, however, remained angry. He could tolerate everything, but not an insult to his appetite. The way a lady is displeased by an insult to her beauty, a man is displeased by insults to his appetite. Babu Sahib was trying to calm him but was also worried at the same time that he might just stay over. His miserliness was revealed; there was no doubt of this now. Now, it was necessary to cover it up once again. He regretted having gone inside to talk about the 'three *ser* of sweets' and that he had spoken in such a loud tone. This wicked fellow was also listening; but now there was no point in repenting. He cursed whoever's ill-favoured face he had seen because of which this misfortune had befallen them If the Pundit went away annoyed from here, then he would definitely defame them and all his work would be undone.

Pondering over this, he went into the house and said to Rangilibai, "This wicked person overheard our conversation. He is sulking!"

Rangilibai said, "When you knew he was at the door, then why didn't you speak softly?"

Bhalchandra replied, "When difficulty arrives, it is never alone. How was I to know that he would be there, with his ears tuned to whatever we were saying?"

Rangilibai said, "God knows whose face we saw…"

Bhalchandra, "This wicked fellow was sleeping in the morning. If I had known, I wouldn't have looked in that direction. Now, we will have to pacify him by giving him something."

Rangilibai said, "Uhh, let it be. What do you care when you did not agree to the marriage? Let him think whatever he wants to. Let him say whatever he wants to."

Bhalchandra said, "My dignity will not be spared like this. Come, give me ten rupees. I will give it to him as a farewell gift. God, now do not show his ill-favoured face again."

Rangilibai, with the greatest hesitation, took out ten rupees. Babu Sahib took it and kept it at Punditji's feet. Punditji thought to himself, 'What a miser! I will rub your nose in the dirt, so that you will never forget. You think that you will fool me by giving me ten rupees. Do not be mistaken. I know you in and out.' He kept the money in his pocket, blessed him and went his way.

Babu Sahib stood, lost in thought for a long time. He was thinking, 'I don't know if he still thinks I am a miser or whether I successfully covered it up. I wonder whether this money has been wasted.'

* * *

4

Kalyani had a bad time. After the death of her husband, this was the first truly bitter experience she had in her currently adverse circumstances. What could be more dreadful for a poor widow than her young daughter being dependent on her? Sons could go to school barefoot; household work could also be done by oneself; one could eat simple fare and survive; one could live in a straw hut; but a young girl could not be made to remain sitting at home. Kalyani would often get so enraged that she would feel like going herself and painting his face black, violently tug out his hair, tell him that he had revoked his promise; tell him that he was no son of his father. Pundit Moteram had revealed his deceit; it was the bare, naked truth that was out now.

She sat, steeped in this anger, when Krishna came by and said, "In how many days will the groom's wedding guests arrive, *Amma*?"

Kalyani said, "Are you dreaming of the wedding party?"

Krishna said, "Chander was saying that it will arrive in two-three days. Will it not come, *Amma*?"

Kalyani said, "I told you once. Why are you pestering me?"

Krishna said, "The wedding guests are arriving in everyone's house. Why won't it come to our house?"

Kalyani said, "The person who was supposed to bring these guests to your house, there was a fire in his house."

Krishna was amazed. "Is it true, *Amma*? Then the whole house must've burnt down. Where would they be staying now? Where is my sister going to stay?"

Kalyani said, "Oh, you crazy girl! You do not understand the matter at all. There was no fire. They will not marry their son here."

Krishna said, "Why so, *Amma*? Initially, it was fixed there, wasn't it?"

Kalyani said, "He is asking for a lot of money. I do not have any to give."

Krishna said, "Are they very greedy, *Amma*?"

Kalyani retorted, "What else if not greedy! A butcher, cruel and traitorous!"

Krishna said, "Then, *Amma*, it is really good that *Didi* was not married into that house. How would *Didi* have lived with him? This is something to be happy about, *Amma*, why do you grieve?"

Kalyani looked at her daughter lovingly. How true her words sounded! Innocent words have such a touching way of explaining a problem. Really this was something to be happy about – that no relationship was established with such a wicked family; there was nothing to be sorry about. Kalyani wondered what Nirmala's condition might have been, dwelling amongst such inhuman people. She would have cursed her destiny. If a bit of extra ghee was put in the dal, there would be uproar in the house; if extra food was cooked, the mother-in-law would make a huge issue of it. The son was also greedy like that. Something good happened, otherwise the poor girl would have cried throughout her life. When Kalyani got up, her heart felt much lighter.

The marriage, however, had to be performed, and if possible, this year itself. Else, fresh preparations would be required all over again the next year. Now, neither a good home nor a good groom was a necessary precondition. Where would the unfortunate girl get a good house or groom now? Somehow, the burden that her daughter represented had to be lifted off her head. Somehow, she had to be taken over to the other side; even though she may be then dumped in a well. This girl may be beautiful, talented, clever and from a good family, but if there is no dowry, then all her virtues were vices; if there was dowry, then all vices were virtues. The human being has no value, only dowry does. How complicated the play of destiny is!

Kalyani was no less to be blamed than fate could be. Being a woman and weak, and a widow, did not free her from any of the blame. Sons were much dearer to her than her daughters. Boys were the oxen pulling the plough, and therefore the foundation of home and family. They had the first right to the best food; whatever was left over was given to the daughters – the cows. She had a house, some cash, jewellery worth thousands, but she had to bring up two boys and educate them. The other daughter would also be ready for marriage in another four-five years. That is why she could not give a big amount as dowry – the boys would also require some of it. If she gave away everything, the boys would think poorly of their father.

It had been fifteen days since Pundit Moteram had returned from Lucknow. The very next day, he had gone in search of a groom. He had promised that he would show those people from Lucknow that they were not the only good families in the world; there were many like them.

Kalyani had started counting the days. Today she had decided to write a letter to him, and sat down, pen and inkpot in place, when Pundit Moteram entered.

Kalyani said, "Come in, Punditji, I was about to write a letter to you. When did you return?"

Moteram replied, "I arrived early this morning, but just then, I was invited to a Seth's house. I had not eaten well for a long time. I thought I would also take care of work also, right there and then. I am coming from there. There was a feast for five hundred Brahmins there."

Kalyani said, "Did anything materialise or did you just keep travelling all over?"

Moteram said, "Why won't anything materialise? Well, is this something to be said? I have spoken to five different families. I have got information about them all. You can select anyone out of the five. Look at this proposal, the father of this boy is a servant in the postal department, drawing a salary of one hundred rupees. The boy is presently studying in college. But there is surety of service, though they have no property. The boy seems to be sincere. The family is also good. The matter will be settled in two thousand, though they are asking for three."

Kalyani said, "Does the boy have any brothers?"

Moteram said, "No, but he has three sisters and all of them are unmarried. The mother is alive. All right, now see the second proposal. This boy earns fifty rupees in the railway department. He does not have parents. He is really a good-looking, sincere, fit and healthy, and active young man. The family background is doubtful – some say the mother was of the barber community, some say, Thakur. The father was an attorney in some estate. There is some land at home, but there is a debt of several thousand attached to it. There is no 'give and take' involved here. The boy must be around twenty years old."

Kalyani said, "If there wasn't a stigma on the family, I would accept it. If there is a fly in the cup, one cannot swallow it after seeing it there."

Moteram said, "Here, look at the third proposal. He is the son of a landholder, earning profits of several thousand rupees yearly. They also do a little farming. The boy is only slightly educated, but clever in court work. He is marrying a second time; it has been two years since the first wife died. There is no child from her, but their way of life is inferior to ours. The grinding and crushing is all done at home."

Kalyani said, "Are they demanding some dowry?"

Moteram said, "Don't ask about it. They want four thousand. All right, now this fourth proposal – the boy is a lawyer, and he is around thirty-five years. He earns around three to four hundred. The first wife is no more. He has three sons from her. He has built his own house and also bought some property. Here, also there is no issue of 'give and take'."

Kalyani said, "What is the family background like?"

Moteram said, "Excellent, they are of old noble stock. Now, look at this fifth proposal. The father owns a printing press; the boy has studied till B.A., but works in the press. He must be eighteen. There is no property other than the press, but they do not owe anything to anybody. The family background is neither good nor bad. The boy is very good-looking and of good character. But the matter will not be settled for less than a thousand, though they are demanding three thousand. Now tell me, which groom do you like?"

Kalyani said, "Whom do you like out of them all?"

Moteram said, "My preference is for two of them. One, who is in the railways and the other, who owns the press."

Kalyani said, "But you said there is a problem with the first family?"

Moteram said, "Yes, there is a fault. You select the one who is in the press."

Kalyani said, "Where will I get a thousand rupees from to give to them? One thousand is your guess, they might want more. You know the condition of the house. We are fortunate enough that we can get food, somehow. Where will the money come from? The landlord says four thousand; the postmaster also raises the question of two thousand. Let them be. Now, only the lawyer is left. Thirty-five is also not that old an age. Why don't we select him?"

Moteram said, "You think over it at length. I am here to obey and carry out whatever you decide. Whereever you tell me to go, I will go there and return after arranging it. But do not worry about the one thousand – the boy with the press is a gem. The girl will prosper with him. Just the way she is both beautiful and has good qualities, similarly, the boy is also good-looking and gentle."

Kalyani said, "*Maharaj*, I also like him. But from whose house will the money come? Who is going to give it? Is there anybody that generous? Those who are well-off, who could have done something, vanished after eating and drinking, when nothing was left after his death. Now, nobody comes here, instead, they feel hurt that they were turned out. Why should I beg for something that is anyway beyond my reach? Who doesn't love their children? Who doesn't want to see them happy? But only when it is within one's control. You can get the wedding arranged with the lawyer with God's blessings. The age is slightly more, but life and death are in God's hands. A man of thirty-five years is not said to be old. If the girl's fate is to enjoy a happy life, then wherever she goes, she will be happy. If she has to experience sorrow, she will know sadness wherever she goes. Our Nirmala loves children. She will consider the children as her own. You find an auspicious time and formalise the engagement."

* * *

5

Nirmala got married. She came to her in-law's house. *Vakil Sahib's* name was Munshi Totaram. He was a fat, prosperous-looking man with a dusky complexion. His age was not more than forty but the hard work involved in practising law had turned his hair grey. He did not get the time to exercise – to the extent that since he never went anywhere, even for a walk, he had developed a paunch. Due to the increased grossness of his body, he suffered from some ailments every other day. Indigestion and piles had established themselves as his chronic problems, therefore, he was quite cautious. He had three sons. The eldest, Mansaram was sixteen years old, the younger one, Jiyaram, was twelve and Siyaram, the youngest, seven. All of them studied in English medium schools. There was no other woman in the house, except *Vakil Sahib's* widowed sister. She was the mistress of the house. Her name was Rukmini and she was above fifty years of age. There was no one in her in-law's house, thus, she stayed here permanently.

Totaram was competent in the department of marital science. He tried to keep Nirmala pleased by showering her with gifts to make up for his innate defects. Though he was quite frugal by nature, he always brought a gift for her each day. When he had to spend, he did not care about the expense involved. A little milk was bought for the boy, but for Nirmala – dry fruits, sweet pickles, sweets, she lacked nothing. He had never gone out for walking or for any show or recreation, but now, during his holidays, he would take Nirmala to the cinema, circus or theatre. He would spend a portion of his invaluable time by sitting in her company, playing the gramophone.

However, for reasons unknown, Nirmala hesitated in sitting near Totaram and talking and laughing with him. Perhaps, the reason was that, till now, a similar man had been her father. She would pass by him stealthily, her body pressed against the wall, her head down. Now, a man of the same age was her husband. So, she considered him an object of respect, rather than someone she should love. She would try to avoid him at all times, and on seeing him, her happiness would flee to a distant place.

Vakil Sahib's knowledge of matrimonial science had taught him that one should speak of love and related matters with women. One should bare one's heart out; this was the main mantra by which ladies were enthralled. That is why *Vakil Sahib* never left any stone unturned in his exhibition of love; such talk filled Nirmala with disgust. The same words from the lips of a young man that would have maddened her with love now left her feeling wounded, as though pierced by an arrow when she heard the *Vakil Sahib* speak them. There was no passion, no joy, no intoxication, and no soul in them. There was only artifice, deceit and dry, lifeless word play. She would not have minded the scented oil, walks and other recreation, wearing ornaments, dressing up and did not mind wearing ornaments; what she minded was sitting near Totaram. She did not want to display her beauty and youth to him, because his eyes were not those that could really see, in her opinion. She did not consider him worthy enough to relish their charm. A bud blooms only when touched by early morning breeze – both possess an equal essence. For Nirmala, could he be like that morning breeze?

After a month had passed, Totaram made Nirmala his treasurer. Returning from court, he would hand over his entire day's earnings to her. He thought that Nirmala would be deliriously happy on seeing the money. Nirmala would do this work with great interest. She would note the income and expense of every *paisa*; if ever he got less money, she would inquire why it was less today. She would talk about household related matters. She would consider him fit only for these kinds of conversations. As he would utter something amusing, her face would became pale.

When Nirmala stood in front of the mirror, adorned with jewellery and saw the reflection of her loveliness and radiance, her heart would be wracked with sensual desires. That moment, a flame would rise in her heart. The thought of putting this house on fire would leap to her mind. She would be angry with her mother, but she would be the most furious with the innocent Totaram. She was constantly burning in this mental agony. A grandee who rides a horse would never like to ride a mule, even though he might then have to go on foot. Nirmala's condition was somewhat like that horse rider. She wanted to sit on a mule and fly away, absorbing the bliss of the exhilarating pace; if the mule would whine and fuss about, then what hope would be left? It was possible that she could forget her condition for some time by playing with the children. She would be refreshed and happy, but Rukmini Devi did not let the boys go anywhere near her as though she were a witch who would swallow them.

Rukmini Devi's behaviour was the strangest of its kind in the entire world. It was difficult to gauge what made her happy and what angered her. If there was something that made her happy once, then the next time the same thing would make her furious. If Nirmala remained confined to her room she would say, "I don't know where this ill-omened creature comes from!" If she would climb onto the roof or speak with the maids, she would lament, "She has no shame, no dignity. The wretch has burned and swallowed her shame! Now, will she dance in the marketplace in a few days?" From the time *Vakil Sahib* had started giving his earning to Nirmala, Rukmini was determined to be critical of her. She felt that very little remained now for a final disaster to occur. The boys felt the need for money every now and then. Till the time she had held the purse strings, she would divert their attention. Now, she would send the boys straight to Nirmala. Nirmala did not like the boys eating stall food, so, she sometimes refused to give money. Rukmini would then get the chance to sharply point out, "Now you are the mistress of the house, why should the boys live? Who will ask after the motherless boys? They used to eat rupees worth of sweets, now they are dying for a sixteenth part of a *paisa*." If Nirmala would give away money without asking her, then *Deviji* would bring out another meaning in her actions. "Why should she bother if the boys live or die? She couldn't care less. Who else but a mother will explain why too many sweets are not to be eaten? Whatever happens, it will fall on my shoulders, how is she affected?"

If this would have been the limit, Nirmala would have accepted the situation quietly. However, *Deviji* suspiciously used to follow Nirmala like a police detective. If she was on the roof, then surely she must be ogling someone; if talking to a maid, then surely she was condemning her. If Nirmala ordered something from the market, then surely it must be a luxury item. She regularly tried reading her letters. She would try to eavesdrop on her conversations. Nirmala trembled thinking of the doubled-edged sword Rukmini yielded. It came to the point where she had to tell her husband, "Will you kindly explain to *Jijji.* Why is she always after my life?"

Totaram got annoyed and said loudly, "Has she said anything to you?"

"She says something or the other daily. It's difficult to utter anything. If she is envious that I am now the mistress of the house, then, give the money to her only. I don't want it. Let her be the mistress. I only want that nobody should taunt or rebuke me."

Saying this, Nirmala started crying. Totaram got a fine chance to express his love. He said, "I will scold her right away. I will tell her clearly, if she can stay here by keeping quiet, then she should, otherwise she should go her way. She is not the mistress of the house, you are. She is there just to assist you. If she troubles you instead of helping you, then there is no need for her to stay. I had thought she was a widow, an orphan. She will eat a bit of food and just stay here. When the other servants eat in the house, then she is welcome – she is my sister, after all. A lady was also required to look after the boys, so we kept her, but this doesn't mean that she will rule over you."

Nirmala then said, "She teaches the boys to go and ask their mother for money, every now and then. The boys then come and really trouble me. It becomes difficult to rest for even a moment. If I scold them, she runs straight to me with fiery eyes. She thinks that I envy the boys. God alone knows how much I love children. After all, these are my children, why will I envy them?"

Totaram trembled with anger and said, "You beat the boy who troubles you. I also see that the boys have turned into hooligans. I will send Mansaram to a boarding house. The other two, I will deal with them today."

At that time, Totaram was going to the court; it was not the time to scold or rebuke anyone. However, when he returned from the court, he immediately said to Rukmini, "Why, Sister, do you intend to stay in this house or not? If you want to then be silent. What is this, that you have made another's life miserable?"

Rukmini understood that her sister-in-law had struck, but she was a lady who could not be easily subdued. One, she was older than Nirmala. Then, she had spent her entire life serving in this house. Who dared to force her out of the house? She was surprised at her brother's meanness. She said, "So, will you keep me on as a maidservant? If I have to be a maidservant, then I will not be one in this house. If you wish that I should just stand and watch while someone sets fire to this house, see someone taking a wrong step and remain silent, let anyone do whatever they wish and I should be still as a clay statue, then I cannot do this. What has happened to make you so angry? All your wisdom has also gone, because a young girl has you firmly in the palm of her hand? Are you letting her dictate you? You didn't ask me if what she said was true or not. She pulled the wire and like a wooden soldier, you pulled your sword and stood ready to attack."

Totaram said, "I have heard that you always find faults, keep taunting her at every turn. If you have to instruct her, do it lovingly, using kind words. Taunts are not instructive; instead they have the effect of burning sarcasm."

Rukmini said, "Fine, so it is your wish that I should not speak up in any matter, so be it. Then don't say later on, 'You were in the house, you could have given proper advice!' When my words are poisonous, then have I been bitten by a mad dog and gone mad, that I will continue to speak? Let me also see, how will the young *Bahu* run the house."

In the meanwhile, Siyaram and Jiyaram came back from school. Immediately, they both went to *Buaji* asking for food.

Rukmini said, "Why don't you go and ask your new mother? I am not allowed to speak."

Totaram said, "If you step into that house, I'll break your legs. You are always full of mischief."

Jiyaram was slightly impertinent. He said, "You do not say anything to her. You always scold us. She never gives money."

Siyaram supported the statement, "She says, 'I'll cut off your ear, if you trouble me".

Nirmala spoke from the room. "When did I say that I will cut off your ear? Have you started lying, too?"

On hearing this, Totaram picked up Siyaram, holding him by his ears. The boy screamed loudly and started howling.

Rukmini came running and freed the child from Munshi's grasp, and said, "Let him go, will you kill the boy? Oh ho! His ears have gone red. It is true when they say that on getting a new wife, a man becomes blind. If this is the state now, then only God can save this house."

Nirmala was feeling happy over her victory, but when Munshiji held the boy by his ears and picked him up, she could not bear it. She ran to free the child, but Rukmini had reached before her. She said, "First you set a fire, then run to put it out! When you have your own sons you will realise then. How can a stranger know what a child's pain is?"

Nirmala said, "He is standing right here. Ask him, what had I said to provoke anything? I had just said that the boys trouble me for money constantly. Apart from this, if I said anything else, then may I lose my eyesight!"

Totaram said, "I am not blind, I can clearly see how mischievous the boys are. All three of them have become stubborn and hooligans. I will send the eldest to the hostel today."

Rukmini said, "Up till now you did not think of their mischievousness, how has your eyesight become so sharp, today?"

Totaram said, "You are the one responsible for their impertinence."

Rukmini said, "So, I am the knot of poison? It is because of me that your house is ruined. Fine, then I am leaving. They are your sons. Kill them or chop them. I will not speak."

Saying this, she went away from the room. Seeing the child cry, Nirmala was overwhelmed. She embraced him and carrying him in her arms went to her room. There, she tried to kiss him and coax him, but the boy started crying, sobbing away. His ignorant heart could not find a mother's love in Nirmala's affection, the mother's love from which God had kept him away. That was not mother's love, it was only sympathy. He felt this was something upon which he had no right, and which was being given to him as charity. His father had previously hit him once or twice, when his mother had been alive. Then his mother never wept holding him in her embrace. She would be displeased and stop talking to him, to the point that he would after sometime forget everything and run to the mother. He understood being punished for being naughty, but he could not understand being fondled after being beaten. Motherly love had severity in it, but mixed with some mildness. This love had sympathy, but not that severity, which is a secret message of intimacy. Who worries about a healthy organ? However, when the same organ undergoes pain then every effort is made to protect it from hurt and blows. Nirmala's pitiful crying was reinforcing the message that the boy was an orphan. He cried for a long time sitting in Nirmala's lap and went to sleep, crying. Nirmala tried to put him on the cot, but the boy in his sleep put both his arms around her neck and clung to her, as though there was a pit below, into which he might fall, should he let go. Fear and doubt were etched on his face. Nirmala again picked up the boy in her arms, but could not put him on the cot. This moment, while carrying the child in her arms, she felt a satisfaction which she never had till now. For the first time, today she felt the pain in her heart, without which her eyes would not have opened or revealed the path of her duty. Now, the path could be clearly seen.

* * *

6

That day, after giving such weighty evidence of his boundless love for her, Munshi Totaram had hoped that he had stamped an indelible impression on Nirmala's tender heart, but this expectation was not fulfilled in the slightest. Instead, if she had previously sometimes spoken to him, smiling, she was now completely absorbed in caring for the children, concerned only with them. When he came home, he would find the children sitting with her. Sometimes, he saw her serving them food; sometimes, dressing them; at other times, playing with them or telling them a story. Nirmala's thirsting heart, brought to despair by lack of desired love, considered this support as fortunate. Her imaginations of motherhood were slaked by laughing and talking with the children. The hesitation, disinterest and unwillingness she had in talking with her husband, to the extent that she wished to get up and run away – was replaced by the true, simple hearts of the children that made her happy. Initially, Mansaram had been shy and hesitated in coming near her, but now he also sat with her sometimes. He was almost the same age as Nirmala, but mentally, five years younger. Hockey and football constituted his entire universe; it was where his imagination roamed free and it represented the green, lush garden of his desires. He was an active boy with a lean, trim body; he was good-looking with a pleasant, smiling countenance, and shy. The only relationship with his home was one of food – the remainder of the day, no one knew where he wandered. Nirmala used to forget her worries when she heard him talking about games. She would find herself wishing that those childhood days would return, when she played with her doll and arranged her wedding – it was, oh, it was only a little while ago.

Munshi Totaram, like any solitude-loving individual, was an amorous being. For some days, he took Nirmala for walks, theatre shows and tried to please her with some recreation or other activities, but when he observed it bore no results, he took resort to solitude. After a day of difficult mental work, his heart would crave pleasure and enjoyment, but when he entered his pleasure-garden the sight was one of drooping flowers, wilted plants and whirling dust – then he felt like destroying it. He could not understand why Nirmala stayed indifferent towards him. He had tested all the principles of marital science, but was unable to fulfil his heart's desire. He could not think of what he should do next.

One day, he was sitting, worrying over marital issues when his friend from school days, Nayansukhram came to meet him. After greeting him and sitting down, he smiled and said, "These days, you must be enjoying the pleasures of youth, embracing the new wife? You are very fortunate! There is no other better solution to refreshing sulking middle age than getting married. Here, my life has become a real headache. My wife is so badly stuck to me like glue, that I cannot pry her apart from me. I'm thinking about a second marriage. If there is some way out, then try to fix it for me. As a commission, I will treat you to paan made by her hands."

Totaram spoke seriously, "Don't do such a foolish thing, otherwise you will repent it. Girls are happy only with boys. You and I are not of any value for them now. Truly speaking, I am repenting after marrying. It is a bad burden around my neck. I had thought that I would enjoy the pleasures of life for another three or four years, but just the reverse happened. Now I am entangled insolubly – all my own doing."

Nayansukhram said, "What are you saying? What is the difficulty in establishing control over girls? A little walk here and there, some shows and recreation, sprinkle praises of their beauty. That's it – you will set the tone and enjoy yourself."

Totaram replied sadly, "I have tried everything I know and have lost."

Nayansukhram said, "All right! Did you try bringing some fragrant oil or flowers for her? Did you take her to eat *chaat*?"

Totaram said, "Oh, yes, I have done all this. I have tried and tested every principle of marital science. It is all futile talk."

Nayansukhram said, "All right, now listen to my suggestion. Change your appearance. I know of a doctor who uses an advanced electrical technique that wipes out all signs of aging. No grey hair or wrinkle dare remain after he finishes his work. I don't know what kind of magic he does that even a man's garb is changed completely."

Totaram said, "What is his fee?"

Nayansukhram said, "I have heard that is around five hundred rupees."

Totaram said, "Oooh! He must be a fraud, bluffing and taking advantage of fools. He must be applying a mudpack that leaves the face smooth and shiny for a few days. I don't have faith in these doctors who advertise. If it was a matter of five to ten rupees, then I would have tried just for the sake of a good joke. Five hundred rupees is a big amount."

Nayansukhram said, "Five hundred rupees is not a big amount for you. It is one month's salary. Brother, if I had five hundred rupees, this would be the first thing I would do. The value of one hour of youth is far more than five hundred rupees."

Totaram said, "Oh ho, tell me about some cheap prescription, some traditional herbs, which will work without laxative and bleaching effects and make my complexion clear. Electricity and radium are best only for the rich. Let them be happy with it."

Nayansukhram said, "Then, take on the raiment of a pleasure-loving man. Throw away this loose coat. Wear a tight, long, fine muslin *achkan*, pleated trousers, a gold chain around your neck, a *jaipuri* turban on your head, *surma* in your eyes and apply henna oil to your hair. It is absolutely necessary that your paunch is reduced. Tie the cummerbund twice. You will be slightly uncomfortable, but the *achkan* will look its decorative best. I'll get a hair dye. Learn about fifty to hundred songs and drop one or two lines at the right moment. Your talk should be charmingly enticing. It must appear that you are not concerned about godly or worldly matters – for you, only your beloved exists. Keep looking for opportunities to display manly valour and youthful courage. At night, raise a false alarm – Thief! Thief! Dash out alone into the dark after him with your sword Yes, but do ascertain it is the right moment. It should not happen that some real thief comes along and you run after him – the whole game will be up, and you will make a fool of yourself. If this happens, bravery lies in lying still, holding your breath, which would give an impression that you did not know anything. The moment the thief escapes, you must jump out with your sword, saying 'Where is he? Where did he go?' and run around. Not for long, just test what I say for a month. After this, if she doesn't start boring you, then whatever fine you charge, I'll pay."

At that moment, Totaram laughed at what was said, like any well-mannered gentleman should, but some of what was spoken of stuck in his mind. There was no doubt that he had been influenced by the talk. He changed his appearance gradually, so that people would not notice it. First, he started with his hair, then came the turn of *surma*, to the point that in a month or two, his appearance had altered completely. The proposition of learning songs was laughable, but there was no harm in boasting about his courageousness.

From that day on, he would strike up a conversation with Nirmala, wherein he spoke of some incidence of his bravery. Nirmala started suspecting he might be inflicted by lunacy. What was there to be surprised about if a man's foppery led all to suspect that the signs displayed might be those of lunacy? This same man, who after having a plain meal of *moong* dal and two chapattis of thick flour, was still in need of Solomon salts could not have been considered otherwise. What other effect would his madness have had on Nirmala? What happened was that she became compassionate towards him. Hatred and disgust are directed towards those who are fully in their senses; a lunatic is an object of compassion. While talking to him, she would joke with him, make fun of him, the way people usually respond to mad people. Yes, she took care that he would not understand what was being done. She thought the poor soul was repenting for his sin. 'This entire farce is for my benefit – that I should forget my suffering. Ultimately, destiny cannot be changed, so, why should I make him suffer?'

One day, Totaram at his foppish best, returned from his stroll around nine o'clock at night and spoke to Nirmala, "Today, I had an encounter with three thieves. I had gone towards Shivpur. It was already dark. As I reached the railway track, three men with swords appeared from God-knows-where. Believe me they could have been three black Gods. I was all alone, with just this stick in my hand whereas all three of them brandished their swords at me.

I lost my senses and understood that life accompanied me only till this moment. Then I thought, if I have to die, then why not a hero's death? In the meantime, a man challenged me, 'Keep aside all that you have on you and quietly go away.'"

"I held my stick aloft and said, 'I just have this stick and its value is equal to a man's head.'"

"As I uttered these words, all three drew their swords and pounced on me. I fended off all their blows with this stick. The three of them attacked, annoyed and angry, the air rang with the clash of swords on stick, and moving like lightning, I cut off their attack For about ten minutes, they tried all the sword play they knew, but there was not a scratch on me. I was helpless because I had no sword in my hand. If there had been one, I would have not left anyone alive. Well, how much longer should I go on? At that time, it was worth seeing how efficient I was. I was also surprised at where that agility came from. When the three of them saw that they could not win, they sheathed their swords, and patting my back, said, 'Young one, we haven't met such a brave fellow like you. The three of us loot three hundred-people strong villages as easily as beating a drum, but today you have defeated us. We acknowledge your iron strength. Saying this, all three vanished from sight.'"

Nirmala smiled gravely and said, "The stick must be bearing many sword marks?"

Munshiji was not ready for anyone doubting his word, but it was necessary to reply. "I fended them off so successfully that they missed the stick. There are two-four hits on the stick that slid across, and didn't leave any marks on the stick."

He had not even completed his sentence when suddenly a distraught Rukmini came running in and stood there, breathing heavily. She managed to say, "Tota? Is Tota here? There is a snake in my room. It is under my cot. I got up and ran here. The wretch must be around six feet. It is hissing and its fangs are out. Come along, bring that stick with you."

Totaram's face paled, and he grew cold and started perspiring. Somehow masking his feelings, he said, "A snake? Here? You must be mistaken? It must be a rope."

Rukmini cried, "Oh! I've seen it with my own eyes. Come along and see for yourself. It is there! Being a man, you fear it?"

Munshi came out of the house, all right, but came to the verandah and stopped. His feet were not moving. His heart was pounding. 'The snake gets angry very quickly. If I get bitten, I will lose my life for no reason,' he thought, but he said, "I'm not afraid. It's just a snake, not a lion. But a stick will not effectively deal with a snake. I'll get somebody. I will get a spear from somebody's house."

Saying this, Munshiji jumped up and went outside rapidly. Mansaram was eating his food. There Munshiji went away; here Mansaram left eating, picked up his hockey stick, entered the room and immediately pulled the cot forward. The snake stayed where it was instead of running away. It reared its head, with its fangs out. Mansaram quickly picked the bed sheet and flung it over the snake, and delivered three-four deadly blows in quick succession with the hockey stick. The snake died, writhing under the sheet. Then he picked it up, and with the dead snake draped over the stick, he went out. Just then, Munshiji entered with many men. He saw Mansaram and on spotting the suspended dead snake, he shrieked. Regaining control, he said, "I was coming. Why were you in such a hurry? Give it here. Someone will throw it away."

Saying this, with a display of courage he stood at the door of Rukmini's room and looked all over the room, carefully. Then, twisting his moustache he approached Nirmala and said, "By the time I returned, Mansaram had killed it! The silly boy ran with the hockey stick. A snake should always be killed with a spear. This is the boy's shortcoming. I've killed many such snakes. I kill them by playing with them. I killed many by simply crushing them in my fist."

Rukmini said, "Go on, today I've seen your manliness."

Being ashamed, Munshiji spoke, "All right! I may be a coward, but I am not asking you for a reward. Go and tell *maharaj* to serve food."

Munshiji went for dinner and Nirmala stood on the doorstep, thinking, 'Oh God! Has he truly got some deadly disease? Do you want to worsen my condition? I can serve him, respect him, can sacrifice my life at his feet, but cannot do something beyond my power! It's not within my control to erase the age gap. What he expects from me, I have finally understood! Aah! I hadn't understood it at the start, otherwise, why would he try such severe measures and farces?'

* * *

7

From that day onwards, Nirmala's attitude and behaviour changed. She decided to concentrate only on her duty, forgetting herself completely. Till now, she had not focussed on her duty, despairing in an agony of disappointment. Panic, like a flame flickered in her heart, whose unbearable pain had rendered her almost unconscious. The intensity of that pain was reducing. She realised that there was no happiness for her in this life, so why should she destroy her life by dreaming about it? Not every person in this world slept on a bed of roses, and she was one of those unfortunate ones. God had also chosen her to carry a burden of sorrow, and this could never be taken off her head. She knew that even if she wanted to, she could not get rid of it, whether darkness spread before her eyes due to its weight. If her neck started to break or it became impossible to take a step forward, she still had to carry that burden. How long can a prisoner facing a life sentence cry? Who pities him even if he cries? Who feels sympathy for him? By crying, she would affect her own work, because of which she would face greater difficulties.

The next day when *Vakil Sahib* came home from the court, he saw Nirmala's smiling form standing at the door of his room. His eyes were thoroughly satisfied on seeing her pleasing beauty. Today, he saw how beautiful she was, like a lotus in full bloom. A big mirror hung on the wall of the room. It was usually covered by a curtain. Today, its cover was lifted. As *Vakil Sahib* entered the room, his eyes fell on the mirror. He could see his face clearly and what he saw hurt him to the quick. The glow on his face had faded after toiling all day. In spite of eating a varied and nutritious diet, there were wrinkles on his face. His stomach also protruded, like an obstinate horse, in spite of being reined in and tightened. Standing in front of the mirror, but looking the other way, Nirmala stood there. There was so much difference between both their faces. One was like a palace, embedded with gems and the other, a ruin. His dilapidated condition was intolerable and filled him with loathing, and he could no longer look into the mirror. He moved away. It was no surprise then that this beautiful lady would dislike the sight of him. He did not have the courage to look at Nirmala. Her peerless beauty seeped into his heart and settled there, rankling like a thorn.

Nirmala said, "Why did you take so long today? My eyes are hurting from watching for you the whole day."

Looking towards the window, Totaram replied, "I don't get time to even to take a breather because of so many cases. There was another case just now, but I came back home, excusing myself with a headache."

Nirmala said, "So, why do you take on so many cases? Do only that much work as you can manage easily. Don't give your life for your work, that's no way to work. Don't take so many cases. I do not crave for money. If you are relaxed and live well, then we will get ample money."

Totaram said, "I cannot spurn Lakshmi, if she visits me."

Nirmala said, "If Lakshmiji arrives with a gift at the cost of your flesh and blood, then it is better she doesn't arrive. I am not hungry for money."

At this moment, Mansaram also came back from school. Walking under the hot sun had brought beads of perspiration to his face; his fair face had a ruddy glow and his eyes sparkled. Standing at the door, he said, "*Ammaji*, give me something to eat. I have to go to play."

Nirmala went and brought a glass of water and some nuts in a plate, and gave it to Mansaram. When Mansaram ate and started to leave, Nirmala asked, "By when will you return?"

Mansaram said, "I can't say. We have a hockey match with the British. The barracks are quite far from here."

Nirmala said, "Then, come back early. The food will get cold, and then you will say you are not hungry."

Mansaram looked at Nirmala with simple affection and said, "If I get late, then understand that I will eat there, and there is no need to wait for me." When Mansaram left, Nirmala said, "Earlier, he never used to come home. He used to feel shy talking to me. If anything was required, he would ask someone else to fetch it and stay outside. He has started coming in, since I called him in and spoke to him."

Totaram said, with a trace of envy in his voice, "Why does he come to ask you for things to eat? Why doesn't he ask *Didi*?"

Nirmala had mentioned this, hoping she might earn some praise. She wanted to show how she cared for his sons. This was not some artificial love – she really loved them. In her own temperament, the feelings of the children were still uppermost; she had the same eagerness, the same love for amusement, that restless naughtiness. Spending time with the boys brought these child-like characteristics to the fore. Commonly-felt wifely-envy had not been born yet and not understanding the reason of her husband's displeasure, she said, "What do I know? I don't know why they don't ask her? When they come to me, I don't scold them. If I do this, then the only thing that will happen is that people will talk – 'She envies the boys!'"

Munshiji did not reply to this, but today he did not talk to the pleader's clients. Instead, he went straight to Mansaram and took his test. This was the first time in his life when he had taken such interest in the education and progress of Mansaram or any of the other boys. He would never have any time to raise his head from his work. It was nearly forty years ago that he had studied any of those subjects. Since then he had never even glanced at them. He studied his law books and read his letters, apart from this, nothing else was perused. He could not get the time to study their subjects, but he strode on ahead to test Mansaram on those very same subjects. Mansaram was intelligent and hardworking, too. In spite of being the games captain of the school team, he always stood first in his class. He could faithfully remember any lesson he read once. In his excitement, Munshiji could not think of any difficult questions which would make a clever boy think before answering. Those that he asked, Mansaram answered with the greatest ease. The way a soldier gets irritated with his futile attacks, and attacks with greater intensity – the same way, *Vakil Sahib* reacted on hearing Mansaram's answers. He wanted to ask such a question whose answer Mansaram could not give. He wanted to see which his weak aspect was, unable to be satisfied with his prowess. He was desirous to see what he could not do. An experienced examiner could have easily found Mansaram's weakness, but could *Vakil Sahib* do that, equipped with only his half a century's forgotten education? At last, when he could find a suitable excuse through which he would vent and thus, justify his anger, he said, "I see you loitering here and there throughout the day. I consider your character to be more important than your intellect, and your loafing around is unacceptable to me."

Mansaram said, fearlessly, "I do not go anywhere, except for an hour in the evening to play. You can ask *Ammaji* or *Buaji*. I am not fond of roaming aimlessly, myself. Yes, the principal calls me specifically to play, so it's compulsory for me. If you do not like my going out to play, then I will not go from tomorrow."

Munshiji saw that the talk was turning in an unexpected direction, so he spoke in a shrill voice, "How can I believe that you do not roam anywhere except to go to play? I regularly hear complaints about you."

Mansaram said with annoyance, "Which great fellow has complained to you, let me also hear it."

Vakil Sahib said, "Someone, but that is of no concern to you. You should believe me to know I would make no false accusation."

Mansaram said, "If anybody comes and says to my face that he saw me roaming around aimlessly, then I will never show my face."

Vakil Sahib said, "Who has the interest to complain about you, in front of you, at the cost of incurring your enmity? You will take a few of your friends and wander about, breaking the tiles on his roof! Not one, but several people have complained to me and I have no reason to disbelieve what my friends tell me. I want you to stay in the school all the time."

Mansaram's face fell. "I have no objection in staying there. Tell me when, and I will go."

Vakil Sahib said, "Why are you so dejected? You don't like it there? It seems as if you are terribly afraid of going there. After all, what is the matter? Do you have a problem there?"

Mansaram was not eager to stay in the boarding house. However, when Munshiji mentioned the same thing, and asked for a reason, he cloaked his hesitation behind a façade of happiness. He said in a pleased tone, "Why should I be sad? For me, the boarding house is the same as my house. There is no problem. And if there is one, I can bear it. I will go from tomorrow. Yes, if there will not be a place vacant, then I am helpless to do anything about it."

Munshiji was a lawyer. He understood that the boy was looking for an excuse so that he did not have to go there, and he would also not be blamed for it, also. He said, "There is place for all the others, so won't there be place for you?"

Mansaram said, "Many boys did not get a place and they are staying in rented houses. Recently, a boy left the boarding house and there were fifty applications for that place."

Vakil Sahib did not find it appropriate to argue over the matter. He ordered Mansaram to be ready the next morning, and asked that his buggy be readied. He went for his walk. For a few days now, he had been going for regular evening walks. Some experienced person told him that there was no better mantra than this for a long life. After he left, Mansaram came to Rukmini and said, "*Buaji, Babuji* had told me to stay at school from tomorrow."

Rukmini asked in amazement, "Why?"

Mansaram said, "How do I know? He started saying that I loiter here and there like a loafer."

Rukmini said, "Didn't you say that you do not go anywhere?"

Mansaram replied, "Of course I did. But he should also believe me."

Rukmini said, "This must be by the grace of your new *Ammaji*, what else?"

Mansaram said, "No, *Buaji,* I do not doubt her. She, poor thing, never says anything, even by mistake. If I ask for anything, she gives it to me immediately."

Rukmini said, "What do you know about female character? This fire has been set by her. Wait, I will go and ask."

Rukmini went fretfully to Nirmala. How could she let slip such an occasion where she could put her to shame her with sarcastic remarks, drag her over thorns, pierce her with taunts and make her cry? Nirmala respected her, and gave way to her, without answering back. Nirmala wanted Rukmini to teach her things, and correct her where she erred, and keep looking after household matters, but Rukmini remained distant and unfriendly.

Nirmala got up from the cot and said, "Come, *Didi,* come and sit."

Rukmini kept standing and said, "I ask you, do you want to expel everyone from this house and live alone?"

Nirmala said, timidly, "What happened, *Didiji*? I did not say anything to anybody."

Rukmini said, "First you turn out Mansaram from the house, and on top of that, you say that 'I did not say anything to anybody!' Of what there is left, you can't even bear to see this much!"

Nirmala said, "*Didiji*, I touch your feet and swear that I don't know anything. My eyes will burst, if I even opened my mouth regarding this topic."

Rukmini said, "Why do you swear uselessly? Till today, Totaram never spoke to the boy. Mansaram had once gone to his maternal parental home for a week. He was so anxious that he went to fetch him and brought him back. Now he is turning out the same Mansaram and keeping him in school. If anything at all happens to the boy, if one hair is awry, then you'll be responsible. He has never stayed outside, he forgets about eating and dressing. He sleeps wherever he is sitting. Though he has grownup, he is still a young boy. He will have a hard time in school. There, who will bother if he has eaten, where has he kept his clothes, where is he sleeping? When there is no one to worry about him in this house, then who will care about him outside? I have warned you, the rest is up to you!"

Saying this, Rukmini left the room.

As soon as *Vakil Sahib* returned from his stroll, Nirmala immediately broached the topic. These days she was studying English: Mansaram taught her. If he went away, then would her study not suffer? Who else would teach her? *Vakil Sahib* did not know about this till now. Nirmala had thought that when she would know some English, then she would surprise *Vakil Sahib* with her knowledge. She had also learnt some from her own brothers. Now she was studying regularly. *Vakil Sahib* burnt with jealousy and said with a frown, "Since when is he teaching you? You never told me."

Nirmala had seen this aspect of his only once before, when he had beaten Siyaram unconscious. The same look but far more menacing and dangerous was visible today. She said nervously, "This doesn't affect his studies. I study only when he is free. I ask him if it is all right, otherwise I tell him to go. I stop him for ten minutes, mostly when he goes to play. I, myself, do not want his studies to be harmed in any way."

The matter was not grave; there was nothing in it really, but *Vakil Sahib*, hopeless and plunged in worry, fell back on his cot, cogitating over the matter. It was far worse than what he had thought – the matter had forged ahead. He cursed himself. Why had he not arranged for the boy to stay in boarding school right in the beginning? He realised the secret why his queen was so happy these days. Earlier, the room was never so decorated, she was also not so dressed up and choosy, but now, the complete reversal was clear to see. His first angry reaction was to turn Mansaram out of the house right away, but the mature person in him advised that temper was inadvisable now. If she sensed it, it would be a disaster. Instead, he decided to gauge her feelings. He said, "I know that he is not at all affected by teaching you for two-four minutes. But, he is an idler. He gets an excuse not to do his own work. Tomorrow if he fails, then he will say clearly, 'I keep teaching throughout the day.' I will keep a lady teacher for you. It will not be a big expense. You did not tell me earlier. What would he be teaching you, anyway? He must be running off after teaching you two-four words. This way you will not learn anything."

Nirmala immediately denied this accusation. "No, it is not so. He teaches me with great interest and his skill is such that you develop interest in learning. You come one day and see how well he explains. I feel that the lady teacher will not teach with so much interest."

Munshiji, pleased at his tactful and successful questioning, twisted his moustache, and said, "He teaches you once a day or several times?"

Nirmala still had not understood the slant of the questions, "Earlier he taught only in the evening, but now for many days, he comes once to see the handwriting, also. He says that he is the best in the class. He came first in this examination, then how do you say that he is not interested in studies? That is why I emphasise this; otherwise, *Didi* will think that I have caused all this trouble. I will then have to listen to taunts with no fault of mine. She just scolded me a few minutes back."

Munshiji thought, 'I understand very well. You are young and you are trying to fool me. Taking advantage of *Didi* for your own good to get your own purpose fulfilled.' Aloud, he said, "I do not understand why the boy fears going to the boarding school. The other boys are happy there, amongst their friends. To the contrary, he is crying. The past few days he was studying with great interest that is why he stood first in class. But these past few days, he is more interested in roaming around. If I will not nip in the bud, then later on I will not be able to tackle it at all. As for you, I will appoint a lady teacher."

The next day, in the morning, Munshiji left after getting dressed. Many clients were sitting in the living room. One of them was Raja Sahib from whom Munshiji got thousands annually. However, Munshiji left him sitting there, promising to return in ten minutes. He sat in his buggy and reached the school. There, he met the Principal, who was a courteous gentleman. He greeted *Vakil Sahib* with great respect, but he informed that he did not have a place vacant in the hostel. All the rooms were occupied. The Inspector Sahib had sternly urged that first his boy must be given a room, then the others. Therefore, if any place did become vacant, then also, Mansaram would not get a place, as there was a huge pile of applications of boys from outside. Munshiji was a lawyer; day and night he dealt with many such people, who in greed would make the impossible possible, and the unattainable, attainable. He thought he might get results by giving some money to someone – he talked about this possibility with the clerk. The clerk laughed and said, "Munshiji, this is not a court. This is a school. If the slightest hint of this reaches the Principal's ears, then he will get extremely angry and immediately expel Mansaram. It is possible, he might complain to the officers." The poor Munshiji, shamefaced, returned home greatly annoyed by ten o'clock. At the same time, Mansaram left for school. Munshiji looked at him harshly as if he were his enemy and went inside the house.

After this for ten to twelve days, it became a routine for *Vakil Sahib* to meet principals of some schools, either in the morning or evening, to try to get Mansaram admitted into the boarding house, but none of the schools had any place. He got a negative reply from all the places; now there were just two options – either keep Mansaram in a separate, rented house or get him admitted in some other school! Both the options were easy. There was often a vacancy in the *mofussil* school, but now Munshiji's doubts had calmed down slightly. From that day, he never saw Mansaram entering the house. He also did not go out to play. Before going to school and after returning from school, he would sit in his room. These were hot summer days, sweat dripped from the body even in the open, but Mansaram did not come out of his room. His self-respect had been badly hurt; he was desperate to get rid of the accusation of being a vagabond. He wanted to wipe off this black mark from his conduct.

One day, Munshiji was sitting and eating food, when Mansaram also came to eat after bathing. Of late Munshiji had not seen his naked body. After many months, his eyes fell on it and he was shocked. A skeleton stood before him. The face still held the glow of youth, but the body had dissolved to extreme thinness, almost thorn-like. He had to ask, "These days, are you not well? Why are you so weak?"

Mansaram tied his dhoti and said, "My health is perfectly all right."

Munshiji said, "Then why are you so thin and weak?"

Mansaram replied, "I'm not thin or weak. When was I fatter than this?"

Munshiji said, "Half of the body doesn't exist anymore, and you say 'I am not weak'. Why, *Didi*, was he like this?"

Rukmini was in the courtyard, pouring water over the *tulsi* plant. She said, "Why will he be weak, now he is properly taken care of? I was a rustic who didn't know how to feed the boys. I had spoilt their habits by letting them eat food sold on stalls. Now an educated woman, adept in household work is feeding them, taking care of them like tender leaves! Her enemies will be weak!"

Munshiji said, "*Didi*, you do a lot of injustice. Who said you are spoiling the boys? Any work that can't be done by others, you should do it yourself. It's not as if you have no relation with this house. She is still a girl, how can she take care of the boys? This is your work."

Rukmini said, "I did it till I considered it mine. When you consider me a stranger, then why should I care and bother to cling to you? Ask them, for how many days have they not had milk? Go and look in the room, the sweets sent for breakfast are fermenting! Mistress thinks 'I have kept the items of food. If no one eats them, should I put it into their mouths?' So brother, this is the way those boys are looked after, those boys, who have never seen the happiness of love and care. Your sons were properly looked after, now they will not be happy to live like orphans. I speak frankly. What will be achieved by feeling bad? On top of that, I heard that arrangements are being made to keep him in school. The poor boy is not allowed to come inside the house. He is scared to come to me, and anyway, what do I have that I can feed him with?"

In the meantime, Mansaram got up after having two chapattis. Munshiji said, "Have you finished eating? It hasn't been more than a minute since we sat. What did you eat, you took just two chapattis?"

Mansaram said, hesitantly, "There was dal and vegetable also. If I eat much my throat starts burning and I get acidic belches."

When Munshiji got up after eating, he was very worried. If the boy kept getting weak like this, then he would catch some terrible disease. He was really angry at Rukmini at this point of time. She only felt envy because she was not the mistress of the house. She did not think whether she possessed the right to be one. One who did not know how to keep accounts; how could she be the mistress of the house? She was the mistress for a year and she had not saved even a single penny. With his salary, Rupkala used to save two hundred to two-hundred-fifty rupees. Under her administration, the same salary could not even meet the expenses. It was no matter, but indulgent affection had spoilt the boys. Why is that such grownup boys eat only when someone feeds them? They should be concerned about it themselves.

The whole day, Munshiji kept thinking over the matter. He also consulted a few friends. People said, "Don't hinder his games, and don't imprison him now. There is less chance of his character being destroyed if he is in an open environment than in a closed room. Definitely protect him from bad company, but not to the extent that he is not allowed to go out of the house. In adolescence, seclusion is very dangerous."

Munshiji now realised his fault. He returned home and went to see Mansaram. He had just come back from school and was still in his school clothes. He stood there, with a book open in front of him, but gazing out of the window. He was fixedly looking at a beggar, who was begging carrying her son in her arms. The son was so happy in his mother's arms; as if he was sitting on a royal throne. Mansaram cried upon seeing the child. Thoughts ran through his troubled mind. 'Is this child not happier than I am? Is there any object in the infinite Universe, which would make him happier than this lap? Even God cannot create a thing like this. God, why do you give birth to such boys whose fate it is to bear the sorrow of parting from their mother? Today, who is more unfortunate than me in the world? Who is conscious about my food and drink, life and death? Even if I die today, who will feel sorrow in their hearts? Father now likes to make me cry, he doesn't want to see my face also. Preparations are being made to expel me from the house. Ah, Mother! Today your son is being called as loafer! The same father, in whose hands you placed your three sons' care, today calls me 'loafer' and 'wicked'. I'm not capable enough to stay in the house.' Tormented by all this, Mansaram burst out crying, in deep agony.

Totaram entered the room right at that moment. Mansaram immediately wiped his tears and stood with his head bent. Probably, this was the first time that Munshiji had stepped in his room. Mansaram's heart started pounding thinking, 'Let's see today what trouble descends.' Munshiji saw him crying; then for a moment his love was startled from its deep slumber. He said fearfully, "Why do you cry, son? Did anyone say anything to you?"

With great difficulty, Mansaram held his tears from overflowing and said, "No, I am not crying."

Munshiji said, "I hope your *Amma* did not say anything?"

Mansaram said, "No, she doesn't even talk to me."

Munshiji said, "What should I do, Son? I married so that the children would get a mother, but this wish was not fulfilled. So, she doesn't talk to you at all?"

Mansaram said, "No, she hasn't talked to me for months now."

Munshiji said, "She possesses a strange nature. I do not know what she wants. If I had known of her temperament, I would have never married. She raises some issue daily. She told me that he is missing throughout the day, and I don't know where he is. What did I know about what she had in her mind? I thought you were in bad company, roaming around aimlessly the whole day. Which father will not be grieved, seeing his dear son loitering around? Therefore, I decided to put you in the boarding house. That's it, nothing else, Son. I didn't want to stop you from playing. Seeing you in this condition causes me great heartache. Yesterday I came to know that I was mistaken about it. Play at your pleasure. Go out to play in the mornings and evenings. You will be benefitted by the fresh air. If you require anything, tell me, you need not say anything to her. Just think that she is not in the house. Your mother left you and went away, but I am still there."

The boy's simple, innocent heart thrilled to hear his father's words and his heart filled with love for his father. He felt as if God was standing before him. Agitated by his disappointment and anguish, he had imagined his father to be merciless and a lot of other things. He had no complaint against the stepmother. Now he realised that he had been unjust to his God-like father. He felt devotion flowing in his heart and he cried putting his head on his father's feet. Munshiji was overwhelmed with compassion. The son, for whom his heart became restless even if he was away from his sight even for a moment; whose modesty, intellect and character was praised by everyone; why had he become so hardhearted towards him? He had started considering his own son as his enemy and was even ready to banish him. To pull Nirmala towards him, he had to step back from his son. The distance between son and father started increasing. Now, Nirmala had become a wall between them. The result was that today, he was deceiving his once inseparable son. Today, after thinking a lot, he had a strategy in hand by which he would remove Nirmala from the middle and pull his other arm towards him. He had started his game–but whether it would have a desirable result or not, who knows?

From the day Totaram had decided to send Mansaram to the boarding house even after Nirmala's ardent requests, she had left studying English. She went to the extent of not talking to him anymore. She had sensed Totaram's impulsive disbelief to some extent. 'Oh! What a suspicious temperament! God should take care of the dignity of this house. His mind is full of such corrupt thoughts. He thinks that I am so far gone?' She thought over this and cried for many days. Then she started thinking, 'Why does he have doubts like these? What is it in me that is not acceptable?' Even after thinking a lot, she could not find anything objectionable. Then, she concluded, it was probably her studying from Mansaram; talking and laughing with him that caused these doubts. She would stop studying, and even by mistake, she would never talk to him or look at his face.

However, this renunciation and penance on her part would not solve the problem. While talking to Mansaram, her sensual imagination was excited as well as satisfied. While talking to him, she experienced endless, deep happiness, which she could not express in words. She did not have the shadow of illicit love or desires. She could not think of a profane love for Mansaram even in her dreams. The natural desire of talking to a friend that every individual has; this was the unknown solution of the blissful satisfaction she felt. Now, this need went unfulfilled and unsatisfied desires started burning in Nirmala's heart, flickering and paining. Time and again, her mind would be tormented with an unknown agony. She lost interest in all her work and would wander all around in search of an unknown lost object; keep sitting in one place for hours. Yes, when Munshiji would come, she would smile and talk about various things, drowning all her desires in despair.

One day, when Munshiji left for court after eating his meal, Rukmini made many sarcastic remarks, pointedly to Nirmala. "You knew you had to bring up children, then why didn't you tell your family members that you would not get married here? You could have gone where there was just a man. He would be happy with your choice of ornamentation and beauty and would praise his luck. Here, how will an old man go crazy over your complexion, figure, beauty, expressions? He married you to care for the boys, not for sensual pleasures." In this way, she liberally sprinkled salt on Nirmala's wounds for a long time, but Nirmala did not utter a word in response. She wanted to present proof of her innocence, but could not do it. If she said she was doing what her husband wished, then the secret would be disclosed. If she accepted her fault and amended it, then there was a fear as to what the result might be. Though she was straightforward, and had no hesitation or fear in speaking the truth, but at this delicate juncture, she had to seal her lips. There was no option other than this. She could see that Mansaram grew more detached and sad; she also saw that he was getting weaker, day-by-day, but there was a restriction on his speech and activity. When a thief's house is robbed, how cheated must he feel? At this moment, Nirmala's condition was the same as that of the thief.

8

When something happens against our expectations, only then we become sad. Mansaram had never expected that Nirmala would complain about him. Therefore, he was in deep agony, thinking, 'Why does she complain about me? What does she want? Just this – he eats from my husband's salary, money gets spent on his studies, his clothes – she must want that I do not stay at home. Their money will be saved if I don't stay. She used to be so pleased with me. I've never heard any harsh words from her. Is she being crafty? It's quite possible. A hunter spreads grains after he lays the net to trap birds. Ah! I did not know that there was a net under the grains – this motherly love was just a drama to get me banished from home.'

'Fine, but why does she mind my staying here? The person who is her husband, is he not my father? Is this father-son relation less intimate than that between male-female? When I don't envy her supreme governance, and she does whatever she wants, when I don't utter a word, then why does she wish to deprive me of my father's love? Why can't she give me a finger-length piece of land from her empire? Why can't you see me sitting under a shadow of a tree, even though you are staying in a palace?'

'Oh, yes, she must think that when he grows up, he will inherit my husband's property, so she wants to expel me right now. How can I make her believe that she need not fear it? How shall I tell her that Mansaram will take poison and die before doing something to her disadvantage? Whatever problems I may face, I will never trouble her and become a thorn in her heart. Though father has given birth to me and may love me a lot, but don't I know that from the day father married her, we no longer have a place in his heart? Now we can keep lying around here as orphans. We have no rights in this house anymore. Possibly, due to our previous *sanskaras*, our state here is better than that of other orphans – but we are orphans. We became orphans the very same day *Ammaji* died. Whatever little right we had over this house; the marriage took care of that. I never kept any special relationship with them. If father would've complained about me in those early days, then probably I wouldn't have felt so bad. I would have been prepared for the shock now. At that time, if needed, I could have found a labourer's job! But they hurt me at a bad time. Even a predatory animal is considerate, and it will only harm a man who is careless. That is why I was shown so much courteousness. If I took a little longer than expected to reach for a meal, then call after call would resound; fresh *halwa* was made for breakfast; I was asked regularly 'Are you in need of money?' That's why that watch worth a hundred rupees was bought.'

'But couldn't she think of any other complaints, besides branding me a vagabond? After all, where did she see me loitering around? She could have said that he is not interested in studies and constantly asks for money for some reason. Why did this particular excuse occur to her? Probably, this was the severest blow she could hurt me with. In the first instance, she shot the *agni-baan*, the inescapable arrow – just so, that I would fall from grace in the eyes of my father? Keeping me in a boarding house was just an excuse. The aim was to remove me, like a fly from the milk. The expenses would be stopped after two-four months, then, who cared whether I lived or died? If I had known that the inspiration came from her, then I would have arranged a place, somehow, even if it was impossible to. I would have found a place in the servant's room; at least, I would get ample space to lie on the verandah. Anyway, there is no love now. When there is no love, then it is being shameless to be here just to eat. Now, this is not my house. I took birth here, played here, but now this is not mine. Father is also not my father. I am his son, but he is not my father. All the relations in this world are bound by love. Where there is no love, there is nothing. Alas, *Ammaji*! Where are you?'

Thinking thus, Mansaram started crying, and as the old memories of his mother came flooding back, more tears flowed. He cried *'Ammaji, Ammaji'* many times as if she stood there, listening. For the first time, he experienced the sorrow of being bereft of his mother. He had a high self-esteem and was courageous, but since he had been brought up in comfort, with great care – this situation seemed to be miserable, one in which he considered himself without support.

It was ten at night. Today, Munshiji had gone out for dinner. The maid had come twice to call Mansaram for dinner. The last time she did, Mansaram irritably told her, "I am not hungry. I will not eat anything. You come and irritate me, again and again." Therefore, when Nirmala wanted to send her again for the same purpose, she did not go saying, "*Bahuji*, he will not come if I call him."

Nirmala said, "Why won't he come? Go and say that the food is getting cold. He should eat at least a few morsels."

The maid said, "I have said all this, but he doesn't come."

Nirmala said, "Did you say that she is still sitting up for you?"

The maid said, "No, *Bahuji*. I did not say this, why should I lie?"

Nirmala said, "All right, then go and say that she is sitting and waiting for you. If you not eat, then she will wind up the kitchen work and go to sleep. My dear Bhoongi, listen, just go once more," she laughed and coaxed, "if he doesn't come, then carry him on your lap."

Bhoongi frowned and went, but returned promptly and said, "Oh, *Bahuji,* he is crying. Has anyone said anything?"

Nirmala got up startled, and walked two-three steps forward as if a mother had heard a news of her son falling into a well. Then she suddenly stopped herself, and said to Bhoongi, "Crying? Didn't you ask why is he crying?"

Bhoongi, "No, *Bahuji*, I did not ask why. Why should I lie?"

Nirmala thought, 'He is crying. Sitting alone, crying in the still of the night? He must be remembering his mother. How will I go and explain things to him? Alas! How? Here one is defamed for the smallest thing. God! You are the witness. If I had said anything to him even by mistake, then he should come before me. What shall I do? Inside, he must be thinking that she must have complained to his father about him. How shall I convince him that I have never uttered a single word against him? If I wished ill upon such a noble boy, then there cannot be a more monstrous female than me in this world.'

Nirmala used to see that Mansaram's health was deteriorating day-by-day, he was getting weaker, his clear, glowing face was fading, and his body was shrinking. She knew the reason for this, but she dared not say anything to her husband about this. Seeing all this, her heart would be torn, but she could not open her mouth. At times, she would get irritated at why Mansaram had taken this one trivial issue so much to heart. Had he become a loafer, simply because her husband had called him one? It was different with her; the slightest suspicion could destroy her, but why did he care so much about such things?

She had an intense desire to go to him, calm him and get him to eat. The poor boy would remain hungry the whole night. 'Oh God! I am the root cause of this turbulence. There was peace in this house before I came. The father loved his sons more than his life, and the children loved their father. All the obstacles appeared after I entered the house. What will be the end? God alone knows. God doesn't grant me death, also. The poor boy is alone and hungry. Earlier, too, he got up leaving food on the plate, and what is his diet? He eats as much as a two-year-old,' she thought in alarm.

Nirmala went out. She went against the wishes of her husband. Her heart trembled, terrified to go to appease the person who was her son, by relation of marriage. She first looked towards Rukmini's room. She lay fast asleep after a hearty meal. Then she went towards the outer room, which was quiet, too. Munshiji had not come in yet. Stepping carefully, she reached Mansaram's room. The room was open; Mansaram was sitting with his head bent over a table – there was a book in front of him. He looked like a live statue of grief and worry. Nirmala wanted to call, but her voice died in her throat.

Suddenly, Mansaram lifted his head and looked towards the door. He failed to recognise Nirmala in the dark. Startled, he cried out, "Who is it?"

Nirmala said, in a trembling voice, "It is me! Why aren't you coming for dinner? It is so late."

Displeased, Mansaram turned his face away and said, "I am not hungry."

Nirmala said, "I've heard this three times from Bhoongi."

Mansaram retorted, "Then hear it a fourth time from me."

Nirmala said, "You did not have anything in the evening also, then why won't you be hungry?"

Laughing sarcastically, Mansaram said, "If I'll be very hungry, then where will it come from?" Saying this, Mansaram tried to close the door of the room, but Nirmala opened the door and entered the room. Nirmala's eyes were filled with tears; she held Mansaram's hand, and in a pleading, sweet voice, said, "Come along and eat something on my request. If you don't come, then I will go to sleep without eating, too. Have just two morsels. Do you want me to die, starving the whole night?"

Mansaram was in a quandary. He thought, 'She hasn't eaten yet and was waiting for me. Is she a Goddess of love, affection and humanity or an illusory statue of envy and evil?' He remembered his mother. When he was angry, then she used to come to appease him and did not get up from there till he went. He could not refuse the request, and said, "You had so much trouble because of me. I am sorry for it. Had I known you were sitting and waiting for me, I would have eaten then."

Nirmala said scornfully, "How could you think that you would remain hungry and I would eat and sleep peacefully. Just because I am your stepmother by relation, does that make me selfish as well?"

Suddenly, Munshiji's coughing was heard. It came from the men's room. It seemed as though he might come this way – to Mansaram's room? Nirmala's face went pale. She immediately stepped out of the room, and not finding the opportunity to enter, said in a harsh tone, "I am not a maid to keep sitting up so late at night at the kitchen's door! Whoever doesn't want to eat, should at least say so beforehand."

Munshiji saw Nirmala standing there. 'This misfortune! What has she come here to do?' he thought, but he said, "What are you doing here?"

Nirmala spoke in a harsh tone, "What I am doing, I am crying over my destiny. I am the root cause of all the problems. Somebody is angry here; somebody is lying there, sulking. Who all will I appease and till what extent should I do so?"

Munshiji was slightly astonished and said, "What is the matter?"

Nirmala said, "He doesn't come to eat, what else? I sent the maid ten times to ask, and had to come myself. It's very easy for him to say, 'I am not hungry'. Here, I am the housemaid for everyone. The whole world is ready to defame me. Somebody may not be hungry, but who will stop people from saying that the witch doesn't give food."

Munshiji said to Mansaram, "Why don't you eat? Do you know what the time is?"

Mansaram stood motionless. He watched the mysterious happenings, without being able to instinctively understand the underlying complicated tracery of emotions. The eyes which were filled with tears of humility a moment earlier, spewed flames of jealousy so suddenly – from where did they arise? A moment ago, the same lips were pouring out nectar, why was poison flowing out now? He answered in a semi-dazed condition, "I am not hungry."

Munshiji frowned and said, "Why are you not hungry? If you were not hungry, then why didn't you say so in the evening? Who would sit the whole night and wait for you to eat? You never had this habit before. Since when did you learn to sulk? Go and eat."

Mansaram said, "No, Sir, I'm not at all hungry."

Totaram ground his teeth and said, "All right, when you feel hungry, then you eat."

Saying this, he went inside. Nirmala also went behind him. Munshiji went to lie down. She finished clearing up the kitchen, and washed her mouth. She ate paan and went in smiling. Munshiji asked, "You have eaten, haven't you?"

Nirmala replied, "What could I do! Why should I stop eating and drinking for anyone?"

Munshiji said, “I don’t know what has happened to him. I cannot understand anything. He is getting leaner and thinner, day-by-day. He stays in his room the whole day.”

Nirmala did not say anything; she kept thinking, dipping into the vast ocean of her worry. ‘What would have Mansaram comprehended from the sea-change in my attitude? Would he have wondered why I got angry when his father appeared? Would he have understood the reason for it, also? The poor boy was coming to eat, but I do not know from where this person burst into the scene? How shall I explain the secret to him? Is it even possible to explain it to him? Into what calamity have I fallen?’

In the morning, she woke up and busied herself with household work. Suddenly, at nine o’clock, Bhoongi came in to say, “Mansaram Babu is loading all his belongings on the carriage.”

Nirmala asked in confusion, “Loading… in the carriage! Where is he going?”

Bhoongi said, “I asked, so he said; ‘Now I will stay in school only.’”

Mansaram had got up early in the morning and gone to meet his school’s Principal. The arrangement was made even though the Principal had said, “There is no place here, there are applications of many boys, before I can consider yours.” However, when Mansaram had said, “If I will not get a place, then probably, I won’t be able to study and might not take the examination,” the Principal, then, had no other option, but to make room for him. There was hope that Mansaram would pass with a first division. Teachers were confident that he would make his school proud. How could the Principal ignore such a boy? He emptied his office room, and that is why, upon his return, Mansaram immediately started loading his luggage onto the carriage.

Munshiji said, “Why the hurry? Leave in two or four days. I want to arrange a good cook for you.”

Mansaram said, “The cook there makes very good food.”

Munshiji said, “Take care of your health. You should not lose your health because of your studies.”

Mansaram said, "Nobody can study there after nine o'clock and everybody has to follow a routine."

Munshiji said, "Why are you leaving the bedding behind? On what will you sleep?"

Mansaram said, "I am taking the blanket. I do not need the bedding."

Munshiji said, "Till the time the servant is loading your baggage, go and eat something. You did not eat anything last night also."

Mansaram said, "I will eat there only. I have told the cook to prepare food. I will get late if I eat here."

Jiyaram and Siyaram, who were at home, were also insisting that they would go with their brother.

Nirmala was trying to divert their attention by saying, "Small boys do not stay there. You will have to do all work yourself..."

All of a sudden, Rukmini appeared and said, "*Maharani*! Do you have a heart of stone? The boy did not eat at night and is going without eating anything and you are talking to the boys? You don't know him. Consider that he is not going to school, but taking exile. He will not return now. He is not one of those boys who forget a hurt incurred while playing. His hurt sets like stone, lining his heart."

Nirmala said in a desperate voice, "What shall I do, *Didiji*? He doesn't listen to anybody. You go and call him. He will come if you do so."

Rukmini said, "What has happened, that he is almost running away? He has never felt dejected before in this house. He had never liked any place, except his home. You must have said something to him or complained about him. Why are you sowing thorns for yourself? *Rani*, you will not be at ease after ruining the house."

Nirmala said, crying, "If I would have said anything, my tongue will split. Yes, I am defamed because I am a stepmother. I beg you, please go and call him back."

Rukmini said loudly, "Why don't you go and call him? Will you become less important? If he was your own, would you keep sitting?"

Nirmala's state was exactly like that of a wingless bird who wanted to fly on seeing an approaching snake, but it cannot fly, so, it jumps and falls down, fluttering its useless wings. Her heart was in torment, but she could not step outside.

In the meantime, both the brothers came inside and said, "*Bhaiyaji* has left."

Nirmala stood stock-still. She was a statue, with no life. The train of thoughts fled in the direction of Mansaram. 'Gone? He did not even come inside the house. He did not even meet me. He went away. So much hatred for me? Even if I meant nothing to him, what about his *Bua*? He should have come to meet her, at least? Oh, I was here. How would he step inside? I would have seen him! That is why he left.'

* * *

9

After Mansaram left, the house became desolate. Both the younger sons studied in the same school as their elder brother. Nirmala asked them everyday how Mansaram was. She hoped that he would come home on a holiday, but when the holidays passed by and he did not come, Nirmala started getting worried. She had prepared *moong dal laddu* for him. On Monday morning, she sent Bhoongi to school with the *laddus*. Bhoongi returned around nine o'clock with the *laddus* as Mansaram had sent all of them back.

Nirmala said, "Has he become better than before?"

Bhoongi said, "Not better, but weaker than before."

Nirmala said, "Is he feeling unwell?"

Bhoongi replied, "I did not ask, *Bahuji*, why should I lie? Yes, the servant over there is my brother-in-law. He was saying that 'Your *Babuji's* diet is nothing.' He gets up after having two chapattis, then doesn't eat the whole day. He keeps studying all the time."

Nirmala said, "Didn't you ask why he was returning the *laddus*?"

Bhoongi said, "I did not ask, *Bahuji*, why should I lie? He said 'Take it, there is no point keeping them here.' So, I brought them back."

Nirmala said, "He didn't say anything else? Didn't you ask why he didn't come yesterday? It was a holiday."

Bhoongi said, "*Bahuji*, it slipped out of my mind to ask him this. Why should I lie? Yes, he said that 'Now you must never come here and neither get anything for me and tell your *Bahuji* not to send me any letters. Do not send any messages through the boys, also.' And he said something which I am not able to repeat," Then she started crying.

Nirmala said, "What was it, tell me?"

Bhoongi said, "What should I say, *Bahuji*? He says 'My life is cursed!' He said this and cried."

Nirmala released the long, slow breath that had cooled her body. She felt as if her heart was sinking. Each part of her being was crying in deep, endless grief. She could not remain sitting there, so she went to her bed, lay down, covered her face and started weeping bitterly. Just one thought echoed in her mind, 'He also knows now!' Oh, what will happen now? The fire of doubt in which she was being burnt to a cinder, was now roaring with a hundredfold force. She did not worry about herself. What happiness would she desire deeply in life, when she had no hope of happiness? She had convinced herself by the thought that this was the repentance for deeds done in her past lives. Which man would be so shameless, so as to live in this state for many days? She had sacrificed her entire life and all her desires on the altar of duty. The heart would cry, but she had to appear happy, face wreathed with smiles. She had to talk pleasantly to the person whose face she did not want to see. Who could know the deeply felt pain and disgust she felt while embracing the body, whose touch felt like the cold touch of the snake? At that time, she wished that the earth would split open and swallow her. Till now, however, her farce was confined only to herself. She had left worrying about herself, but now the problem had become extremely terrifying. She could not bear to see Mansaram's pain with her own eyes. Her soul would tremble with fear when she thought of the effects of this accusation on a thoughtful, courageous boy like Mansaram. Now, she would no longer sit quietly, no matter how much doubt it might raise, no matter whether she might have to commit suicide. She was desperate to protect Mansaram. She decided to be bold and throw off the cover of shame and hesitation.

Every morning, once he had eaten his food, *Vakil Sahib* would always meet her before leaving for the court. It was now time for his arrival. Nirmala stood at the door waiting, thinking that he must be on his way. What had happened? He was going outside. He used to order for the carriage to be readied from inside, but it stood, ready. 'So he will not come today, but leave from outside! No, this will not happen,' she thought. She told Bhoongi, "Go and call *Babuji*. Say there is some urgent work . . . he should listen."

Munshiji was just about to leave. He came inside after getting the message, but did not enter the room and asked from a distance, "What is it? Tell me quickly as I have to go for some urgent work. A few minutes earlier, there was a letter from the Principal that Mansaram has got fever. It will be better to take him home for treatment. So, I will go to court from there only. Have you anything special to say?"

It was as if a thunderbolt had fallen upon Nirmala. She struggled with her tears just as she tried to speak – both were ready to flow. She was in shock and the turmoil was reflected in her lost, choked voice and the threatening torrent of tears. It was difficult to judge whether she would first speak or cry. At last, the tears flowed, overtaking the feeble voice that emerged. She barely managed to utter, "There is nothing special. Are you going there, now?"

Munshiji said, "I had asked the boys yesterday. They said that he was sitting and studying yesterday. They did not know what happened today."

Nirmala said, shaking with anger, "You are doing all this."

Munshiji frowned and said, "I am doing it? What am I doing?"

Nirmala said, "Ask your heart."

Munshiji said, "I thought he couldn't study with interest here, so there he would surely study with the boys. This wasn't something bad, and what else did I do?"

Nirmala said, "Think hard, had you sent him there only for this? You had nothing else in mind?"

Munshiji hesitated slightly, and to hide his weakness, he tried to smile and said, "What else could it be? You think over it yourself!"

Nirmala said, "All right, you are right. Now you be so kind as to bring him here today. If he stays there, his illness will get worse. The way *Didiji* can take care of him in his sickness, no one else can."

The next moment she said, bending her head down, "If you do not want to get him here because of me, then send me to my house. I will stay there comfortably."

Munshiji did not answer this. He went outside and in a second, the vehicle turned onto the road leading to the school. Oh Mind! You work so mysteriously and are so full of secrets and so impenetrable! How quickly you change colours? You are adept in this art. Even the fireworks wheel takes time to change colours, but you do not take a moment to change. Where there earlier was love, suspicion again resettled itself firmly.

He thought, 'Did he by any chance make an excuse?'

* * *

10

Mansaram remained plunged in deep anxiety for two days. Every now and then, he would remember his mother; neither food appealed to him nor was he interested in studying. He had changed completely. Two days had passed and in spite of staying in the boarding house, he had not done the homework given to him before he became a boarder. As a result, he had to stand on the bench. What had never happened before had occurred today. He had to bear this unbearable insult, also.

The third day, he was engrossed in these worries and was trying to explain to himself, 'In this wide world, is it only my mother who has died? Stepmothers are all of the same type. It is nothing new that is happening to me. Now I should work hard like a man, with redoubled efforts, and keep Mother and Father pleased, the way they need to be. This year if I get the scholarship, then I need not depend on home for anything. So many boys attain high designations just on their own strength. It is a man's duty to overcome obstacles and grasp opportunities that come his way. What will happen by crying and cursing destiny?'

In the meantime, Jiyaram came and stood there.

Mansaram asked about things were at home. "The new *Ammaji* must be really happy?"

Jiyaram said, "I don't know the state of her mind, but since you have come here, she has not eaten a single morsel. Whenever we see her, she is crying. However, she laughs in *Babuji's* presence. When you came here, I also packed my books in the evening. I wanted to come and stay here with you. That witch Bhoongi went and told *Ammaji*. *Babuji* was sitting and *Ammaji* snatched the books in front of him and cried, 'Who will stay in the house, if you will also leave? If you all are leaving the house because of me, then I will go somewhere else.' I was already angry, and when *Babuji* was not present, I became angry with her and said, 'Why will you go? This is your house. Stay here comfortably. We are the strangers. If we are not here, then you will be very comfortable.'"

Mansaram said, "Very well said! You said the right thing. She must have got even angrier and would have complained to *Babuji*."

Jiyaram said, "No, nothing of that sort happened. The poor thing sat on the ground and started crying. I also felt very bad for her and I started crying. She wiped my tears with her *sari* and said, 'Jiya, I swear and God is my witness, that I did not say a word to your *Babuji* regarding your brother. My destiny has a black mark on it and I am enduring it. Then I don't know what all she said. I couldn't understand it all. There was something about *Babuji*."

Mansaram asked, perplexed, "What did she say regarding *Babuji*? Do you remember anything?"

Jiyaram said, "I don't remember what she said. As if my memory is very good! But the meaning I could guess from her words was that she had to pretend in front of *Babuji* to keep him happy. She spoke of vice-virtues, but I could not follow what she meant as I could not understand what she was talking about. Now I am ready to believe that she did not want to send you here."

Mansaram said, "You do not understand the meaning hidden in these moves. They are very deep and clever strategies."

Jiyaram said, "It may be according to you, but not according to me."

Mansaram said, "When you cannot understand geometry, then how will you understand these matters? You remember that night, when she had come to call me for dinner, and I was ready to go on her request? At that time, immediately after seeing *Babuji*, she changed her behaviour completely. Can I ever forget that?"

Jiyaram said, "This is what I also cannot understand. Yesterday, when I went back from here, she started asking me about your state. I said, 'He was saying that he will never set foot in the house again.' I did not lie. You had said this to me. On hearing this, she started crying bitterly. I really repented at having said it. Time and again, she would say, 'Will he leave the house because of me? Is he so angry with me? He left and did not meet me also! The food was ready, but he did not come to eat. Alas! How can I tell him, what kind of calamity I face?' Just then, *Babuji* came in. She immediately wiped her eyes and went to him, smiling. I cannot understand this matter at all. Today, she requested me earnestly to get you along with me. Today I am going to pull you out and take you home. In two days, she has become so thin. When you see her, you will pity her. So, you will come, won't you?"

Mansaram did not reply. His legs were trembling. Jiyaram ran on hearing the attendance bell; but he lay on the bench, and took such a long breath as if he had not breathed for a long time. Words of unbearable pain escaped his lips, "Alas! God!" Apart from this name, he felt his life was without a foundation, worthless. Who could imagine that this single breath had so much despair, such sensitivity, such compassion, and was filled with such needy prayer? Now he had understood the whole mystery, and time and again, his oppressed heart would cry out in pain. 'Alas, God! Such a terrible accusation!'

Can a calamity bigger than this be imagined in one's life? Can anything meaner than this be imagined in this world? Till now, no father must have laid such a heartless accusation on his son. Such a son, whose character was praised by everyone, who was regarded as an ideal for other boys, who never let profane thoughts anywhere near him – on him, such an awful blemish! Mansaram felt as though his heart was bursting.

The next bell also rang. The boys came to their rooms, but Mansaram, resting his face between his hands, was staring fixedly at the ground, as if all of him had drowned, as if he could not show his face to anybody. He would be marked absent in school, he would be fined, but he was not worried by these things. When he had been robbed of everything, what fear was left for these small, trivial matters? 'If I live even after such a horrible accusation has been laid on me, then I curse my life!' he thought, finally.

In that grief-stricken state, he cried, "Mother, where are you? Your son, whom you loved dearly, faces a terrible dilemma. His father is running a knife across his own son's neck. Alas! Where are you?"

Mansaram calmed himself and started thinking, 'Why am I being doubted? What is the reason? What did he perceive in me that caused this doubt? He is my father, not my enemy, who would blame me so easily without any reason. He must have surely heard or seen something. He loved me so much. He would not eat without me, and he has become my enemy. This cannot happen without any reason.'

'All right, which day was the seed of distrust sown? The decision of putting me in the boarding house happened quite late. That night, when he came to my room to give me a test, that day his mood was different and he was angry. What happened that day which he had disliked? I had gone to ask my new Mother for something to eat. *Babuji* was also sitting there. Yes, now I remember, that very moment his face went red with anger. From the very day, new *Amma* stopped studying with me. If I knew that father did not like me visiting the house, talking with *Ammaji* and teaching her, then would this situation have arisen? And new *Amma*! What must she be going through?'

Till now, Mansaram had not thought about Nirmala. His hair stood on end as he thought about Nirmala. 'Alas, how will her simple loving heart bear this shock? Oh! I was under such illusion. I took her love as her skilful artifice. How did I know that she had to behave harshly with me in order to quell father's suspicion? Aah! I have been so unjust with her. Her state must be even worse than mine. I came here, but where will she go? Jiya says that she hasn't eaten for two days and cries all the time. How will I go there to explain? Why is she taking this calamity upon herself for this unfortunate wretch? Why does she ask about me all the time? Why does she call me home again and again? How should I say, Mother, I have no complaint against you. My heart is clear and feels no anger towards you?'

'She would be sitting and crying right now. What a great misfortune all this is! What is happening to *Babuji*? Did he marry for this? Did he bring her home just to kill her? Has he plucked this tender flower, just to crush it?'

'How will she be freed from this situation? How will the face of that innocent lady be radiant again? She is being punished just because of her loving behaviour towards me. This is the award she is receiving for her gentleness. Will I just keep sitting and watch her bearing the cruel blows? I will have to sacrifice my life, if not to defend my self-respect, but in respect of the safety of her life. There is no other way of deliverance. Ah! What desires I had in my heart! I will have to now turn them into ashes. A chaste women is being suspected, and that too because of me. I will have to protect her with my life, this is my duty. This is real heroism. Mother, I will wash out this stain with my blood. My welfare and yours lies in this.'

He was plunged in these thoughts throughout the day. In the evening, both his brothers came to request him to come home with them.

Jiyaram pleaded, "Why don't you come with us? My dear brother, come, let's go."

Mansaram replied, "I am not free that I can go with you, whenever you want."

Siyaram said, "And anyway, it is Sunday tomorrow."

Mansaram said, "I have work on Sunday, also."

Jiyaram said, "All right then, will you come tomorrow?"

Mansaram said, "No, I have to go for a match tomorrow."

Siyaram said, "*Ammaji* is making *moong laddu*. You will not get even one, if you will not be there. We will eat the *laddu*s together, Jiya, and will not give him."

Jiyaram said, "*Bhaiya*, if you will not come tomorrow, then probably *Ammaji* will come here."

Mansaram said, "Really! No, why will she do this? If she comes here, then it will be a great problem. Tell her that I had gone to watch a match."

Jiyaram said, "Why will I start lying? We will say that you were sitting and sulking. Just watch, will I bring her along or not?"

Siyaram said, "I will say that you did not go to study today. You were just lying there, sleeping."

Mansaram got rid of the messengers by promising to visit the next day. When both of them had left, he again plunged in worry. He slept fitfully the entire night, turning this way and that. The day of vacation also passed – he just sat there, fearing that *Ammaji* might really come along. On hearing a vehicle rattling by, his heart would thud. Had she arrived?

There was a small dispensary in the boarding house. A doctor used to sit there for an hour in the evening. If any boy was sick, he would give him medicine. Today when he sat there, Mansaram, pondering over something, the doctor approached him. He knew Mansaram very well. As he saw him, the doctor said with surprise, "What has happened to you? It looks as though you are melting away. Hope you haven't developed a taste for the bazaar food, have you? What has happened to you? Come over here!"

Mansaram smiled and said, "I have a disease called 'life'. Do you have any medicine for it?"

The doctor said, "I need to take a few tests. Your face has changed totally. You cannot be recognised anymore."

Saying this, he caught Mansaram's hand, and examined his chest, back, eyes and tongue, one by one. Then he said in a worried voice, "I will meet *Vakil Sahib* today. You have got phthisis. All symptoms point towards it."

Mansaram said very eagerly, "In how many days will my life be completely finished, Doctor?"

The astonished doctor said, "What are you saying? I will meet *Vakil Sahib* and advise him to send you to a hill station. God willing, you will get well very soon. The disease is only in its first stage now."

Mansaram said, "Then there will be a delay of a year or two. I cannot wait that long. Listen, I do not have phthisis or any other ailment. Please don't uselessly bother *Babuji* with this. At the moment, I have a headache. Give me some medicine, something that will help me sleep. I haven't slept for two nights."

The doctor opened the cupboard that housed poisonous medicines, and poured a little out of a bottle. He gave this to Mansaram, who said, "This seems to be a poison. If somebody drinks it, will he die?"

The doctor said, "No, he will not die, but surely his head will spin."

Mansaram said, "Is there any medicine here, which kills the person who consumes it, immediately?"

The doctor said, "Not one or two, there are many such medicines. This bottle you are looking at? If just one drop of it enters the stomach, it will be fatal. Death will be instant."

Mansaram said, "Doctor, those who consume poison, they must suffer greatly."

The doctor said, "All the poisons do not cause suffering. There are a few that kill a man instantly. This bottle has a poison that renders the person unconscious. Then he does not regain consciousness ever."

Mansaram thought, 'Then it is so easy to take one's life. Why are people so scared? How will I get this bottle? If I get to know the name of the medicine and want to buy it from a druggist in the town, he will never give it to me. Oh, there is no problem in getting hold of it. At least, I learnt how easy it is to kill oneself.' Mansaram became very happy, as if he had been awarded a prize. His heart had been relieved of its burden. The clouds of worry that were rolling just over his head dispersed. After several months, his mind felt light and his pace quickened. The boys were going to the theatre. They had taken permission from the supervisor. Mansaram also went with them. He was so happy it seemed as though there was no creature happier than him in the entire world. He was in splits of laughter watching the mimicry in the theatre. He was the first one to clap and call 'once more' out loud. He would openly enjoy listening to the song and cry, 'Oh ho ho' out loud. The spectators' eyes would turn towards him again and again, wondering who was raising such a hue and cry. The actors of the theatre would also stare at him; they were eager to know who this admirer and sentimental person was. His friends were amazed at his indiscipline. He was a calm and serious boy. Why was he laughing so much? Why was there no limit to his amusement?

On returning from the theatre at two o'clock at night, his elevated spirits did not subside. He toppled over a boy's cot, closed the doors of many boys' rooms from the outside, and laughed, listening to them knocking inside. Even the Secretary of the boarding house got up from his sleep, hearing the hue and cry, and he expressed his regret at Mansaram's mischief. Who knew that a strong revolt was going on, deep in his heart? The pitiless blow of suspicion had crushed his shame and self-respect. He did not fear even the shadow of rejection and insult. This was no happy amusement; it was the tender, crushed cry of a soul in torment. When all the other boys had gone to sleep, then he also lay on his cot, but sleep did not come. After a moment he got up and packed all his books in his trunk. He thought, 'When I have to die, then what will happen by studying? A life which has such hindrances and such tortures, surely, death is far better than this.'

He kept thinking and soon it was dawn. He had not slept for a single moment for three nights now. This time when he got up his legs were shaking and his head was spinning. His eyes burnt, and the entire body was turning lifeless. The sun had risen, morning was fast approaching, and he did not possess even that much energy, that he could get up and wash his hands and feet. All of a sudden, he saw Bhoongi, along with a servant, coming towards him with something tied in a handkerchief. His heart became still. He thought wildly, 'Oh God? She has come! Now what will happen? Bhoongi must have not come alone. The buggy must be certainly standing outside?' Here he was not even able to get up, but on seeing Bhoongi, he ran to her and said in a nervous voice, "Has *Ammaji* also come?" Only when he was told that *Ammaji* had not come did his mind become calm.

Bhoongi said, "*Bhaiya*! Why didn't you come yesterday? *Bahuji* kept waiting for you. Why are you angry with her? She says that she didn't complain at all about you. Today she was crying and she asked me to bring these sweets to you and say, 'Why did you leave the house because of me?' Where should I keep this *thali*?"

Mansaram said dryly, "Slam it on your head, you witch! You have come with sweets! I warn you, don't ever come here again. Here, with a gift! Go and tell her, it's your house, you stay there. Tell her; here he lives in great comfort. He eats well and enjoys himself. Are you listening, say it clearly in front of *Babuji*, do you understand? I am not afraid of anyone; they can do whatever they feel like, so that no wish is left unfulfilled in their hearts. If they say so, I can go to Allahabad, Lucknow or Calcutta. For me, any other town is like Banaras. What is there for me here?"

Bhoongi said, "*Bhaiya*, keep the sweets, otherwise she will die crying. Believe me, she will die crying."

Mansaram said, suppressing the rising tears, "I don't care even if she dies! What great comfort has she given me that I should repent her death! They have destroyed me. Tell her not to send any messages to me. I need nothing."

Bhoongi said, "*Bhaiya*, you used to say, I eat a lot here and enjoy myself, but your body isn't half of what you were. You are so weak now, not even half the weight of what you were before."

Mansaram said, "Your eyes deceive you. See if I don't become fat like an ox in two or three days. Tell her to stop this weeping and wailing. Wait and see what I do if I hear that she cries and doesn't eat! When I have been turned out of the house, then she should live peacefully. Here she tries to show she cares! I have studied such female characters very deeply."

Bhoongi went away. Mansaram had started feeling cold while talking to her. To keep up this act, the extent to which he had to suppress his feelings had been unbearable for him. His self-esteem was compelling him to end this ill-treatment as soon as possible, but what would its result be? Will Nirmala be able to endure this blow? Till now, while imagining his death he had never thought of any other person, but now, all of a sudden, he realised that his life was also tied to the life-thread of another's. Nirmala would think that it was her brutality that took his life. Would her heart not burst thinking thus? Her life was still in danger. Would a gentlewoman, trapped in the cruel hands of suspicion, be able to live for many days if she considered herself a murderess?

Mansaram lay on the cot and covered himself with a bed sheet, but he was still shivering, right to his heart. A few moments later, he was running high temperature and lost consciousness. In this unconscious state, he had different kind of dreams. He would start and wake after every few minutes; his eyes would open, and he would again faint.

He was startled to hear *Vakil Sahib's* voice all of a sudden. Yes, it was *Vakil Sahib's* voice. He threw off the cover, got off the bed and stood on the ground. A strong feeling arose in his heart – he would die at this moment, how truly happy his father would be. Probably that was why he was there; to see how much longer he had to die. *Vakil Sahib* caught his hand to support him, and said, "How are you, boy? Why didn't you keep lying down? Lie down, why did you stand up?"

Mansaram replied, "I am very well. You have been troubled in vain."

Munshiji did not reply. Tears rose to his eyes seeing the condition of his boy. That well-built boy who would gladden one's heart on sight was now terribly lean and thin. He had become so weak in five to six days that it was difficult to recognise him. Munshiji slowly made him lie on the cot and covered him carefully with the bed sheet. He started thinking about what should be done now. He wondered whether the boy would slip away, out of his hands. On thinking about this, he was so overcome with grief that he sat on the stool and cried bitterly. Mansaram was also crying, with his face covered with the bed sheet. A few days ago, the father's heart would swell with pride on seeing him, but today, even on seeing his horrible condition, he was juggling with the merits and demerits of taking him home. 'Can the treatment not be carried out here? I will sit here all the time. The doctor is also here. There will be no problem,' he thought, as he perceived hurdles after hurdles in taking him home. The biggest fear was that there Nirmala would sit next to him all the time, and he will not be able to stop it. This was unbearable for him.

In the meantime, the Secretary entered the room and said, "I think it is best that you take him along with you. You have the vehicle, so there won't be any discomfort. Proper care would not be possible here."

Munshiji said, "Yes, I had come here with this thought. But his condition seems to be critical. If there is the slightest carelessness, I fear delirium."

The Secretary said, "There will definitely be some difficulty in taking him from here. But you can understand better that the comfort he would get at home isn't possible here. Apart from this, it is against the rules to keep any sick boy here."

Munshiji said, "If you say so, I'll take permission from the Principal. I don't think it is advisable to move him from here in this condition."

The Secretary heard the Principal's name mentioned, so he assumed that the Munshiji was threatening him. He got annoyed and said, "The Principal doesn't do anything against the rules. How can I take such a big responsibility?"

Munshiji's quandary persisted. 'Now what will happen? Will I have to take him home? The excuse to keep him here was the doubt that his sickness might be aggravated in taking him home. There is no excuse for taking him from here. Maybe I could keep him in the hospital. Whoever will hear of this will say that he was kept in the hospital to save the doctor's fee – but now, there was no other option left. If the Secretary was ready to take a bribe, then probably he would take two to four month's salary worth, but do people of principles have such intelligence and cleverness? If at this moment, some person would suggest some such objection due to which Mansaram need not be taken home, then he would be obliged to him, lifelong. There was no time to think, also. The Secretary was hovering around him, like the devil himself. Perforce Munshiji called both the servants and they started picking up Mansaram. He was semi-conscious and got startled. He uttered, "What is it? Who is it?"

Munshiji said, "No one, Son. I want to take you home. Come, I'll pick you up."

Mansaram said, "Why are you taking me home? I will not go there."

Munshiji said, "You cannot stay here. It is against the rules."

Mansaram said, "Whatever may happen, but I won't go there. Take me somewhere else, under a tree, in some hut. Keep me wherever you want to, but don't take me home."

The Secretary said to Munshiji, "Don't be bothered by what he says. He is not in his senses."

Mansaram said, "Who is not in his senses? Am I not in my senses? Do I abuse anybody? Do I bite? Why am I not in my senses?

Leave me lying here only, whatever will happen will happen here itself. If I have to go, then take me to the hospital. I will stay there. If I have to live, I'll live. If I have to die, I will die, but I will not go back to home in any condition."

After gaining strength from this insistence, Munshiji again started requesting the Secretary. The Secretary was a man of principles, and did not listen to any pleading or reason. He asked Munshiji that if it is was an infectious disease, and it spread to other boys, then who would be answerable to them? Munshiji's court-like legal arguments were defeated by this one reason.

At last, Munshiji said to Mansaram, "Son, why are you refusing to come home? There will be all sorts of comfort." Munshiji said this because he had to, but he was scared that Mansaram might really agree. He was looking for an excuse to keep Mansaram in the hospital, with the complete responsibility of this decision resting on Mansaram. This had happened in front of the Secretary, he was witness to the fact that Mansaram was adamant upon going to the hospital. Munshiji had no share in the blame, if any was laid.

Mansaram said with irritation, "No, no! Hundred times – no! I will not go back home. Take me to the hospital and stop all the family members from coming to see me. Nothing has happened to me. I am not sick at all. You leave me – I can walk on my own feet." He got up and went towards the door like one intoxicated, but his legs staggered. If Munshiji would not have caught, he would be badly hurt. With the help of both servants, Munshiji took him to the *baggi* and made him sit inside.

The vehicle trundled towards the hospital; whatever Munshiji wished would happen, happened. Even in the moment of grief, his mind was dissatisfied. The son was going to the hospital by his own wish. Was this not proof that he had no love for his home? Did this also not prove that Mansaram was innocent? He had doubted him without reason.

However, after sometime, a feeling of depression overtook his mind, in place of the satisfaction he had felt earlier. He was taking his dearly beloved son to the hospital and not to his home. His huge home did not have a place for his own son, when his condition was dire, and his life was hanging by a thread. What irony!

After a moment, unbidden, suddenly, a question wormed its way into Munshiji's mind, 'Had Mansaram, by any chance, gauged my feelings? Is that the reason why he hates his home so much? If this is so, then it will be disastrous.'

Just dwelling on this grievous misfortune, Munshiji's hair stood on end and his heart palpitated. The shock went thudding, straight to his heart. If this was the reason of the fever, then God alone was his saviour. At this time, Munshiji's state was pathetic. He comprehended, for the first time, just how the fire he had lit for his own cold, shivering hands was now spreading in his whole house. His mind was frightened by the tender pity, repentance and doubt welling up inside him – if his secret crying could emerge, then those who listened would have been moved to tears. If his tears flowed, they would flow endlessly. He looked with fatherly love and affection at the pale face of his son; driven by pain, he embraced him and cried so much that his breathing and crying turned into hiccups.

The hospital gate came into view.

* * *

11

When Munshi Totaram reached home in the evening after attending court, Nirmala asked him. "You met him? How is he?" Munshiji saw that there was not the slightest sign of sorrow or worry on Nirmala's face. She had dressed up and worn more jewellery than she usually did. She would usually not wear a necklace, but today it adorned her neck. She did not prefer the long, dangling earrings, but today, the *jhumar* were also shining beneath the fine silk *sari* and above the black hair. Munshiji turned his face away and said, "He is sick, what else shall I tell you?"

Nirmala said, "You had gone to get him here."

Munshiji said irritably, "When he did not want to come, could I have forcibly picked him up and brought him here? I urged him to come home but mere mention of the word 'home' would make his fever rise. He stubbornly insisted that he would die there, but would not go home. At last, I was helpless and I had to take him to the hospital. What else could I do!"

By this time, Rukmini also arrived and stood at the verandah. She said, "He is stubborn by birth. He will not come here no matter what, and wait and see, he will also not get well there."

Munshiji said timidly, "Sister, it would be very good if you went and stayed there for two or four days. He will be consoled by your presence. My dear sister, please accept my request. If he is alone, he will cry his life away. He just cries and repeats 'Alas, *Amma*! Alas, *Amma*!' I am going there, please come with me. He is not in a good state. Sister, he doesn't have that appearance anymore. Let's see, what God does now."

Saying this, tears ran down Munshiji's face, but Rukmini said in a firm voice, "I am ready to go. If my staying there will save my dear one's life, then I will go, even if I have to walk on my head. But keep this in your mind, he will not recover there. I know him very well. He doesn't have any disease. It is just the shock of being turned out of his house. This pain has appeared in the form of fever. Not only one, you can give him one lakh medicines and even if you can show him to the Civil Surgeon, nothing will have any effect."

Munshiji said, "Sister, who turned him out of the house? I sent him there, because I was concerned about his studies."

Rukmini said, "You may have sent him for whichever reason you had, but he has been hurt by it. I am nowhere in the picture, and I don't have the right to say anything. You are the master. Your wife is the mistress. I am merely an unfortunate widow who survives on your food. Who will listen to me and who cares about what I say? But this much I have to say. Mansa will get well only when he comes to the house and when your heart is the same as it was in the earlier days."

Saying this, Rukmini went away from there. She knew and understood the secret of the temperaments and acts played out before her experienced eyes, and all the anger was poured out only on innocent Nirmala. This time, too, she barely managed to stop herself from saying that till the time the lady of the house stays here, the state of the house will go from bad to worse. She said nothing more, but the implication was not hidden from Munshiji. After she left, Munshiji bent his head and started thinking. At this moment, he was so angry with himself that he wanted to batter his head against the wall and end his life. Why had he married? What was the need to have got married? God had given him, not one, but three sons. He was close to fifty years of age, then, why did he get married? Was God willing to destroy him by using this excuse? He lifted his head and saw the beautiful, clear hearted Nirmala, still as a statue, and left for the hospital. Gazing upon Nirmala's flawless beauty had calmed his mind. After days, he felt this peaceful.

Can a heart, torn apart with love, remain peaceful and unmoved in such a state? No, never. A wounded heart cannot be concealed by skill. He was extremely agitated over how weak and misguided his mind had been. Without reason, he had let doubt enter his mind, and such a terrible mishap had occurred. In his mind, there was no fear regarding Mansaram's feelings. However, in its place, a new doubt had cropped up. 'Had Mansaram sensed it? Knowing so, is this why he persistently refuses to come home? If he has sensed it, then it will be a grave misfortune.' Just thinking about it made his heart quail with fear. His body felt loose, and his bones seemed to move, in order to quell the disturbing interior uproar. Panicking, he told the coachman to speed up. Today after many days, the black cloud, with its tentacles clutching his heart had burst, and the light inside was jostling and impatient to emerge from the darkness. He put his head out to see whether the coachman was asleep as he had never felt the horse was going so slowly before.

On reaching the hospital, he rushed towards Mansaram. He saw that the doctor was standing in front of him, immersed in worry. Munshiji got very nervous and his hands and feet froze. He could not utter a word. Then he spoke in a choked, heavy voice, with the greatest difficulty. "What is his condition like, Doctor?" Saying this, he started crying. The doctor took a moment to reply. At this delay, his heart sank to his feet, and he slumped on to the cot, put the boy's head on his lap and started whimpering and sobbing, like boys do. Mansaram's body was burning like a hot, iron griddle. Mansaram opened his eyes once. Oh, what a terrible and helpless look it was. Munshiji embraced the boy and asked the doctor, "What is the state, Sahib? Why are you silent?"

The doctor said in a sceptical tone, "Whatever his condition is, it is plain for you to see. He has a temperature of 106 degrees, what else can I tell you? The fever seems to be mounting. I am doing whatever I can. God is our saviour. Since you've been gone, I haven't moved from here. I was not able to eat my food, also. His condition is so delicate that you can't say what will happen in the next minute. This is a very high fever, he is unconscious. Time and again, he gets a fit-like delirium. Did anyone in the house say anything to him? He just says '*Ammaji*! *Ammaji*! Where are you?' This is the only thing he utters."

While Doctor Sahib was saying this, Mansaram got up and sat up, pushing Munshiji from the cot. He said in a high, delirious voice, "Why do you scold? Kill me. Kill me. Kill me right now! You cannot find a sword? Do you have a rope noose? I will put it around my neck! Aahh! *Ammaji*, where are you?" He became unconscious and fell down.

For a moment, Munshiji gazed at Mansaram's lifeless form with grief-stricken eyes. Then, he suddenly caught hold of Doctor Sahib's hand and requested him with immense humility, "Doctor Sahib, save this boy. For God's sake, save him, otherwise I'll be completely destroyed. I am not a rich man, but I'll do whatever you'll say, only save him. Call the best doctors and take their opinion. I'll pay for all the expenses. I cannot bear to see his condition like this. Alas, my good, worthy son!"

Doctor Sahib said gently, "Babu Sahib, I'm telling you the truth. I'm doing all that I possibly can. Now you are asking me to take suggestions from other doctors. I'll call Dr. Lahiri, Dr. Bhatia and Dr. Mathur. I'll call Vinayak Shastri also, but I don't want to give you false assurances – his condition is critical."

Distressed even more, Munshiji started crying, "No, Doctor Sahib, do not utter such words. His enemies should be in a critical condition. God should not be so angry with me. Send trunk calls to the doctors of Calcutta and Bombay. I'll be your slave for the rest of your life. He is the brightest lamp of my family. He is the basis of my life. My heart feels like it is bursting. Give him some medicine, which will make him conscious. Let me hear with my own ears what he has to say. Let me hear what is troubling him. Alas! My child!"

Doctor Sahib said, "Try to console your heart. You are a mature man. Lamenting and gathering an army of doctors will not bear any result. Sit quietly, while I call the people from the city. Let's see what they say? Please stay calm don't lose your composure."

Munshiji said, "All right, Doctor Sahib! Now I'll not say anything, I will not even open my mouth. You do whatever you want. The boy is in your hands. Only you can protect him. I just want that he regains his senses, recognises me, and is able to understand my words. Is there any medicine like *sanjivini buti*? Then, I would say a few words to him."

Saying this, Munshiji lost his composure and said to Mansaram, "Son, open your eyes a little. How are you feeling? I'm sitting next to you, crying. I have no complaints against you. I have nothing in my heart against you, it is clear."

Doctor said, "You have again started talking nonsense. Oh, Sahib, you are not a boy, you are mature. Please be patient."

Munshiji said, "All right, Doctor Sahib, now I'll not speak. This was a mistake. You are free to do what you want to. I have left everything upon you. Is there any way, by which I can make him understand that my heart is clear? You tell him, Doctor Sahib, tell him that his unfortunate father is sitting and crying. His heart has no complaints against you. It was only a misunderstanding that has been cleared now. That's all, just say this much. I do not want anything else. I am sitting quietly. I will not open my mouth, but please will you tell him this much?"

Doctor Sahib said, "For God's sake, Babu Sahib, be patient, otherwise I'll be compelled to tell you to go home. I am going to the office to write letters to the doctors. Sit here quietly."

Heartless doctor! Which father will be patient after seeing his son in such a terrible state? Munshiji was a man with a serious nature. He also knew that there was no point in crying like this, but it was also impossible for him to remain seated quietly at this moment. If the disease had a natural cause, then he would have been quiet, he would explain to others, he would call the doctors himself. However, could he be patient even now after knowing that the fire was set by him, purely by him? Can any father be so hardhearted? He cursed himself! He was wondering why this wrong feeling had occurred to him. Without any definite proof, how had he imagined such a terrible scenario? All right, then what should he have done in that situation? He could not decide whether he could have done anything else, other than what he had done. Realistically speaking, tying the marriage knot had been like chopping off his own feet. Yes, this was the root cause of all the chaotic misfortune.

He thought further, 'But I did not do anything different. All men and women marry. They spend their life happily. We marry, keeping bliss and comfort in mind. In my neighbourhood, hundreds of men have married twice, thrice, four times, even seven times, and are much elder than me. They lived comfortably while they lived. None of them died before their wives did. After marrying a second and third time, they again became widowers. If their state would have been like mine, then who would want to marry again? My father married at the age of fifty-five and he was sixty when I was born. Yes, it is true that there is a lot of difference between then and now. Earlier, women were not literate. A woman worshipped her husband, no matter what kind of person he was. This was the case

– that men behaved shamelessly even after being aware of everything; this must be the reason, for sure. When a man cannot be happy with an older lady, then how can a girl be happy with an old man? But I wasn't that old. Nobody, after seeing me, will say I am more than forty. Whatever it is, after youth has passed, one has to be somewhat shameless after marrying a young girl, there is no doubt in it. Women are shy by nature. It is totally different for promiscuous women, but generally, a woman is calmer than a man. After getting married to the husband of her choice, she may joke around with other men, but her heart remains pure. But after marrying a mismatch, even though she will not raise her eyes to even look at anybody, she will always be sad. The former is a strong wall; it will not break when an iron rod is used against it. The latter is a weak wall and will stand only till the rod doesn't smash against it.'

Pondering over these thoughts, Munshiji dozed off. These thoughts immediately flowed into a dream. He saw his first wife standing in front of Mansaram. She was saying, "Husband, what have you done? You killed my son so cruelly. He, whom I had nourished with my blood, you laid such a terrible accusation on him, my noble boy! Now what are you being sorry for? You washed your hands off him. I'm snatching him from your merciless hands and taking him away with me. You were never so suspicious! Did you embrace suspicion soon after you got married? Such a hard blow to such a tender heart! Such a terrible blemish! Anyone who lives after bearing such an insult would be very shameless. My son cannot bear it." Saying this, she picked up the boy and walked away! Munshiji was crying as he tried to snatch Mansaram from her, when his eyes opened he saw Dr. Lahiri, Dr. Bhatia and half a dozen other doctors, standing in front of him.

* * *

12

Three days had passed and Munshiji had not come home. Rukmini would go to the hospital morning and evening to see Mansaram. Both the boys would also go, but how would Nirmala go? Her feet were shackled. She would be anxious to know how Mansaram was. If she asked Rukmini, all she heard were taunts, and on asking the boys, she would get to hear nonsensical, irrelevant chatter. She was growing desperate to go herself and see him once. She feared that suspicion would have rendered Munshiji's love for his son cold, and wondered whether his narrow-mindedness was hindering Mansaram's recovery? Doctors are nobody's relatives, they just want money – they did not care if the dead went to hell or heaven. She had the strong desire to go to the hospital and give a bag with one thousand rupees in it to the doctor and say, "Save him, this packet is a gift," but she neither had the money nor the courage. Still, if she could reach there even now, Mansaram would get well. The care and concern he needed, was not being given him there, otherwise would the fever not have abated in three days? This was not a physical fever, but a mental one. The fever would be gone when the mind was at peace. If she sat there the whole night and Munshiji would not take it otherwise, then surely Mansaram would believe his father's heart was clear, and then he would recover quickly, but was this possible? Would Munshiji be able to remain happy seeing her there? Does his heart still harbour some suspicion? When he was leaving for the hospital, it felt as though he was repenting his mistake. It should not happen that she should go there and the flames of suspicion would rise again and become the reason for his son's death.

Three days passed, overlain by this confusing dilemma. Neither was food cooked in the house nor did anyone eat anything. Puris would be bought from the market for the boys; Rukmini and Nirmala would go to sleep hungry. Neither felt like eating.

On the fourth day, Jiyaram returned from school and came home after a visit to the hospital. Nirmala asked, "Oh, *Bhaiya*, did you go to the hospital? What is his state today? Did your brother get up or not?"

Jiya said in a weepy tone, "*Ammaji,* today he didn't even say anything or move at all. He lay quietly on the cot. He beat the cot with his hands and feet forcefully."

Nirmala's face went pale. She asked nervously, "Was your *Babuji* there?"

Jiyaram said, "Of course, he was there. Today he was crying a lot."

Nirmala's heart started beating heavily. "The doctors were there, weren't they?"

Jiyaram said, "The doctors were also there. They were discussing something. The senior-most one, the Civil Surgeon, was saying in English that the patient's body needed some fresh blood. At this, *Babuji* said 'Take all the blood you need from my body.' At this, the Civil Surgeon laughed and said, 'Your blood will not do. We need blood of some young men.' At last, he injected some medicine in *Bhaiya's* arm with a syringe. The needle must not have been less than four fingers wide, but *Bhaiya* did not move one bit. I was so scared that I closed my eyes."

Great, noble resolutions are born in fury. On one hand, Nirmala was becoming frail due to fear and on the other hand, there was the glow on her face accompanying the firm, unshakeable decision in her mind. She had taken the decision of giving fresh blood from her body. If her blood could save Mansaram's life, then with great happiness, she would happily give up even the last drop. Now, it would not matter what anybody thought, she would not care anymore. She said to Jiyaram, "You run and get an *ekka*. I will go to the hospital."

Jiyaram said, "There will be many people there at this moment. Let it be dark."

Nirmala said, "No. You get it right now."

Jiyaram said, "What if *Babuji* gets angry?"

Nirmala said, "Let him. You go right now and get the *ekka*."

Jiyaram said, "I will say that *Ammaji* had asked for the carriage."

Nirmala said, "Tell him that."

While Jiyaram had gone to fetch the carriage, Nirmala quickly combed her hair and made a bun, wore fresh clothes, wore her ornaments, ate paan and stood at the door.

Rukmini was sitting in her room. Seeing Nirmala apparently ready to go out, she said, "Where are you going, *Bahu*?"

Nirmala said, "I'm going to the hospital."

Rukmini said, "What will you do there?"

Nirmala said, "Nothing, what can I do? God is the one who does things. I want to see him."

Rukmini said, "I'm telling you not to go."

Nirmala said softly and politely, "This time I will go, *Didiji*. Jiyaram was saying that his state was not good right now. My conscience cannot agree and I feel restless. Will you come along?"

Rukmini said, "I have already seen him. Now, just understand, there is hope for saving his life only when fresh blood is provided to him. Who will give him blood and why? There is a fear for his life in that also."

Nirmala said, "That is why I am going. Will my blood not work?"

Rukmini said, "Why not, the blood of a young person is required, but it's better to throw Mansaram in the water than to save his life with your blood."

The *ekka* came and stood at the door. Nirmala and Jiyaram both sat in it and the *ekka* went its way.

Rukmini stood at the door and kept crying for a long time. Today for the first time, she felt pity for Nirmala. If she could have, she would have kept her tied. She was not able to see where her compassion and sympathy took her, whereas it was clear now, as invisibly in the future as it lay, to Rukmini. Aah! This was all instigated by ill-fortune. This was the path of destruction.

When Nirmala reached the hospital, lamps had been lit. The doctors had left after giving their advice and opinions. Mansaram's fever had abated slightly. He was staring at the door. He was gazing at the open sky as if he was waiting for God to arrive. He did not know where he was, from which direction he might arrive; he had no knowledge of this.

Suddenly, his gaze fell upon Nirmala. He sat up with a shock. His meditative state was disturbed. His lost consciousness came to life again. He was now aware of his situation and condition, like one recalls some long forgotten thing. He looked steadily at Nirmala and turned his face away.

All of a sudden, Munshiji spoke in a loud voice, "Why have you come here?"

Nirmala was shocked speechless. What could she say about what she had come here to do? Was she able to reply to such a simple, straight question? What had she come here to do? Simple as it seemed, who would have confronted such a complicated question? A member of a family is sick – she was here to see him; was this not clear without being asked about? Then, why the question?

She stood like a person struck dumb, as if she had become senseless. She had judged from the two boys' narration of their father's sorrow and repentance that his heart was clear now. This, she now realised, was only an illusion. Yes, it was a great illusion. If she had known that the downpour of tears had not extinguished the fire of suspicion, then she would never have come here. She would die in torment, but she would not have stepped out of the house.

Munshiji again asked the same question, "Why have you come here?"

Nirmala replied, fearlessly, "What have you come here to do?" Munshiji's nostrils flared in anger. Angrily, he got up from the cot and caught her hand. Agitatedly he said, "There is no need for you to come here. When I call you, then you come, understood?"

Oh! What misfortune occurred! Mansaram, who could not even move, stood up and fell at Nirmala's feet, crying, "*Ammaji*, you needlessly took such pains for this unfortunate one. I will never forget your love. I pray to God that I take birth from your womb in my next birth, so that I can pay back my debt to you. God knows that I haven't considered you as my stepmother. I always took you as my mother. You are not much older than me, but you were in the place of my mother, and I always looked upon you as such . . . .

Now I cannot speak, *Ammaji*, forgive me! This is our last meeting." Nirmala, controlling the flow of her tears, said, "Why do you say such things? You will be fine in a few days."

Mansaram said in a faint voice, "Now there is no desire to live or strength to speak."

Saying this, Mansaram lost all his strength and lay there on the floor. Looking at her husband with fearless eyes, Nirmala said, "What have the doctors suggested?"

Munshiji said, "All of them are intoxicated, having eaten bhang. They say fresh blood is required."

Nirmala said, "If we get fresh blood, then can his life be saved?"

Looking at Nirmala pointedly, Munshiji said, "Neither am I God, nor do I consider doctors to be God."

Nirmala said, "Fresh blood is not such an unobtainable thing?"

Munshiji said, "The stars of the sky are also not unobtainable? It is a bad situation, we stand right on the precipice edge and anything can happen."

Nirmala said, "I am ready to give my blood. Call the doctor."

Munshiji said with surprise, "You!"

Nirmala replied, "Yes! Will my blood not be of any use?"

Munshiji said, "You will give your blood? No, your blood is not required. There is a threat to life in this."

Nirmala said, "When will my life be of some use then?"

Munshiji said with tears in his eyes, "No, Nirmala, it's become more precious in my sight now. Till today, it was a thing of my enjoyment and use, but, from today it is an object of worship. I have done grievous injustice to you. Forgive me!"

* * *

13

Whatever had to happen, happened; despite all efforts, nothing worked. Mansaram bade farewell after showing a glimpse of his noble character. He departed from this illusionary world, while Doctor Sahib was trying to take Nirmala's blood to give to him. Perhaps his soul had waited so long for Nirmala only. How could he have left this world, without proving her innocent? Now, his aim had been fulfilled. Munshiji believed that Nirmala was innocent, but when? When the hand had released the arrow from the bow; when the traveller had put his foot in the stirrup and left for his journey!

Bowed down with grief at his son's loss, Munshiji's life had become like a burden. From that day on, there was no smile on his lips. His life seemed worthless to him. He would go to court, not to pursue the cases, but only to divert his mind. He would get restless and return from there in an hour or two. He would sit to eat, but could not put even a morsel in his mouth. Nirmala would cook delicious dishes, but Munshiji would not eat more than two-three morsels. He felt as if the food would come out of his mouth. As he went towards Mansaram's room, he felt his heart breaking into pieces. Where once all his hopes were burning bright, the lamp was extinguished; there was only darkness now. He still had two sons, but when the cream of the flock, the mother cow, had died, what hopes remained for the calves? When a fruit-bearing tree in all its glory falls, then what hopes could be laid on the small saplings? It is customary that young and old die, but the true agony lay in the cold, hard fact that he had taken his son's life. The moment he recalled this, he felt his chest might burst and his heart would tumble out.

Nirmala had true sympathy for her husband. She was concerned with keeping him happy to the extent she could, and would ensure never to refer to past incidents. Munshiji hesitated to talk to her about Mansaram. At times, he felt like pouring out everything that was in his mind to Nirmala, but shame would hold him back. This way he did not get the comfort which one gets by sharing one's pain and sorrow with others. The resulting sore had spread inside and had become toxic. Day-by-day, he was melting away, becoming thinner and weaker.

Since a few days now, Munshiji and the doctor, who had treated Mansaram, had became friends. The well meaning doctor would sometimes try to explain things to Munshiji; at other times, would force him to accompany him for a walk. His wife, Sudha, had come a few times to meet Nirmala. Nirmala had also gone to her house a number of times, but whenever she returned from there, she would remain sad for many days. Doctor Sahib used to get just two hundred rupees and in this income, too, they both spent their life happily. There was just one maid in the house; the lady had to do a lot of the household work herself. She had worn a few ornaments, but there was the kind of love between them that did not care a straw for money. Seeing her husband, the wife's face would glow. The man, too, would be pleased and satisfied upon seeing his wife. Nirmala's house had more wealth compared to them – she was always laden with jewellery; she did not have to do any household chores, but in spite of being well-off, she was sad. Sudha, even though she had much less, was happy. Sudha had such things in her house, which Nirmala did not possess, in front of which, her own wealth seemed meagre – up to the extent that she was hesitant to wear her jewellery while visiting Sudha's house.

One day, when Nirmala visited Doctor Sahib's house, she was in a particularly sad mood. Sudha was prompted to find out the reason. "Sister, you are very sad today. Is *Vakil Sahib's* health all right?"

Nirmala replied, "What shall I say, Sudha? His state is deteriorating day-by-day. I am unable to say anything in the matter. I don't know what God wills, and what will happen?"

Sudha said, "My *Babuji* says it's necessary for him to go somewhere else for a change in the environment, otherwise he will be inflicted with some grave disease. He told *Vakil Sahib* a number of times, but he refutes, saying, he is fine where he is and he has no problems. Now you must explain to him today."

Nirmala said, "When he doesn't listen to the doctor, then will he listen to me?"

Saying this, Nirmala's eyes filled with tears, and the doubt and fear that were disturbing her for several months now escaped from her lips. Till now, she had hidden the doubt, but was unable to stop herself today. She said, "Sister, the symptoms don't appear to be good. Let's see what God does."

Sudha said, "Today you must stress upon him that he needs a change of place. He will forget many things by staying away for two or four months. I feel his grief will be lessened if he changes his house. But you won't be able to go out anywhere. Which month is it now?"

Nirmala said, "I am in my eighth month. The worry is also killing me. I had never prayed to God for it. I don't know why this problem was hung around my neck. I am really unfortunate, Sister. My father died one month before my marriage. My bad days started since his death. Earlier my marriage was fixed somewhere else but they turned their back on us. Poor *Ammaji* was helpless and married me into this family. Now my younger sister is going to get married. Let's see which shore her boat ends up at."

Sudha said, "Why did those people refuse, when your marriage had already been fixed?"

Nirmala said, "That they would know better. Father was no longer alive, so who would give them the bundle of gold?"

Sudha said, "This is meanness! Where were they from?"

Nirmala said, "Lucknow. I do not remember the name, but he was some big officer in the distillery."

Sudha asked, in a serious tone. "And what did his son do?"

Nirmala said, "Nothing. He was studying somewhere, but he was a good boy."

Sudha said, with her head bent down, "Didn't he say anything to his father? He was young, couldn't he pressurise his father?"

Nirmala said, "Now what do I know about this, Sister! Who doesn't like a bundle of gold? The pundit who had gone from our side with the message said that it was the boy who was refusing. The mother was very good. She explained to both the father and the son, but she could not prevail upon them."

Sudha said, "If I would have got the boy I would have taught him a lesson."

Nirmala said, "Whatever was written in my fate has already happened. Poor Krishna, what will she have to go through?"

In the evening, after Nirmala had left, Doctor Sahib came home.

Sudha said to him, “Why, dear, what will you call a man who, after his marriage is fixed, establishes relations elsewhere because of greed?”

Sinha looked at his wife inquisitively, and said, “This should not be done, what else?”

Sudha said, “Why don’t you say it is utter cheapness, it is wickedness of the first order?”

Sinha said, “Yes, I do not disagree with that also.”

Sudha said, “Whose offence was bigger? The groom’s or his father’s?”

Sinha could not understand what Sudha meant by these questions. He said with surprise, “Well, it depends upon the circumstances. If he is obedient, then it will be taken as the father’s crime.”

Sudha said, “Even being obedient, wouldn’t the young man have any duty? If he required a coat for himself, then he would certainly get it made, after setting up a great hue and cry, even after his father’s objection. Couldn’t he convey the importance of this matter to his father? I say that the groom and his father both are culprits, but the groom is more to be blamed! The old man thinks, ‘I have to bear all the expenses. The more I can extract from the girl’s side, the better.’ But it is the duty of the groom, if he has not sold himself to selfishness, to show his own strength. If he doesn’t do this, then I’ll say that he is greedy and cowardly, too. Unfortunately, my husband is also one of them and I can’t understand in what words to condemn him.”

Sinha stammered and said, “That . . . that . . . that was a different case. It wasn’t a matter of give and take, it was totally different. The father of the girl had died. What could we do in this situation? We also came to know that the girl had some defect. It was a totally different matter, but who told you this tale?”

Sudha said, “Go on, say that the girl was one-eyed, had a hunch, was a barber’s daughter, and was a harlot! Why did you leave this much unsaid? Well then, let me hear it, what was her defect?”

Sinha said, “I had not seen her. I had heard from somewhere that she had some defect.”

Sudha said, “The biggest shortcoming was that her father had died and she couldn’t give a big amount. Why do you hesitate to accept this much? I won't bite your ears! Even if I say something, you will listen from one ear and take it out from the other. If I overdo it, then you can take the help of the stick. The female species is kept in place by a stick. If that girl had any defect, then I'll say Goddess Lakshmi is also not without defects! You were unfortunate, that's all! What else? I had to be in your life."

Sinha said, "Who told you what kind of a girl she was? As you are convinced by hearing about her from someone else, so were we."

Sudha said, "I was not convinced by hearing of it. I have seen with my own eyes. Why should I praise her so much? It is enough to say I haven't seen such a beautiful lady."

Sinha asked in a confused manner, "Is she somewhere here? Tell me the truth, where did you see her? Did she come to your house?"

Sudha said, "Yes, she came to my house, not once, but many times. The wife of *Vakil Sahib* is the same girl, whom you discarded because of defects!"

Sinha said, "Really?"

Sudha said, "Absolutely! If, today, she comes to know that you are the same great person, then perhaps she will not step into the house again. Such a gentle lady, so adept in the household work and such a beautiful lady – there must only be a couple of other such ladies in this town. You praise me but I am not worth being her maid also. She has everything that God could give her, but when the partner is such a mismatch, then what is the point of having everything? Blessed is her patience that she is spending days with the silly, dried-up old lawyer. I would have taken poison quite early on. But the heart does not express its grief merely by speaking. She laughs, talks, wears jewellery and fine clothes, but her entire being cries."

Sinha said, "She must be complaining a lot about *Vakil Sahib*."

Sudha said, "Why will she complain? Is he not her husband? All that she possesses in this world is *Vakil Sahib*! Whether he is old or diseased, he is her master. Women from good families do not criticise their husbands. That is the work of sluts. She is tormented by his condition, but doesn't utter a word."

Sinha said, "What occurred to *Vakil Sahib* that he married at this age?"

Sudha said, "What will happen to the poor spinsters if such people aren't there? You and your companions will not discuss marriage without that big bundle, then where will these poor ladies go? You have committed a terrible injustice and you will have to repent for it. May God keep her husband alive! But if something happens to *Vakil Sahib*, the poor girl's life will be destroyed. Today, she was crying so much. You are really very heartless. I will get my Sohan married to some poor girl."

Doctor Sahib did not hear the last sentence. He fell into deep, worried thought. Certain questions were rising in his mind and making him restless – if something happens to *Vakil Sahib*, then what? Today he could see the dangerous form of his selfishness. In fact, this offence had been committed by him. If he would have emphatically told his father that he would not have married elsewhere, then could he have married him off, without his consent?

Suddenly, Sudha said, "If you say so, shall I fix your meeting with Nirmala? Let her also see your face. Though she won't say anything, but perhaps, with one look, she would reproach you and you will never be able to forget it. Tell me, shall I set up a meeting tomorrow? I will give her a brief introduction to you."

Sinha said, "No, Sudha, I beg you, don't do such a terrible thing. Otherwise, I tell you truly, I will really run away, leaving the house."

Sudha said, "Why do you fear to eat the fruit of the thorn that you've sown? At least, take a look at the person's suffering, on whose neck you placed the dagger! My *Dadaji* gave you five thousand, isn't it! Now you will get five to six thousand for your younger brother's marriage. Then there will not be any man richer than you in this world! Eleven thousand is a lot. Oh, my God! Eleven thousand! It will require months to pick it all up to keep it away. Even if the sons start squandering it, it will last for three generations! Are you all discussing marriage proposals with anyone?"

The doctor became so ashamed at all this mockery that he could not raise his head. His clever wordplay disappeared, and a small, childish face that emerged looked as though it were beaten. At the same time, someone called Doctor Sahib from outside. The poor fellow ran for his life. Today he was acquainted with just how adept women are in sarcasm and mockery.

While sleeping at night, Doctor Sahib said to Sudha, "Nirmala has a sister, doesn't she?

Sudha said, "Yes, we were discussing her. She has started worrying for her. She had gone through what was destined in her life, now she is consumed by worry for her sister. The mother now has even less than before, so she will also be forcibly tied to some such old fellow."

Sinha said, "Nirmala can help her mother."

Sudha said in a harsh tone, "At times, you say such senseless things. If Nirmala can do a lot, it won't be more than two to four hundred. What else can she do? *Vakil Sahib* is in a bad shape, and she has the rest of her life, looming like a mountain before her. Then who knows their state? He has been at home for the past six months – money doesn't fall from the sky. They must have ten or twenty thousand, but that too in the bank, not with Nirmala. If our expenses are two hundred rupees a month, then won't theirs be four hundred rupees?"

Sudha slept but Doctor Sahib tossed and turned sides for a long time. Then after thinking of something, he got up and started writing a letter.

* * *

14

All three things happened at the same time – Nirmala gave birth to a girl, Krishna's marriage was fixed and Munshi Totaram's house was auctioned. The birth of a girl was a commonplace event, even though in Nirmala's sight, it was an important one; the rest of the incidents were completely out of the ordinary. How did Krishna's marriage get fixed in such a prosperous house? Her mother did not have a *paisa* by way of dowry, and in the family of old Sinha Sahib who had retired with his pension and was known in his family as being an excessively greedy person! How did he agree to get his son married into such a poor house? People found it difficult when they first heard it. And even bigger surprise was the auctioning of Munshiji's house. People considered Munshiji to be a big man, even if they did not think he had lakhs. How did his house get auctioned? The reality was that Munshiji had taken a loan from a moneylender and mortgaged a village. He had hoped he would pay it back in a year or two, and would establish firm possession of the village in five to ten years. In the belief that the landlord would be unable to pay back the capital plus interest, Munshiji had taken the case. The village was a large one – he could have earned four to five hundred from it. However, what he had thought remained only a thought. Even after trying to regain courage and energy, he was unable to go to the court. The grief of losing his son had left no energy in him. Who could be such a heartless father, who after running a sword across his son's neck, would be able to pacify his mind?

The moneylender did not receive interest for a year, and neither did Munshiji visit him after his repeated messages. Instead, the last time, he reverted with the message, 'We are nobody's slave, let the moneylender do whatever he wants!' Hearing this, the moneylender got angry and filed a case against him. Munshiji did not even go to the court in his own defence. All of a sudden, judgment was passed. There was no money in the house and in a few days, Munshiji had to testify. He could not arrange for the money. At last, the house was put on auction. Nirmala had gone for her delivery. Her heart became still on hearing this news. Even after having no other happiness in life, she was free from financial worry. If money is not of the utmost importance in a man's life, then it is the next most important thing. Now, this worry was added to the other things she already lacked. She sent a message through a maid to save the house by selling off her jewellery, but Munshiji did not accept the proposal.

From that day, Munshiji was gripped by increasing worry. The wealth he thought he would enjoy by marrying again, that same wealth remained just a memory of the past. He could not face Nirmala now because he was so ashamed. Today he could gauge the degree of injustice he had done to Nirmala, and the birth of a girl had completed it – it had destroyed everything.

After twelve days from the delivery, Nirmala came home to her husband with the newborn baby. In spite of all she lacked, she was still so pleased as if she had no worries at all. Embracing the girl to her heart, she had forgotten all her worry. Seeing the bright and joy-filled eyes of the baby, her heart was ecstatic with happiness. All her miseries had disappeared with the abundant joy of motherhood. She wanted to be satisfied and happy by putting the baby on her husband's lap, but Munshiji hesitated on seeing the little girl. His heart did not gush with joy to hold the child, but once he looked at it with a sympathetic gaze, he bent his head down – the baby's face was exactly like that of Mansaram's.

Nirmala misinterpreted his emotion. With a hundredfold love, she embraced the child, as if saying to him, 'If you find her such a weighty burden, then I won't even let your shadow fall on her. This gem that I have got after such hard penance; doesn't your heart burst by showing such disrespect towards it?' That very moment, she went to her room, the baby clinging to her chest, and she cried for a long time. She did not make the slightest effort to try and understand her husband's dejection; otherwise, she may not have considered him so hardhearted. She did not have the burden of responsibility that had fallen on her husband's shoulder, did she? If she had tried to think hard on this, then she would have understood this much.

Munshiji realised his mistake in one second. The heart of a mother is so absorbed in love that the future's worry and hurdles do not make her feel any fear at all. She experiences a phenomenal energy inside her, which defeats all the hurdles in front of her. Munshiji came running inside the house and taking the baby in his arms, said, "I remember, Mansa was also like this – exactly like this."

Nirmala said, "*Didiji* also says the same thing."

Munshiji continued, "The same big eyes and red lips. God has given me my Mansaram in this form. The same forehead, the same face, the same hands and feet! God, your play is endless!"

Suddenly, Rukmini also joined them. As she saw Munshiji, she said, "See, Babu, is this Mansa or not? He has come back. No matter what anyone might say, I will not listen. Clearly, it is Mansaram. It's nearly one year since he left all of us."

Munshiji said, "Sister, each part of the body is simila to his. God has given me my Mansaram." He looked at the child and said, "Why dear, you are Mansaram, aren't you? Do not think of leaving, I will again pull you back. You ran away so mercilessly. At last, did I or did I not catch you? That's it, I have said it now. Do not ever mention going away and leaving me again. See, Sister, how intently she is staring at me?"

That very moment, Munshiji started building a palace of desires. Love pulled him back into this world. Human life! You are momentary, but your imaginations have such a long life! The same Totaram, who was growing detached from this world, who day and night summoned death, now had the support of a straw. He was trying with all his might to reach the other shore.

However, has anyone reached the shore with the help of a straw?

* * *

15

Though Nirmala had no relief from the tribulations of her own household, when she received news of Krishna's wedding, there was no way she could stop herself. Her mother had requested her to come. The greatest attraction was that Krishna's marriage had been arranged in the same household where Nirmala was earlier supposed to be wed. It was amazing how they had agreed to the marriage without a dowry this time.

Nirmala had been very worried about Krishna and had thought, 'She will be tied to someone forcibly, just like me.' She dearly wanted to help her mother out somehow, so that a suitable match could be arranged for Krishna. However, here, with her husband staying home from work, and the moneylender seizing their property, she was facing financial constraints of her own. In this situation, her mind was at peace on hearing this news. She made arrangements to leave. Her husband came to see her off at the station. He loved the little girl dearly. He would not let go of her, and was even ready to go with Nirmala. However, Nirmala did not think it right for him to stay at his in-laws' house for a month before the wedding. Nirmala had not told her mother about her tale of troubles yet. What was the use of upsetting her mother by crying over what had already passed? Her mother had always believed that Nirmala was living happily. Now that she saw Nirmala's face, she was aghast, deep down in her heart. Girls do not come from their in-law's looking thin and weak; and then a girl like Nirmala, who had all the material comforts of a happy life? How many girls had she seen, who went from their parents' house looking wan like the sickle moon, but returned as radiant as the full moon.

She had imagined that Nirmala would be glowing, her body would have filled out and become healthy, the beauty of every part of her body enhanced. Now that she saw her, she was not even half of what she had been. Neither was there the bubbling, enticing youthfulness nor the heart-warming, pleasing expression on her face. The youth and beauty that come from a happy, fulfilled lifestyle were nowhere to be seen. Her face was pale, expression crestfallen, limbs were lifeless; though only in her nineteenth year, she seemed to have aged.

When mother and daughter had their fill of crying and calmed down, her mother asked, "Well, don't you get anything to eat there? You were so much better before your marriage. What ailed you there?"

Krishna laughed and said, "She is the mistress of the house, isn't she? Mistresses worry about everything in the world. When will they eat?"

Nirmala replied, "No, *Amma*, the water does not suit me. My health remains uncertain."

Her Mother said, "Your husband will come for the wedding, won't he? I will ask him then, how come he took a young girl in the flower of her youth and brought her to this state? Well, now tell me, why had you sent money here? I never asked you for it. Even if I may be far gone, but it is never my intention to use my daughter's money!"

Nirmala was stunned, "How much money was there, mother? I did not send any."

Her Mother said, "Don't lie to me! Hadn't you sent five hundred rupee?"

Krishna said, "If you hadn't sent it, then did it fall from the sky? Your name was written clearly. The stamp was also of that area."

Nirmala replied, "I touch your feet and swear I did not send the money! When did this happen?"

Mother replied, "Oh, it must be about two months or two and a half months ago. If you didn't send it, where did the money come from?"

Nirmala said, "How would I know? But I did not send the money. At our place, since his eldest son died, he hasn't gone to court. My hands are tied as it is, so where would the money come from?"

Mother said, "This is very surprising. Is there any other relative or kinsman there? Could your husband have hidden it from you and sent it?"

Nirmala said, "No, *Amma*, I don't believe that."

Mother said, "We should find out about this. I spent the entire amount on Krishna's clothes and jewellery. This is the problem."

There was a sudden altercation between both the boys, and Krishna went there to settle the matter. Nirmala turned to her mother and said, "I was very surprised to hear about this wedding. How did it happen, *Amma*?

Mother said, "Whosoever hears of it here bites their fingers in astonishment. The same people who had turned away from a settled decision of marriage, and that, too, for the lust of a little money! It is incredible that they are now ready for marriage and that too, without taking a thing. They sent the proposal themselves. I wrote back clearly saying that I had nothing to give them except for an accomplished girl who would serve them well."

Nirmala asked, "Didn't they reply to this?"

Mother said, "Shastriji took the letter to them. He would only say that Munshiji did not want anything now. He was also a little ashamed of his earlier breach of promise. I had no expectation of such generosity from him but I've heard that his elder son is a gentleman. He talked his father into agreeing."

Nirmala said, "Didn't the same gentleman want a packet of money earlier?"

Mother replied, "Yes, but now Shastriji said, he is irritated even hearing of dowry. I have heard that he even regrets not marrying here. He broke this engagement for money and though he got a lot of money, he does not like his wife."

Nirmala felt a strong desire to see the man, who after ignoring her, now wished to help in her sister's upliftment. Repentance was very well, but how many people would be ready to repent in this way? Nirmala's heart grew impatient to talk to him, upbraid him with soft words, and showing him her beautiful countenance, make him even more jealous. Both sisters slept in the same room at night. How many girls in the locality had been married, who had fallen in love, whose marriage was conducted with great pomp and show, who got husbands just as they wished for, who got how many and what kinds of ornaments as gifts from the boy's side – all these topics were discussed for a long time. Krishna wanted again and again to ask about things at her sister's house, but Nirmala would not give her the opportunity to ask. She knew that Krishna would ask her about things she was not comfortable talking about. Ultimately, Krishna asked whether her husband would be coming for the wedding.

Nirmala replied, "He has said he will be here."

Krishna asked, "He is happy with you now, isn't he, or is it still the same as before? I used to hear that men love their second wives more than life itself, but I saw the opposite there. After all, what does he get so angry about?"

Nirmala said, "Now, how would I know what is in someone else's heart?"

Krishna said, "I understand it like this – he gets irritated by your acerbic behaviour. You had been angry even when you left here. You must have said something to him there as well."

Nirmala said, "It is not the case, Krishna, I swear it. There is not the least negative feeling in my heart towards him. As far as I am able to, I serve him. Even if there was a deity in his place, I could hardly do more than I do for him. He, too, loves me. He keeps looking at my face again and again, but what can he or I do about things that are beyond our control? Neither can he become younger, nor can I become an old woman. I don't know how many juices and powders he consumes to regain youth, and I have left eating milk, clarified butter, and all such foods in a bid to age faster. I think, perhaps through my thinness alone, I can bridge the gap in the situation. But neither do nutritious diets help him, nor does fasting help me. Since Mansaram has passed away, his situation has worsened."

Krishna said, "You also loved Mansaram dearly?"

Nirmala said, "He was such a boy that whoever saw him would love him. I have never seen anyone with such big, dark eyes. His face always bloomed like a lotus flower. He was so brave that had the opportunity arisen, he would have even leapt into fire. Krishna, I tell you, when he used to come and sit next to me, I would forget myself. I would wish that he would always sit before me, so that I could just look at him. There was no hint of impropriety in my mind. If I viewed him with any other emotion for even a second, then may I go blind! But I don't know why whenever I found him near me, I was extremely happy. That is why I put on the act of studying; otherwise he would not come to the house at all. I know that if I had feelings for him, I could have done anything for him."

Krishna said, "Oh, Sister, be quiet, what are you saying?"

Nirmala said, "Yes, I know, it sounds bad and it is bad, but no one can change human nature. You tell me. If you were married to a fifty year old man, what would you do?"

Krishna said, "Sister, I would take poison and sleep. I wouldn't even be able to look at his face."

Nirmala said, "That's it, then consider that's what happened. That boy never even looked up towards me, but old men are suspicious. Your brother-in-law became his enemy and ultimately took his life. The very day he found that his father was harbouring suspicions about him, he fell ill with a fever that left him only when it took his life. Oh! The image of his last moments hovers before my eyes. I had gone to the hospital, and he was unconscious with fever. He had no energy to get up, but as soon as he heard my voice, he got up with a start. Saying, 'Mother-Father', he fell at my feet." Crying, she continued, "Krishna, at that moment, I felt like taking my own life and giving it to him. At my feet, he lost consciousness and never opened his eyes again. The doctor had suggested transfusing fresh blood into his body, I had rushed there for this purpose, but before the doctors could start the procedure, he had passed away."

Krishna asked, "Would blood transfusions have saved his life?"

Nirmala replied, "Who knows? But I was ready to give my last drop of blood. Even in that state, his expressive face glowed like a lamp. If he had not run and fallen at my feet as soon as he saw me, and some blood had reached his body earlier, then perhaps he would have been saved."

Krishna asked, "So, why didn't you make him lie down immediately?"

Nirmala replied, "Oh silly, you still haven't understood. By falling at my feet and showing our relation to be that of mother and son, he wanted to remove suspicion from his father's mind. It was for that reason alone that he had got up. He gave up his life so that his father's suspicion would be eliminated, and his wish was fulfilled. Your brother-in-law was straightened out from that day. Now I feel sorry to see his condition. The sorrow of losing his son will be the death of him. He is now repenting the wrong he did to me by suspecting me. Now, when you see him, you will be scared. He has become an old man. Even his back seems a little bent."

Krishna asked, "Why are old people so suspicious, Sister?"

Nirmala said, "Go and ask that to old people!"

Krishna said, "I understand. Like a thief, a little fear sits constantly in his heart that he cannot keep this young woman pleased. That is why he must be suspicious of every little thing."

Nirmala said, "You know it, then why do you ask me?"

Krishna said, "That is why the poor man must be bending to your will as well. Onlookers probably think he loves you a lot."

Nirmala said, "Where have you learnt so many things in such a few days? Leave these aside, do you like your groom? You must have seen his photograph?"

Krishna replied, "Yes, it had come. Shall I bring it and show you?"

In a trice, Krishna brought the photograph and placed it in Nirmala's hands.

Nirmala smiled and said, "You are very fortunate."

Krishna said, "Mother, too, liked him a lot."

Nirmala said, "Tell me whether you like him. Don't tell me about other people's opinions."

Embarrassed, Krishna said, "His appearance is not bad. Only God knows about his temperament. Shastriji says that few men are of as good nature and character as him."

Nirmala asked, "Was your photograph also sent from here?"

Krishna replied, "Yes, it had been sent. Shastriji took it with him."

Nirmala asked, "Did they like it?"

Krishna said, "Now, how would I know what they thought? Shastriji said they were very happy."

Nirmala said, "All right, tell me, what gift shall I give you? Tell me now, so that I can get it made."

Krishna said, "Give whatever you want. He loves books. You could get some good books."

Nirmala said, "I wasn't asking for him, I was asking for you."

Krishna said, "I am asking it for myself."

Nirmala looked at the photograph and said, "The clothes appear to be of khadi."

Krishna replied, "Yes, he is very fond of khadi. I have heard that he used to visit remote areas with khadi laden on his back to sell. He is an accomplished speaker, too."

Nirmala said, "Then you will have to wear khadi as well. But you dislike thick cloth."

Krishna said, "When he likes thick cloth, then why will I dislike it? I have learnt how to use a spinning wheel."

Nirmala said, "Really! Are you able to draw thread?"

Krishna replied, "Yes, Sister, I am able to spin a little. Since he is so fond of khadi, I am sure he must be spinning as well. If I am not able to spin, it will be so embarrassing for me."

Soon after, both the sisters fell asleep. About two o'clock at night, her daughter started crying and Nirmala woke up. She saw that Krishna's bed was empty. Nirmala was surprised and wondered where she could have gone so late at night. Perhaps she had gone to drink some water. However, there was water at her bedside, then where could she have gone? She called out Krishna's name a few times, but there was no sign of her. Then Nirmala got worried. Anxieties of all kinds arose in her mind. Suddenly she had a thought – perhaps Krishna was in her own room. When the child fell asleep, Nirmala got up and went to Krishna's room. Her guess was right, Krishna was in her room. The entire household was sleeping and she was sitting at the spinning wheel. She must not have even watched a theatre performance with such intent. Nirmala was stunned. She went inside and said, "Hey, what are you doing, is this the time to spin thread?"

Krishna was startled and bowing her head shyly, said, "How did your sleep get disturbed? I had kept water by the bed."

Nirmala said, "I say, don't you get time during the day, that you are sitting with the spinning wheel so late at night?

Krishna said, "I don't get time during the day."

Nirmala saw the thread and said, "The thread is very fine."

Krishna said, "No, Sister, this thread is still so thick. I want to spin fine thread and make a turban for him. This is my gift to him."

Nirmala said, "You have thought of something excellent. What else could be more valuable in his eyes? All right, now get up. Spin it tomorrow. If you fall ill, everything will end up unfinished."

Krishna said, "No, my Sister, you go and sleep, I will come in a while."

Nirmala did not persist in asking her. She went to lie down, but sleep eluded her. Seeing Krishna's excitement and spirit, an unidentified desire stormed through her heart. Oh! How happy she is right now. Love had made her so restless. Then she remembered the time of her own wedding. From the day the *tilak* had been sent, all her liveliness, all her vivacity had deserted her. She would sit in her room, crying over her fate and praying to God that her life would end. Just like convicts await punishment, so had she awaited her marriage. That marriage, which would end all the hopes and desires of her life; when her wishes would burn to ashes in the fire altar under the marriage canopy!

* * *

16

The month soon passed. The auspicious time for the wedding arrived. The house filled up with guests. Munshi Totaram arrived a day early, and with him came Nirmala's friend. Nirmala had not insisted she come, as much as she, herself, was eager to attend. Nirmala's greatest desire was that she would meet the groom's elder brother, and if possible, thank him for his good sense.

Sudha laughed and said, "Will you be able to say this to him?"

Nirmala replied, "Why, what harm is there in saying so? Now there is a different relation altogether. And even if I can't speak, you are always there to do so!"

Sudha said, "Oh no, I will not be able to do it. I can't talk to an unknown man. Who knows what kind of a person he is."

Nirmala said, "He isn't a bad person, and besides, it's not like you have to marry him. So, what's the harm in speaking with him a little! If Doctor Sahib had been here, I would have taken permission for you."

Sudha said, "Are people who are good at heart also of sound character? No man has any qualms in staring at unknown women."

Nirmala replied, "All right, don't do it, I will talk to him myself. He can stare all he wants. There, are you satisfied now?"

Just then, Krishna walked in and sat down. Nirmala smiled and said, "Tell me the truth, Krishna, why is your heart so restless right now?"

Krishna said, "*Jijaji* is calling you. First go and hear him out, gossip later! He seems very angry."

Nirmala said, "What is it, didn't you ask?"

Krishna replied, "He seems to be somewhat unwell. He's become very thin."

Nirmala said, "You could have sat with him and entertained him a while, why did you come running here? God has been kind, otherwise you, too, would have got a man like him. You should just sit and talk. Old people have more layered conversations. The young are not so inventive."

Krishna said, "No, Sister, you go. I can't bear to sit there."

Nirmala went away. Sudha said to Krishna, "The wedding party must have come by now. Why hasn't the *dwar-puja* begun?"

Krishna replied, "Who knows, Sister? Shastriji is still collecting the required material."

Sudha said, "I have heard that the groom's mother has a very stern temperament."

Krishna asked, "How do you know?"

Sudha replied, "I have heard, that is why I am cautioning you. You will have to quietly swallow whatever she says."

Krishna said, "I am not in the habit of quarrelling. When she will have no cause of complaint from me, will she get angry without reason?"

Sudha said, "Yes, I have heard she is like that. She will fight on false pretexts."

Krishna said, "There is only one thing I know for sure – gentleness can soften the hardest stone."

Suddenly, there was a noise; the wedding party was on its way. Both the beautiful women came and sat before the window. In a moment, Nirmala, too, joined them.

She was excitedly expectant to see the groom's elder brother.

Sudha said, "How will we know who the elder brother is?"

Nirmala said, "If we ask Shastriji, then we will know. All right, the elephant is carrying Krishna's father-in-law. Oh, how has Doctor Sahib reached here? He is on the horse, can't you see?"

Sudha said, "Yes, it is indeed him."

Nirmala said, "He must be friendly with these people. Is he related in any way?"

Sudha said, "Now, if we meet the gentleman, I would ask. I don't know anything."

Nirmala said, "The gentleman who is sitting in the palanquin, he doesn't look anything like the groom's brother."

Sudha agreed, "Not at all. It appears as though his entire body is composed only of his stomach."

Nirmala asked, "Who is sitting on the other elephant? I cannot make out."

Sudha replied, "Whoever it is, it cannot be the groom's brother. Can't you see how old he is – he must be over forty."

Nirmala said, "Shastriji is busy worrying about the *dwar-puja* at the moment, otherwise I would have asked him."

Coincidently, the barber came asking for money. Nirmala had the keys to the trunks. Right now, some money was required for the entrance ceremony, and mother had sent him for it. The barber had also gone with Pundit Moteram when they had taken the *tilak* for the groom.

Nirmala said, "Is the money needed right now?"

The barber said, "Yes, madam, please go and give it."

Nirmala said, "Okay, I'll come along. First tell me, do you recognise the groom's elder brother?"

The barber replied, "Why wouldn't I recognise him? There he is, in the front."

Nirmala asked, "Where? I don't see him."

The barber said, "Oh, there, on the horse – that is him."

Stunned, Nirmala said, "What are you saying, the groom's brother is riding on the horse? Do you really recognise him or are you just guessing?"

The barber said, "Oh, Madam, will I forget so soon? I just served them refreshments and came."

Nirmala said, "Oh, but that is Doctor Sahib. He lives in my neighbourhood."

The barber said, "Yes, yes. That is Doctor Sahib."

Nirmala looked at Sudha and asked, "Do you hear what he ays, Sister?"

Sudha stifled her laughter and said, "He is lying."

The barber said, "All right, just as well a lie. Who will argue with one's superiors? Now if I ask Shastriji, will you believe me then?"

Since the barber was taking so long, Moteram himself came into the courtyard and shouted out, "The honour of this house is in the hands of God alone! The barber came an hour ago, and still hasn't got the money!"

Nirmala said, "Shastriji, please come up here. How much money is required, shall I take it out?"

Shastriji climbed up, mumbling and huffing loudly; he took a long breath and said, "What is it? This is not the time for talking, take out the money quickly!"

Nirmala said, "There you go, I am taking it out. Now, shall I fall flat on my face and touch your feet? First please tell me, which of the guests is the brother of the groom?"

Shastriji said, "Good God! You have sent me so high up in the sky for such a little thing! Doesn't the barber recognise him?"

Nirmala said, "The barber says that it is the person on the horse."

Shastriji said, "Who else shall he say it is? That is indeed him."

The barber said, "I've been saying so for ages, but madam doesn't believe me." Nirmala looked at Sudha with a mixture of love, maternal affection, and gladness and pretended to be insulted, and said, "Oh, so you were the one who was playing this wicked game with me till now! If I had known, I would never have invited you. Oh ho! You are able to conceal things well! You have been playing this prank on me for months, and not once did you even accidentally let a word slip. I would have revealed it in just a few days!"

Sudha said, "If you had found out, then why would you have come to my place?"

Nirmala said, "Wonder of wonders, I have spoken to Doctor Sahib many times. This sin will fall on your head. Krishna, did you see your sister-in-law's mischief! She is such a witch, beware of her!"

Krishna said, "I will wash the feet of such a Goddess and anoint my head with it. I am blessed to have met her!"

Nirmala said, "Now I understand. You must have sent the money as well. Now if you shake your head, I tell you truthfully, I will beat you!"

Sudha said, "You can't call a guest to your house and then insult them."

Nirmala said, "Just you wait and see, how I take care of you! I had written to you just as a token of respect, and you actually ended up coming! What must the bridegroom's party be saying!"

Sudha said, "I told everyone before coming."

Nirmala said, "Now I will never come to visit you. You could at least have given me a hint to be veiled around the Doctor Sahib."

Sudha said, "What harm was there in his seeing you? If he hadn't seen you, how would he have lamented over his fate? How would he have known what a thing he lost simply for a little greed? Looking at you now, *Lalaji* is beset with remorse. He doesn't say anything openly, but in his heart, he regrets his mistake."

Nirmala replied, "I will never come to your house again."

Sudha said, "You can't shake me off so easily. Haven't I seen your house and don't I know the way to your house?"

The *dwar-puja* was over. The guests were sitting and were being served refreshments. Doctor Sinha was sitting next to Munshiji. Nirmala stood at the threshold, and watching them from behind the blinds, was stricken. One was healthy, a God of youth, talent and ability, but the other… it is better not to say anything on this matter.

Nirmala had seen Doctor Sahib several times, but the thoughts that arose in her heart today, had never risen before. Again and again, she wanted to call him and really scold him, taunt him so that he would never forget, leave him in tears, but end up forgiving him. The wedding party had gone to the rest house. Preparations were being made for the meal. Nirmala was busy picking the plates for the meal. Just then, the maid entered and said, "*Bitti*, Sudha *rani* is calling you. She is sitting in your room."

Nirmala left the plates, and shaken, came to see Sudha, but stopped as soon as she stepped into the room – Doctor Sinha stood there.

Sudha smiled and said, “Here, Sister, I called him. Now scold him as much as you like. I am at the door, he can’t run away.”

Doctor Sahib said gravely, “Who would run? Here I stand with my head bowed.”

With joined hands, Nirmala said, “Please always bless us with your mercy. Don’t ever forget us. This is my only request.”

* * *

17

Sudha left after Krishna's wedding. Nirmala, however, stayed on in her mother's house. Her husband would write again and again, but she would not go. She just could not bring herself to go back there. There was nothing there that pulled her to return. Here, her time was spent blissfully, taking care of her mother and younger brothers.

If her husband had come himself, perhaps she would have agreed to go back, but during the wedding, the girls of the locality had poked such fun at him that the poor fellow did not even mention coming back.

Sudha, too, wrote to her many times, but Nirmala made excuses to her, too. Finally one day, Sudha accompanied by a servant, came unannounced.

After they had both embraced, Sudha said, "It seems as though you are afraid of going back there."

Nirmala said, "Yes, Sister, I do feel scared. When I went there after my marriage, it was three years before I returned. If I go there again, my whole life might pass before I come back here. Then, who will invite me, and who will come?"

Sudha said, "What stops you from coming? Whenever you feel like, you can come. Your husband is getting very restless there."

Nirmala said, "Very restless? Perhaps he is unable to sleep at night."

Sudha said, "Sister, you have a heart of stone. I pity his condition. He said there is no one who cares at home, no boy or girl, how should he amuse himself? Since he has moved to the other house, he is very unhappy."

Nirmala said, "God has given him two sons."

Sudha said, "He complains a lot about them. Jiyaram doesn't listen to anyone now. He answers back needlessly. As for the younger one, he is completely influenced by him. The poor man keeps thinking of the eldest son and crying."

Nirmala said, "Jiyaram was not cunning, how did he become so mischievous? He never opposed anything I said – I just had to indicate and he did everything I asked him to."

Sudha replied, "Who knows, Sister! I heard that he accused his father of poisoning his elder brother to death. He called him a murderer. Many times he has taunted his father for having married you. He says such things that make your husband cry. Oh, what more shall I say? He even ran to throw stones at him, one day."

Nirmala fell into grave thought, and said, "This boy has turned out to be very wicked. Who told him that his father poisoned his brother?"

Sudha said, "You are the only one who can put him right."

Nirmala now had a new worry. If Jiyaram had turned out this way, fighting with his own father, why would he take any heed of her? She stayed awake deep in thought for a long time at night. She was missing Mansaram a lot tonight. She could have spent her life happily with him. As for this boy, if he behaved like this before his father, what must his actions be behind his back! The household had gone out of hand. Some debts must still be hanging over their heads, and the state of the income was equally bad. Only God could see them through this. Today, for the first time, Nirmala felt worried about her daughter. Who knew what would happen to that poor thing? God had placed them in this terrible quandary. She had had no need of her. If she had to be born, why was she not born into some fortunate house? The child was sleeping in her embrace. Nirmala clasped her even closer, as though afraid that someone was trying to steal her away.

Sudha's cot was placed near Nirmala's. While Nirmala floundered in the sea of worries, Sudha was lost in sweet and blissful sleep. Did concerns about her son trouble her? Death makes no difference between young and old, then why did Sudha have no fears? Nirmala had never seen Sudha sad, worrying over the future.

Suddenly, Sudha woke up. Seeing that Nirmala was still awake, she said, "Oh, haven't you slept yet?"

Nirmala replied, "I'm just not sleepy."

Sudha said, "Close your eyes, and sleep will come by itself. It's like I pass out when I reach the bed. Even if my husband is awake, I have no idea. I don't know why I feel so sleepy. Perhaps it is some disease."

Nirmala replied, "Yes, it is a very serious disease. It is known as the 'royal disease'. Ask Doctor Sahib to give you some medicines for it."

Sudha said, "After all, of what should I think of lying awake? Sometimes I remember my mother's house; on those days I stay awake longer."

Nirmala asked, "Don't you miss Doctor Sahib?"

Sudha replied, "No, never. Why would I remember him? I know that he must have played tennis, eaten dinner and must be resting comfortably."

Nirmala said, "Oh look, Sohan has woken up, too. When you woke up, why would he stay asleep?"

Sudha said, "Yes, Sister. He has a strange habit. He sleeps when I sleep and wakes when I do. He must have been a *sadhu* in another life. Look at the mark on his forehead. There are similar marks on his arms as well. He was surely a *sadhu*."

Nirmala said, "*Sadhu*s don't mark themselves with sandalwood. He must have been a foolish priest. Why Sohan, tell us, where were you a priest?"

Sudha said, "I will get him married to your daughter."

Nirmala said, "Oh, come on, Sister. You are abusing him. Since when does a brother marry his sister?"

Sudha replied, "I will get them married, no matter what anyone says. Where else will I find such a beautiful daughter-in-law? Would you just check, Sister is his body a little warm or is it just me who thinks so?"

Nirmala felt Sohan's forehead and said, "No, no. His body is hot. When did this fever rise? He is drinking milk, isn't he?"

Sudha said, "When he slept a while back, his body was cool. Maybe he has caught cold. I'll cover him well and put him to sleep. He will be fine by morning."

When morning came, Sohan's condition worsened. His nose started to run, and the fever also rose. His eyes rolled up and head drooped. He would not move his limbs nor would he talk or laugh; he just lay there quietly. It seemed as though he disliked the sound of anyone talking. He started to cough a little. Now, Sudha became worried. Nirmala, too, suggested that Doctor Sahib should be called for, but her old mother said, "There is no work for a doctor or medicine man here. I can see clearly that the child has caught the evil eye. What good will a doctor do?"

Sudha said, "Mother, who would cast the evil eye here? He hasn't even gone out anywhere yet."

The mother said, "No one casts the evil eye, my dear, some people have a bad eye, it affects people on its own. Sometimes, even the mother and father can affect the child thus. Ever since he has come here, he hasn't cried even once. It is always so with spoilt children. Seeing him jump around and play, I had grown worried, lest something bad should happen to him. Don't you see how his eyes have rolled up? This is the surest sign of the evil eye."

The old maidservant and the neighbour's wife both added their assent to this. Mangu came, saw the child's face and said laughing, "Mistress, this is the evil eye, nothing else. Please bring some thin sticks. God-willing, the child will be laughing by sunset."

Five thin pieces of wood were given to him. Mangu bunched them uniformly and tied them together. Then mumbling something, he stroked Sohan's head softly with those tied sticks. As they looked on, the five sticks had become of uneven size. All the women were stunned to see this strange phenomenon. Who could now have doubted that it was the evil eye? Mangu started stroking the child with those sticks again. This time, the sticks became more or less even. Only a little difference was left. This proved that now only a little effect of the evil eye remained. Mangu reassured everyone and promised to return that evening. The child's condition worsened during the day. He was strained by a bad cough. In the evening, Mangu once again showed his play with the sticks. This time, all five sticks were even. The ladies were convinced, but Sohan spent the entire night, coughing. Many times, his eyes rolled over completely.

Sudha and Nirmala sat up all night with him. Anyway, the night passed peacefully. Now the old mother had a new idea. Mangu had not been able to remove the evil eye, so it now became necessary to go to a *maulvi* who could blow the spirits away from the child. Sudha was again not able to send word to her husband. The maid wrapped Sohan in a sheet and took him to a nearby mosque, got the spirits blown away; she went again in the evening, but Sohan's condition did not improve. Night came, and Sudha decided that once the night had passed peacefully, she would send a telegram to her husband.

However, the night did not pass peacefully. By midnight, the child slipped out of her hands. Sudha's life's wealth was snatched from her hands, even as she watched.

The child, the idea of whose marriage had given them such joy two days back, was now making the whole house cry. Where earlier his innocent face had made his mother's heart swell, seeing him today was making her heart burst with grief. The whole house would console Sudha, but her tears would not stop, nor could she control herself. The greatest despair was how she would face her husband. She had not even sent him news of Sohan's illness!

A telegram was sent that night itself, and the next day by nine o'clock, Doctor Sinha reached there in a motor car. Sudha got news of his arrival, and broke down and cried even more loudly. The last rites were performed for the child. Doctor Sahib came in many times, but Sudha did not go near him. How could she? How could she face him? It was because of her foolishness that the most precious jewel of his life had been snatched and drowned in the river. Now, going near him was shattering her heart into a million pieces. Seeing the child in her lap, his eyes used to light up. The child would leap into his father's lap, and when she would call him back, he would cling to his father's chest. A million entreaties and kisses would not make him leave his father's lap. Then his mother would say, "How selfish he is!" Today, who would she take in her lap and go to her husband? Seeing that empty lap, she was afraid she might scream out and start crying. Rather than go before her husband, she would have found it much easier to just die. She did not leave Nirmala's side for a moment, in case she should have to face her husband.

Nirmala said, "Sister, what had to happen had already passed. How long will you keep running away? He will leave tonight. Mother said so."

Sudha looked with tearful eyes and said, "How shall I face him? I am scared that when I go before him, my legs will shake so much that I am bound to fall down."

Nirmala said, "Come, I will go with you. I will take care of you."

Sudha said, "You won't leave me and run, will you?"

Nirmala said, "No, no. I will not run away."

Sudha said, "My heart is overflowing already. I am astonished that despite this thunderbolt, I am still sitting here. He loved Sohan so much, Sister. Who knows what the state of his heart will be? What consolation will I give him if I can't control my own tears? Will he leave this very night?"

Nirmala replied, "Yes, Mother said he hasn't taken leave."

Both friends set off towards the men's' rooms, but at the door, Sudha sent Nirmala away. She entered the room alone.

Doctor Sahib was worried, wondering what Sudha's state must be like. All kinds of fears arose in his mind. He was ready to leave, but he did not want to go. Life seemed to be empty. In his mind he was agitated; if God had to take away the child so soon, why had he given him at all? He had never prayed to God for a child. He could have stayed childless his whole life, but having once had a child, it was unbearable to be deprived of him. Are humans really toys for the Almighty? Is this the value of human life? Is it just a child's playhouse, where its making or breaking has no reason at all? However, even children have such fondness for their little playhouse, their paper boats and their wooden horses. They value their favourite toys more than life itself. If God is a child, then he is an unusual child!

However, the intellect does not accept this form of the Almighty. The Creator of this unending Universe cannot be an unruly child. We adorn him with all those attributes, those which are beyond our limited intellect. Being playful is not one of those great attributes. Is it a game to claim the lives of happy, lively young children? Does God play such a heinous game?

Just then, Sudha softly entered the room. Doctor Sahib stood up and coming close to her, said, "Where were you, Sudha? I was waiting for you."

The room seemed to swim in front of Sudha's eyes. Putting her arms around her husband's neck, she put her head on his chest and started to cry, and in this bout of tears she experienced unending patience and comfort. Clinging to her husband's shoulders, she found a strange vigour and strength collecting in her heart, much like a lamp, wavering in the breeze, finds its refuge behind a cover.

Doctor Sahib cupped her beautiful tear-drenched cheeks in both hands and said, "Sudha, why are you so upset? Whatever Sohan had come to accomplish in this life, he had already done, then why would he stay on? Like a tree grows with water and sunlight, but is only strengthened by a strong gust of wind, similarly, the cruel strokes of unhappiness foster love. It is easy to find people who will laugh with you in happiness, but those who cry with us in sadness are our true friends. The lovers who have not had the chance of crying together, what do they know of the joy of love? Sohan's death has today completely removed our duality. Today, we have seen each other's true forms."

Sudha said, with a catch in her voice, "I was taken in by the sham of the evil eye. Oh! You were not even able to see his face. I don't know where he got such wisdom in those days. When he would see me crying, he would forget his own discomfort and smile at me. Just on the third day of illness, my dear boy's eyes shut. I couldn't even give him any medicines."

Saying this, Sudha's tears welled up again. Doctor Sinha clasped her to his chest, and in a voice trembling with tenderness said, "Dear, till today, there must not be a single household which fulfilled their desire of suitably treating the child or aged person who died."

Sudha said, "Nirmala helped me a lot. I would even take a nap once in a while; but she never so much as blinked. The entire night she would hold him or walk around with him. I will never forget her favour. Will you leave today?"

Doctor Sahib said, "Yes, there was no time to apply for leave. The Civil Surgeon had gone out hunting."

Sudha said, "Do they always go hunting?"

Doctor Sahib replied, "What other work do kings have?"

Sudha said, "I won't let you go today."

Doctor Sahib said, "I don't want to go either."

Sudha said, "So, don't go. Send a telegram. I will leave with you. I will take Nirmala along as well."

Sudha returned from there, with a lighter heart. Her husband's loving and gentle voice had taken away all her grief and guilt. There is endless trust, endless patience and endless strength in love.

* * *

18

When some great trouble befalls us, we have to deal not only with our own sorrow, but also have to bear the taunts of others. People get the much awaited opportunity to discuss our affairs, for which opportunity they remain restless. It was as if Mansaram's death gave society the excuse to make loud comments about them. Who knew the inside story; what was apparently clear was that it was the stepmother's doing. All around, the discussion was that God should be so kind, that young boys would never have to experience living with a stepmother. Such comments floated around: "Whoever wants to ruin their settled home, and run a sharp knife across their dear children's throat, should marry a second time while their children are still around."

"It has never been seen that after a stepmother comes to the house, it was not ruined; that the same father who would give his life for his children, becomes their enemy as soon as the stepmother arrives; his entire mindset changes."

"Such a goddess has not yet been born, who has considered another woman's children as her own."

The difficulty lay in that people were not satisfied with just these discussions. There were some folks who now suddenly developed a special fondness for Jiyaram and Siyaram. They would express much sympathy for the two boys to the extent that a few ladies would recall the mother's patience and temperament and shed a few tears. "Oh dear! How could the poor lady have known that as soon as she died, her boys would face this terrible fate? Where would they even get milk and butter now?"

Jiyaram would say, "Why wouldn't we get it?"

The ladies would say, "Of course, you get it! Oh son, there are ways in which you get something. When watered-down milk for a *ser* a rupee is bought and kept, if you drink it or not, who asks? Otherwise the poor lady would send the servant to bring fresh milk. Your faces clearly tell your tale. The healthy look that milk gives cannot be hidden, that look has now gone."

Jiya had no recollection of the milk he had drunk when his mother was alive, that he could counter this allegation, and neither did he remember how his face looked then. So, he would just stay quiet. It was natural for these well-wisher's words to have their effect. Jiyaram grew increasingly irritated with his family members. When Munshiji came and settled in a second house after the first house was auctioned off, he started worrying about the rent. Nirmala stopped buying butter. When the income was insufficient, the earlier expenses could not be sustained. Both the servants were removed. Jiyaram felt bad about this frugality. When Nirmala went to her mother's house, Munshiji stopped buying milk as well. His worry over the newborn girl preyed on his mind.

Jiyaram said angrily, "By not buying milk you must be collecting funds for the construction of your palace. Stop our food as well!"

Munshiji said, "If you want milk, why don't you go yourself and get it milked from the cow? I find myself unable to pay for the water."

Jiyaram said, "What if some boy from school sees me if I go to get the milk?"

Munshiji replied, "Tell them, I am taking milk for myself. Getting milk is not theft."

Jiyaram said, "It is not theft! If someone saw you bringing milk, wouldn't you feel ashamed?"

Munshiji replied, "Not at all. I have drawn water and lugged sacks of grain with these very hands. My father wasn't a millionaire."

Jiyaram said, "My father is not poor. Why should I go to get the milk? Why did you ask the servants to leave?"

Munshiji said, "Doesn't it even occur to you that my income is not as much as it used to be? You aren't that ignorant."

Jiyaram said, "Well, why has your income gone down?"

Munshiji replied, "Now, if you have no brains, what will I explain to you? Here, I am tired of life. Who will take up new cases? And even if I do, who will prepare for the cases? I don't have the heart for it. Now I am just counting the days of my life. All my desires died along with Lallu."

Jiyaram said, "Well, it was by your own hands, wasn't it?"

Munshiji screamed and said, "Oh fool, it was God's will. Does anyone cut their own throat with their own hands?"

Jiyaram said, "God had not come to get you married a second time."

Munshiji could not bear it anymore. With bloodshot eyes, he said, "Have you come ready for a fight today? And on what basis? Do you pay for my food? When you are so capable, then give me advice. Then I will listen to you. Right now you do not possess the right to give me advice. Learn good manners and politeness for some days. You are not my advisor that I will consult you in everything I do. I have earned the wealth, and I will spend it as I wish. You don't even have the right to open your mouth. If you behave so rudely with me ever again, the result will be bad. If my life did not end with the death of a gem like Mansaram, I will definitely not die without you, do you understand?"

Even this harsh scolding did not serve to move Jiyaram from there. Without any misgivings, he said, "So you want us to keep quiet no matter how much we suffer? I won't' be able to do so. I am not hungry for the prize that my brother got for his manners and politeness. I don't have the courage to eat poison and give up my life. Such manners I salute from a distance."

Munshiji said, "Don't you feel ashamed to say these things?"

Jiyaram said, "Children copy their own elders."

Munshiji's anger cooled. That he could not affect Jiyaram in the slightest, of that he was sure now. He got up and went for a walk. Today, he had received the intimation that quite soon, this household would be destroyed.

From that day, father and son would fight over something or the other everyday. Even as Munshiji would give way, Jiyaram would become even more daring – to the extent that one day, Jiyaram said to Rukmini, "He's my father that is why I am sparing him. Otherwise, I have such friends that if I want, I can have him beaten up openly in the marketplace." Rukmini told Munshiji, who pretended not to be concerned, but a fearful doubt settled in his mind. He stopped going for walks in the evening. This new worry took precedence, and ruled by it, he did not even bring Nirmala home, in case this wicked fellow should behave similarly with her. In fact, Jiyaram had once said in an undertone, "Let's see, how will she enter this house now? If I don't insult her before she reaches the house, then my name is not Jiyaram. What will the old man do?" Munshiji well understood that he could do nothing about him. Had it been an outsider, he would have held him in the grip of the police and the law. What would he do with his own son? It is true – if a man loses, he loses only to his own sons.

One day, Doctor Sinha called Jiyaram and started to counsel him. Jiyaram respected him. He sat quietly and listened to him. In the end, Doctor Sinha asked him, "After all, what do you want?"

Jiyaram said, "Should I say it clearly? You will not mind it?"

Doctor Sinha said, "No, whatever is in your heart, tell me clearly."

Jiyaram said, "Then listen. Since my brother has died, I feel angry looking at my father's face. I feel that he killed my brother, and if he gets the chance, he will kill me and my younger brother as well. If this was not so, then why would he have married again?"

Doctor Sinha stifled his laughter with difficulty and said, "Why would he need to remarry to kill you, this I can't understand. He could have murdered you even without marrying!"

Jiyaram said, "Never! That time his heart was of a different kind. He would give his life for us! Now he doesn't even want to see our faces. His only wish is that no one should live in the house other than those two creatures. He wants to remove us from the path of the sons he will have now. This is those two people's heartfelt desire. By giving us all sorts of discomforts, they want to make us run away. That is why he doesn't take on anymore cases now. If we die today, then you will see what a spring of plenty there will be."

Doctor Sinha said, "If he had to get rid of you, wouldn't he just have blamed you for something and turned you out?"

Jiyaram said, "I am already prepared for such a thing."

Doctor Sinha said, "Let's hear what the preparations are."

Jiyaram said, "When the time comes, then you will see."

Saying this, Jiyaram went away. Doctor Sinha called out to him many times, but he did not even turn around once.

Many days later, Doctor Sinha met Jiyaram again. Doctor Sinha loved the cinema, and Jiyaram was passionate about it. Doctor Sinha drew Jiyaram into a conversation by making some allegations about the cinema, and took him home. It was time for food, and both sat down to eat together. Jiyaram found the food delicious, and said, "At my place, since the cook has been sent away, the food is not enjoyable at all. My aunt cooks strictly vegetarian food. I force myself to eat it, but I don't even want to look at the food."

Doctor Sinha said, "At my own home, when the food is cooked, it is much tastier than this. Your aunt must not even be touching onions and garlic?"

Jiyaram replied, "Yes, Sir, she just boils it and keeps it. Lalaji doesn't care whether anyone eats it or not. That is why he removed the cook. If there is no money, where does the jewellery come from?"

The doctor said, "That is not so, Jiyaram, his income has really gone down. You revile him a lot."

Jiyaram laughed and said, "I revile him? You can make me swear to the fact that I don't even talk to him in the first place. He has taken it upon himself to discredit me. Incessantly, needlessly, he is always after me. In fact, he can't bear my friends. Just think, can anyone stay alive without friends? I am not a ruffian that I will keep company with ruffians, but he troubles me everyday about my friends. Yesterday I made it clear – my friends will come to my house, whether anyone likes it or not. Sir, no one can bear such threats all the time."

Doctor Sinha said, "My boy, I feel very sorry for him. This was the age for him to relax. One, he is old, on top of that, is in grief for his son's death, and his health is also not good. What can such a man do? Whatever little he does is enough. If you can't do anything else, at least you can behave well and keep him happy. It is not difficult to please old people. Believe me, talking pleasantly is enough to make him happy. What does it cost you to ask him, 'Father, how is your health?' Your recalcitrance eats his heart. I tell you the truth, he has cried many times. Suppose he made a mistake by marrying. He accepts this as well, but why are you turning your back on your duty?

He is your father, you should serve him. You should not let a single word pass your lips that could hurt him. Why give him the chance to even think that everyone wants to eat out of his earnings, but no one even asks about how he is? I am much older than you, Jiyaram, but even today, I don't answer back to anything my father says. He scolds me even today, and I bow my head and listen. I know that whatever he says is for my own benefit. Who could be a greater well-wisher than our parents? Who can be free of their debt?"

Jiyaram sat and kept crying. His good feelings had not vanished yet, and he could clearly see how rascally his behaviour was. He had not felt so sorry for many days. Crying, he said to Doctor Sahib, "I am very sorry. I got carried away by the words of others. Now you will not hear the slightest complaint against me. Please ask Father to forgive my mistake. I am really very unfortunate. I have troubled him a lot. Please ask him to forgive my faults, otherwise I will blacken my face and go away somewhere, I will drown myself to death."

Doctor Sinha was delighted by his successful counselling. He embraced Jiyaram and sent him home. When Jiyaram reached home, it was eleven o'clock. Munshiji had just eaten and stood outside. Seeing Jiyaram, he said, "Do you know what time it is? It is almost twelve!"

Jiyaram said with great meekness, "I met Doctor Sinha and went to his house with him. He insisted I stay for dinner, so I was forced to stay. That is why I got late."

Munshiji said, "You probably had to cry on Doctor Sinha's shoulder, or had you some other work?"

A quarter of Jiyaram's meekness evaporated, and he said, "I am not in the habit of crying on people's shoulders."

Munshiji said, "Not at all. You don't even have a tongue in your mouth! The things people say to me about you are probably all made up, I suppose?"

Jiyaram said, "I can't say about other days, but today at Doctor Sinha's place, I said nothing that I cannot say here before you."

Munshiji said, "I am very happy to hear that. Tremendously happy! Have you taken a guru's guidance?"

Another quarter of Jiyaram's meekness disappeared. Lifting his head, he said, "A man can be ashamed of his bad traits without taking a guru's guidance. A guru *mantra* is not essential for one's own betterment."

Munshiji said, "I hope the rascals will not meet here now."

Jiyaram said, "Why do you call anyone a rascal, unless you have proof to do so?"

Munshiji said, "All your friends are rascals and ruffians. Not even one of them is a good person. I have told you many times not to let them gather here, but you never listen. Today I tell you for the last time, if you let those rascals gather here, I will have to take the help of the police."

Yet another quarter of Jiyaram's meekness disappeared. Flaring up, he said, "Very well, take the help of the police. Let's see what the police can do. More than half of my friends are sons of police officers. When you are bent upon improving me, why should I uselessly take the trouble?"

Saying this, Jiyaram went into his room and a moment later, the sweet notes of the harmonium wafted out.

The lamp that had been lit by kindness was snuffed out by a single gust of unkind sarcasm. The stubborn horse had started pulling forward, encouraged by affectionate handling, but as soon as the whip fell on its back, it became stubborn again, and started pushing the cart back.

* * *

19

This time, Nirmala had to return home with Sudha. She wanted to stay a few days more in her mother's house, but how could the grieving Sudha stay alone? Ultimately, she had to come.

Rukmini said to Bhoongi, "Do you see how *Bahu* has blossomed in her mother's house?"

Bhoongi replied, "Sister, girls like food cooked by their mothers."

Rukmini said, "You're right, Bhoongi. Only a mother knows how to feed someone well."

Nirmala felt as if none of the people in the house were pleased at her return. Munshiji showed a lot of happiness, but could not hide his deep-rooted worry. Sudha had named the little girl Asha. Indeed, she was a model of hope. Seeing her, one's worries would just disappear. When Munshiji wanted to take her in his lap, she started to cry. She ran and clung to her mother, as though she did not recognise her father. Munshiji tried to lure her with sweets. There was no servant in the house, so he went and told Siyaram to buy sweets worth two *anna*s.

Jiyaram was also sitting there. He spoke up, "Sweets are never bought for us."

Munshiji got annoyed and said, "You are not little children."

Jiyaram said, "Then are we old? Ask someone else to bring the sweets, and then we will know whether we are young or old. Take out four *anna*s more and thanks to Asha, we, too, will benefit."

Munshiji said, "I don't have the money right now. Go Siya, and come back soon."

Jiyaram said, "Siya will not go. He isn't anyone's slave. If Asha is her father's daughter, then he, too, is his father's son."

Munshiji said, "What useless talk is this? Aren't you ashamed of trying to compare yourself with a little girl? Go on, Siyaram, take this money."

Jiyaram said, "Don't go, Siya! You are no one's servant."

Siyaram was in a dilemma. Who should he listen to? In the end, he decided to do as Jiyaram told him to. His father would, at most, scold him, but Jiya would beat him. Who would he then complain to? He said, "I won't go."

Munshiji said, threateningly, "All right, then don't come to me asking for anything."

Munshiji went to the market himself, and bought sweets worth a rupee. He had felt ashamed to ask for sweets worth only two *anna*s. The sweetshop owner recognised him. What would he have thought?

Munshiji went inside with the sweets. Siyaram saw the large box of sweets, and repented for not having listened to his father. Now how could he go inside to ask for sweets? What a mistake he had made. He mentally started comparing the sting of Jiyaram's slaps against the sweetness of the sweets.

Just then, Bhoongi brought two saucers and placed them before the two boys. Jiyaram said angrily, "Take it away!"

Bhoongi said, "Why are you angry, don't you like sweets?"

Jiyaram said, "The sweets came for Asha, not for us. Take it away otherwise I'll throw it out on the road. We have to beg for every *paisa*, and here sweets are being bought for a whole rupee!"

Bhoongi said, "You take it, Siya Babu, even if he doesn't take it."

Siyaram had just hesitantly put out his hand, when Jiyaram said sharply, "Don't touch the sweets, if you do, I'll break your hand! Greedy fellow!"

Siyaram was scared by one rebuke, and did not have the courage to eat the sweets. When Nirmala heard this tale, she went to cajole the two boys. However, her husband stopped her.

Nirmala said, "You don't understand. This anger is directed at me."

Munshiji said, "He has become audacious. I don't behave too harshly thinking that people will say I am troubling motherless children. Otherwise, I would have dealt with their cheek in a trice."

Nirmala said, "This disrepute is exactly what I am afraid of."

Munshiji said, "Now I will not bother, let anyone say what they will."

Nirmala said, "They were not like this earlier!"

Munshiji said, "Oh, he says when you had sons, why did you remarry! He doesn't even have any qualms in saying that you people poisoned Mansaram. He isn't my son, he is my enemy."

Jiyaram stood hidden at the door. He had come there to hear what discussion took place between the lady and the man regarding the sweets. Hearing Munshiji's last sentence, he could not hold himself back. He said, "If I wasn't an enemy, why would you be constantly after me? What you are saying right now, I realised a long time ago. My brother did not realise it and was betrayed. You won't have your way with us. The whole world is saying that my brother was poisoned. When I say it, why do you get so angry?"

Nirmala was shocked to hear this. It felt as though someone had put live embers on her body. Munshiji tried to scold Jiyaram into silence, but Jiyaram stood there brazenly giving replies as hurtful as bricks, where he got merely stones. It reached the point that even Nirmala got angry with him. That worthless young boy, barely an adult, good-for-nothing, was standing and ranting away as though he took care of running the entire house. Raising her eyebrows, she said, "Stop, that's enough now, Jiyaram. It is evident that you are very able. Now go outside and sit."

Thus far, Munshiji had been a little subdued, but now that he had Nirmala's support, he grew braver. Grinding his teeth, he leapt forward and before Nirmala could catch hold of his hand, he tried to slap him. The slap hit Nirmala's face, and she fell forward. Her head spun. She could never have imagined that Munshiji's dried-up hands had so much strength. She sat with her head in her hands. Munshiji's anger flared up even more, and again he swung his hand. However, this time, Jiyaram caught his hand and pushing him back said, "Talk to me from a distance, why do you want to get insulted needlessly? I am thinking of Mother, otherwise I would have shown you what I can do."

Saying this, he went out. Munshiji stood there, dumb struck. If at this moment a divine thunderbolt had struck down upon Jiyaram, perhaps he would have been heartily pleased. The same son, whom he would once hold in his lap and experience selfless love, now aroused all kinds of negative feelings in his mind.

Rukmini was in her room till then. Coming out now, she said, "When your son is an adult, you should not lay hands on him."

Munshiji bit his lip and said, "I will turn him out of the house. Whether he begs or steals, it has nothing to do with me."

Rukmini said, "Whose honour will be hurt?"

Munshiji said, "I don't care."

Nirmala said, "Had I known that my coming would trigger this storm, I would not have dreamt of coming back. It would still be better for you to send me back even now. I won't be able to bear staying in this house."

Rukmini said, "He has great regard for you, *Bahu*! Otherwise a great calamity would have befallen us today."

Nirmala said, "What worse calamity can befall us, Sister? Even though I tread so carefully, still aspersions are cast on me. I have hardly set foot in the house and this incident occurred. Only God can do something good now."

That night, no one rose to eat dinner; Munshiji ate alone. Today Nirmala had a new worry – how would she go through life? If there had only been herself to consider, she would not have been particularly worried. Now a new problem clutched at her throat. She was wondering, 'What is written in my daughter's fate, oh, Lord Ram?"

* * *

20

How does one sleep if one is worried? Nirmala was tossing and turning on her bed. However much she wanted sleep to come, it was as though sleep had sworn to stay away. She had turned out the lamp, opened the windows and kept the ticking clock in the other room; yet sleep eluded her. Whatever she had to ponder, she had already pondered over – even her worries were exhausted, but she could not sleep a wink. Then she relit the lamp and started reading a book. She must have just read two or three pages, when her eyes shut. The book remained open.

Just then, Jiyaram stepped inside the room. His feet were trembling. He looked up and down the room. Nirmala was asleep; on the shelf near her bedside was kept a small brass box. Jiyaram tiptoed over, slowly took down the box, and quickly went out of the room. At that moment, Nirmala's eyes opened. Shaken, she stood up. Going to the door, she looked out. Her heart skipped a beat. Was that Jiyaram? What had he come to her room for? Maybe she had been mistaken. Maybe he had come from Rukmini's room. What work had he here? Maybe he had wanted to say something to her, but why would he have come at this time to say it? What was his intention? Her heart trembled.

Munshiji was sleeping upstairs on the roof. There was no railing, so Nirmala could not sleep there. She thought of going and waking him up, but she did not have the courage to go. He was a suspicious man, who knew what he might think, and what he might get prepared to do? She went back and started reading the book again. She would ask about it in the morning, and everything would be clear. Who knew, perhaps she had been mistaken! One could be mistaken in a sleepy state. However, even the decision of asking about it in the morning did not bring back her sleep.

In the morning, when she herself took breakfast for Jiyaram, he was shaken to see her. Everyday, Bhoongi would come, then why was she here today? He did not have the courage to look at Nirmala.

Nirmala looked at him with trusting eyes and said, "Had you come to my room at night?"

Jiyaram feigned surprise, and said, "I? What would I go there at night for? Had someone gone there?"

Nirmala said as though she completely believed him, "Yes, I felt as though someone went out of my room. I didn't see his face, but seeing his back, I thought that maybe you had come for some work. How can I find out who it was? I have no doubt that someone entered my room!"

Trying to prove his innocence, Jiyaram said, "I had gone to the theatre last night. When I returned from there, I went to a friend's place and stayed till late. It has only been a little while since I've come home. There were many other friends with me. You can ask whoever you want. Yes, I am very afraid. It should not happen that something is missing, and I am accused of it. No one will catch the thief; it'll all come onto my head. You know Father. He will run to kill me."

Nirmala said, "Why would you be accused? Even if it had been you, no one can accuse you of theft. A thief steals someone else's things; no one steals their own things."

So far, Nirmala had not gazed upon her brass box. She started cooking. When her husband went to court, she went to meet Sudha. They had not met for many days, and she also wanted to discuss the last night's incident. She said to Bhoongi, "Bring the jewellery box from my room."

Bhoongi returned and said, "There is no box there. Where had you kept it?"

Nirmala said in an irritated tone, "You can never do anything in one go. Where will it go to from there? Did you check in the cupboard?"

Bhoongi said, "No, *Bahuji*. I didn't check the cupboard, why should I lie?" Nirmala smiled. She said, "Then go look and come back quickly."

In a moment, Bhoongi returned empty-handed, again. She said, "It isn't in the cupboard either."

Nirmala got up in anger, saying, "I don't know why God gave you eyes. Now see whether or not I bring it from that very room."

Bhoongi also followed her into the room. Nirmala cast her eyes on the shelf and then opened the cupboard and looked. She looked under the bed, then opened the big clothes' trunk and looked there. The little box was nowhere to be seen. She was surprised – where could the box have gone?

Suddenly, that night's incident flashed before her eyes. Her heart leapt. Till now, she had been searching with blithe unconcern. Now, as though she burnt, she started searching everywhere with great vigour. It was nowhere to be seen. She searched where she ought to, and she searched where she ought not to. How could such a big box be hidden in the bedding? However, she still dusted out the bedding. Her face grew paler with every passing moment. Her spirits ebbed, and she felt them sinking to her feet, till finally giving up, she struck a blow on her chest and started crying.

Jewellery is the only property a woman has. She has no rights over any other property of her husband's. These are the only things that give her strength and pride. Nirmala had jewellery worth about five or six thousand. Whenever she wore them and went out, her heart would be full of joy for that period of time. It was as though each article of jewellery was a form of protection against problems and obstacles. Just last night she had thought that she would not stay there, dependant on Jiyaram. May God never bring it to pass that she should have to beg anyone for anything. This was the rudder with which she would steer the boat of her life, and she would manage to settle her daughter at a bank along the way, as well. Why should she worry? No one would snatch these from her. Today, they adorned her, tomorrow they would support her – how much comfort she had derived from this thought. That asset had slipped out of her hand today. Now she had no backing. In this whole world, there was not even the littlest part for her; there was no support for her. With the foundation of her hopes cut off at the roots, she started crying uncontrollably. "Oh God! Could you not even see this much? You had already handicapped my unhappy self, and now you gouged my eyes out." Who would she now spread her hands before, at whose doorstep would she beg? Her entire body was drenched in sweat and her eyes were swollen from crying. Nirmala was crying with bowed head. Rukmini was trying to give her courage, but her tears would not stop, the fire of her grief would not lessen.

At three o'clock, Jiyaram returned from school. On hearing of his return, Nirmala rose as one demented, and coming to the door of his room, said, "Brother, if you played a joke, give it back. What will you get by troubling an unfortunate woman?"

For a moment, Jiyaram felt like a coward. This was his first attempt in the art of stealing. He had not yet attained that hardness which delights in violence. If he still had the box, and if he had enough opportunity to put it back on the shelf, he would never have passed up the chance – but the box had left his hands. His friends had already dispatched it to the pawnshop and sold it for a pittance. What can protect thieves other than untruths? He said, "But, Mother, why would I play such a joke on you? You are still continuing to suspect me. I have told you that I was not at home last night, but you still don't believe me. It is very sad that you think I would fall so low."

Wiping her tears, Nirmala said, "I do not suspect you, Brother! I don't blame you for theft. I thought perhaps it was a joke."

How could she suspect Jiyaram of theft? The world would just say that because the boy's mother is dead, he is being accused of theft. It was her image that would be blackened!

Jiyaram said reassuringly, "Come, I'll look. Who can take it, after all? From where could the thief have come?"

Bhoongi said, "Brother, you are talking of thieves coming. They can come out of mouse holes, then, there are windows all around here."

Jiyaram said, "Have you searched thoroughly?"

Nirmala said, "We have searched the whole house, where else would you have us look?"

Jiyaram said, "You people sleep as though you are competing with the dead."

When Munshiji returned home at four o'clock, he saw Nirmala's state and asked, "How are you feeling? Are you in pain?" Saying this, he took Asha in his lap.

Nirmala was unable to answer, and started crying again.

Bhoongi said, "This has never happened before. I have spent my entire life in this house. Till date, not even a *paisa* has ever been stolen. The world will say it was Bhoongi's work. May God keep the way smooth for me."

Munshiji who was unbuttoning his coat, closed the buttons again and asked, "What happened? Was something stolen?"

Bhoongi said, "All of *Bahu's* jewellery has been taken."

Munshiji asked, "Where was it kept?"

Sobbing, Nirmala recounted the entire incident of the night, but did not mention having seen a man who resembled Jiyaram leaving her room. Munshiji drew in a long breath and said, "God is very unfair. He kills those who are already dying. It appears that bad days have come. But where did the thief come from? There is no sign of a break-in, and there is no way to enter from any side. I haven't committed any sin for which I am being given this punishment. I kept telling you – don't leave the jewellery box on the shelf, but who listens to me?"

Nirmala said, "How was I to know that this catastrophe would break upon us?"

Munshiji said, "You do know that not all days are the same. If I get the same jewellery made today, it will cost not less than ten thousand. My present condition is not hidden from you. It is hard enough to make ends meet, how will we get ornaments made? I will go and inform the police, but don't have any hope of recovery."

Nirmala objected, "When you know that nothing will come of informing the police, why are you going there?"

Munshiji said, "My heart is not convinced, why else? Having sustained such a heavy loss, I cannot sit quietly."

Nirmala said, "If they were to be found, then why would they be gone in the first place? They were not written in my fate, then how could they stay?"

Munshiji said, "If they are in our fate, they will be found. If not, they are gone in any case."

As Munshiji left the room, Nirmala held his hand and said, "I say, don't go. It should happen that we may well lose more than we gain."

Munshiji shook off her hand and said, "You are insisting on it like some child. A loss of ten thousand is not something that I can bear nonchalantly. I am not crying, but only I know what is happening in my heart. This blow has hurt me deeply to the core." Munshiji was not able to say anymore. Words stuck in his throat. He quickly went out of the room and stopped only when he reached the police station. The police officer respected him greatly. He had once successfully fought a case for him when he had been charged with taking bribes. He came along with him to investigate the matter. His name was Alayar Khan.

It was evening. The policeman looked in the front and back of the house. Coming in, he went to Nirmala's room and looked around intently. He surveyed the upstairs ledge. He secretly spoke with a few people from the neighbourhood and then he said to Munshiji, "Sir, I swear to God, this is not an outside job. I swear to God, if it turns out to be someone from the outside, I will give up police work from today. Is there any servant in your house that you are suspicious of?"

Munshiji said, "These days we only have one maidservant."

The police officer said, "Oh, she is mad! This is the work of someone very clever, I swear to God."

Munshiji said, "Then who else is there in the house? There are my two sons, wife and my sister. Out of them, whom shall I suspect?"

The policeman said, "I swear to God, it is the work of someone from the house, whoever it may be! *Inshallah*, I will give you further news of this matter in a few days. I cannot promise that all the stolen goods will also be found, but I swear to God, I will definitely catch the thief."

When the police officer left, Munshiji came and told Nirmala what he had said.

Nirmala was scared, and said, "Please tell the officer not to continue with his investigation, I beg of you!"

Munshiji said, "But why?"

Nirmala replied, "Shall I tell you why? He said that it was the work of someone from within the house."

Munshiji said, "Let him rattle on."

Jiyaram was sitting in his room praying to God. His face was pale and drawn. He had heard that the police officers could tell a thief from his face. He did not have the courage to step outside. He was quivering to know what the two men had spoken of.

As soon as the police officer left, and Bhoongi came out for some work, Jiyaram asked, "What was the officer saying, Bhoongi?"

Bhoongi came closer and said, "The bearded man was saying that it is the work of someone from within the house, not someone from outside."

Jiyaram said, "Didn't Father say anything?"

Bhoongi replied, "He didn't say anything at all, just stood saying 'Hmmm hmmm'. The only outsider here is Bhoongi! Everyone else is family."

Jiyaram said, "I am also an outsider, why only you?"

Bhoongi asked, "Why are you an outsider, Brother?"

Jiyaram said, "Didn't Father say anything to the policeman? That he doesn't suspect anyone in the house?"

Bhoongi said, "I didn't hear him say anything. The poor policeman said that Bhoongi is mad, how can she steal anything? Else *Babuji* would have had me jailed."

Jiyaram said, "Then you are also out of it. I, alone, am left. You tell me, had you seen me in the house that day?"

Bhoongi said, "No, Brother, you had gone to the theatre."

Jiyaram said, "You will testify to it, won't you?"

Bhoongi exclaimed, "What are you saying, Brother? *Babuji* will put a stop to the investigation."

Jiyaram said, "Really?"

Bhoongi replied, “Yes, Brother, she keeps saying that the investigation should be stopped. If the ornaments have gone, let them go. But *Babuji* is not agreeing.”

For the next five or six days, Jiyaram did not eat properly. Sometimes he would eat a few morsels, at other times, he would say he was not hungry. His face remained pale. He would stay up at nights; he spent every moment dreading the policeman’s return. Had he known the matter would stretch so far, he would never have done such a thing! He had thought that some thief would be suspected, and no one would even consider him for a moment, but now it seemed that the case would be solved and his game was almost up. The way the wretched policeman was conducting the investigation was causing a great deal of anxiety to Jiyaram.

On the seventh day, when he returned home in the evening, he was very worried. Until today, he always had slender hopes of being saved. The goods had not been found anywhere yet, but today, there had been news of some of the goods may have been discovered. The police officer and constable may be on their way here. There was no way of escape left. It was possible that by bribing the officer, he might succeed in suppressing any further prosecution. He had the money in his hands. However, would the matter stay quiet? The goods had not been found as yet, but the rumour all over town was that the son had stolen the ornaments. Once they were found, the story would be rife in every street. Then he would not be able to show his face anywhere.

When Munshiji returned home from the court, he appeared very anxious and shaken. He sat down on the cot with his head in his hands.

Nirmala said, “Why don’t you change your clothes?

Munshiji said, “What clothes shall I change? Did you hear anything?”

Nirmala asked, “What is the matter? I didn’t hear anything.”

Munshiji replied, “The goods have been found. Now it will be difficult for Jiya to escape.”

Nirmala was not surprised. From her expression it seemed as though she already knew this fact. She said, “I had asked you from the beginning not to go to the police station.”

Munshiji asked, "You suspected Jiya?"

Nirmala replied, "Why would I not suspect him, I had seen him going out of my room."

Munshiji said, "Then why didn't you tell me?"

Nirmala replied, "This was not something for me to say. You would have felt in your heart that I was making allegations because I was jealous. Would you not have thought so? Don't lie."

Munshiji said, "It is possible, I can't disagree. Even then, you should have told me. I would not have reported the matter. You were concerned about your good name, but did not consider what the outcome would be? I will go to the police station just now. Alayar Khan will be coming any moment now."

Sadly, Nirmala asked, "What now?"

Munshiji looked up towards the sky and said, "Now? As God wishes! If I had a thousand or two thousand for bribes, perhaps the matter could be suppressed, but you know my condition. It is my bad luck, nothing else. I have committed sins, who will bear the consequences? I had a son and look at what happened to him. The second is in this state. He was useless, did wrong things, shirked work, but is my son! Sooner or later he would have matured. I can't bear this hurt anymore."

Nirmala said, "If we can give some money and save our lives, I will arrange for the money."

Munshiji asked, "You can arrange it? How much money can you give?"

Nirmala said, "How much will be required?"

Munshiji replied, "Discussion of the matter may not be possible for less than a thousand. I had charged a thousand rupees for a case I had fought for him. Today, he will compensate himself for that sum."

Nirmala said, "It will be done. Now go to the police station."

Munshiji was very late returning from the police station. He got the chance to talk in solitude after a long wait. Alayar Khan was an old hand at it. With great difficulty, he agreed. Even after taking five hundred rupees, he managed to place a heavy load of obligation on Munshiji's head.

The work was done. Returning home he said to Nirmala, "There you go, we won the day. You gave the money, but my tongue did the work. After a great deal of difficulty, I convinced him. This, too, I will remember. Has Jiyaram eaten?"

Nirmala replied, "Where, he hasn't come home yet."

Munshiji said, "It must be twelve o'clock."

Nirmala said, "I went many times to look. The room is in darkness."

Munshiji asked, "And Siyaram?"

Nirmala replied, "He ate and fell asleep."

Munshiji asked, "Didn't you ask him where Jiya had gone?"

Nirmala said, "He says that he did not tell him anything when he went out."

Munshiji felt a little doubtful. He woke up Siyaram and asked, "Didn't Jiyaram say anything to you about when he would return? Where did he go?"

Siyaram said, scratching his head and rubbing his eyes, "He didn't say anything to me."

Munshiji said, "He has worn all his clothes and gone?"

Siyaram replied, "No, Sir. He wore a kurta and dhoti."

Munshiji asked, "Did he seem happy when he left?"

Siyaram said, "He did not look happy. He would turn around to enter the house but he would return from the threshold. Then he stood under the awning for many minutes. When he started to walk away, he was wiping his eyes. For many days now, he would often cry."

Munshiji took a deep breath as though there was nothing left in life anymore. He said to Nirmala, "On your part, you did it for the best, but even an enemy could not have struck a crueller blow to me. If Jiyaram's mother had been alive, would she have hesitated? Never ever!"

Nirmala said, "Why don't you go over to Doctor Sahib's place? Maybe he is over there. Many boys go there daily, you could ask them, maybe you can find out something. Even though I was so careful, I have still attracted infamy."

Munshiji said woodenly, as though speaking to an open window, "Yes, I am going. What else can I do?"

When Munshiji stepped out, he saw Doctor Sinha standing there. Surprised, he asked, "Have you been standing here long?"

Doctor Sinha replied, "No, I just arrived. Where are you going at this time? It is half past twelve."

Munshiji said, "I was coming towards your house. Jiyaram has still not returned home from his walk. Did he happen to go towards your place?"

Doctor Sinha held both of Munshiji's hands and could only say, "Brother, you must be strong..." before Munshiji collapsed on the ground as though he had been shot.

* * *

21

An annoyed Rukmini knit her brows and said to Nirmala, "Will he go barefoot to school?"

Nirmala was plaiting her daughter's hair. She replied, "What can I do? I don't have any money."

Rukmini said, "Money to buy ornaments can be saved, but giving money for the boy's shoes burns you up! Two of them have already gone. Do you intend to make the last one weep till he dies?"

Nirmala drew in a deep breath and said, "Whoever has to live, will live. Who has to die, will die. I don't go around killing or burning anyone."

These days, Rukmini and Nirmala quarrelled over something or the other, daily. The theft of Nirmala's jewellery had wrought a complete change in her temperament. She saved money now with great desperation, as though clenching every *paisa* with her teeth. So what if Siyaram died crying? He would not get any money for sweets and this behaviour was not reserved for Siyaram only – Nirmala even postponed fulfilling her own needs. Until the old clothes were rent to shreds, new clothes would not be bought. For months altogether, hair oil would not be bought. She used to enjoy chewing paan, but now the betel nut box stayed empty for days on end. She even stopped buying milk for her daughter. The future of her young child took on gigantic proportions that constantly hovered in her mind, troubling her thoughts.

Munshiji had surrendered himself to Nirmala's care and was completely ruled by her. He would not interfere in anything she did. It was not clearly known, but for some reason, he always seemed a little intimidated by her. He now went to court without fail. He had not worked so hard even in his youth. His eyesight had become so poor that Doctor Sinha prohibited him from reading and writing at night. His digestion had always been weak; now it worsened. He had also started complaining of asthma, but the poor man worked from early morning till midnight. Whether or not he wanted to work, whether or not his health was fine; he had to work. Nirmala did not feel the slightest pity for him. The great, terrible worry about the future was destroying all her finer, inner feelings. If she heard a beggar's cry, she would flare up. She did not want to spend even a single *paisa*.

One day, Nirmala sent Siyaram to the market to buy ghee. She did not trust Bhoongi and did not ask her to buy anything anymore. Siyaram did not have the habit of stealing and cheating. He did not know how to falsify accounts. Therefore, he had to do all the market work. Nirmala would weigh each and every thing. If there was the littlest discrepancy in weight, she would return it.

A lot of Siyaram's time was spent going to and fro like this. The shopkeepers would not sell him anything quickly. The same situation occurred today. As far as he knew, Siyaram had bought very good ghee only after checking at many shops, but as soon as Nirmala smelt it, she said, "The ghee is bad. Return it."

Siyaram said angrily, "There is no better ghee in the market. I have bought this after checking in all the shops."

Nirmala said, "So then am I lying?"

Siyaram said, "I am not trying to say that, but the shopkeeper will not take the ghee back now. He had told me to check the ghee in any way I wanted right there as the goods were right in front. But at the auspicious start of the business day, he would not take back the sold goods. I smelt it, tasted it and then bought it. With what face shall I return it now?"

Through clenched teeth, Nirmala said, "The ghee clearly has fat mixed in it, and you say that this is good ghee. I will not take it into the kitchen. You can return it if you want to or eat it if you like."

Leaving the pot of ghee there, Nirmala went into the house. Siyaram was rendered irresolute with anger and disappointment. With what face would he go to return it? The shopkeeper would outright refuse to take it back. What would he do then? The other ten or fifteen nearby shopkeepers and passersby would stand there and watch. He would have to be embarrassed in front of everyone. As it was, none of the shopkeepers in the market gave him any goods easily, but after this, he would be able to go to any shop. He would be scolded from all sides. He quivered with anger and thought in his own mind, 'Let the ghee lie there, I will not go to return it.'

There is no sadder, poorer person in the world than a motherless child. All other sorrows can be forgotten. The boy now sorely missed his mother and thought, 'If Mother had been alive today, would I have had to suffer all this?' His eldest brother had gone, Jiyaram had also gone, why was he left alone to bear the brunt of this problem? A torrent of tears arose from Siyaram's eyes. His throat was constricted by grief and sorrow; he heaved a deep sigh and these words escaped, "Mother! Why have you forgotten me, why don't you call me to you?"

Just then, Nirmala again came towards the room. She thought that Siyaram would have gone by now. When she saw him sitting there, she said angrily, "You are still sitting here? When will the food be cooked?"

Siyaram wiped his tears. He said, "I will get late for school."

Nirmala said, "If you are late one day, there is no harm in it! This work is for the house, isn't it?

Siyaram said, "This happens everyday! I never reach school on time. I don't get time to study at home, either. Nothing is bought before being returned three or four times. I am the one who gets scolded. I am the one who gets embarrassed. What is that to you?"

Nirmala said, "Yes, what is it to me? I am your enemy, after all! If it was someone of your own, then they would feel sad. I pray to God that you are not able to study. I am the one full of all the faults. You are blameless. The name 'stepmother' is a bad one. If your own mother feeds you poison, even that is like nectar. If I was to feed you nectar, it would become poison. Because of you people, my life had been ground to dust and I am ruined. My life is being spent weeping. I don't know why God brought me into this world, but according to you, I am living well, and I get great pleasure out of troubling you. Even God doesn't ask me whether I would like to live, otherwise all the problems would come to an end."

Saying this, Nirmala's eyes filled with tears. She went inside.

Siyaram was scared seeing her cry. He did not feel any regret, but he was worried about what punishment he might incur. He quietly picked up the pot and went to return the ghee, much like a dog entering a new village. Just like that dog, his internal sadness was evident in his entire being. Looking at his abject appearance, even someone with moderate understanding could tell that he was an orphan.

As Siyaram went further ahead, the fear of the coming battle made his heartbeat increase. He decided that if the shopkeeper did not take the ghee back, he would leave the ghee there and come back. The tired shopkeeper would call him back on his own. He even thought of words to upbraid the shopkeeper with. He would say, 'Why, Trader Sir, are you trying to throw dust in my eyes and trick me? Showing the best stuff, you give the worst?' Even having decided this, his feet still crept forward, slowly lifting and dragging themselves forward. He did not want the shopkeeper to see him coming; he wanted to appear before him suddenly. So, he took a roundabout path and went to the shop via another lane.

As soon as the shopkeeper saw him, he said, "I had said I will not take back sold goods. Tell me, had I not said so?"

Siyaram said angrily, "You did not give me the ghee you showed me. You showed me one thing and gave me another, so how will you not take it back? Is this some kind of cheating?"

The shopkeeper said, "If there is any ghee finer than this in the market, I will pay the fine. Pick up the pot and check in a few shops."

Siyaram said, "I don't have so much of free time. Take back your ghee."

The shopkeeper said, "I will not take it back."

At the shop, a *sadhu* with matted hair was sitting and watching this drama. Getting up, he came to Siyaram and smelt the ghee in the pot. He said, "Child, the ghee appears to be very good."

The shopkeeper, getting support, said, "*Babaji*, we don't give him poor quality stuff. Does one give bad goods to known customers?"

The *sadhu* said, "Take the ghee, child. It is very good."

Siyaram burst out crying. What proof did he now have to show that the ghee was bad? He said, "She is the one who says the ghee is not good, give it back. I said that it is good."

The *sadhu* asked, "Who says so?"

The shopkeeper said, "His mother must be saying so. No goods please her. She makes the poor boy run back and forth, again and again. She is his stepmother, that's why! If it was his own mother, she would care a little for him."

The *sadhu* looked at Siyaram with kind eyes, as though his heart was aching to comfort him. In tender tones, he said, "How long has it been since your mother passed away, child?"

Siyaram said, "It is the sixth year now."

The *sadhu* said, "Then you must have been very small at the time. God, how strange your divine dramas are. You denied this sweet, innocent lad his mother's love. What a terrible thing you do, God! A six-year-old child had to encounter a demonic stepmother! You are great, oh, kind God. Shopkeeper, have mercy on the child – take back the ghee, otherwise his mother will not let him stay in the house. By God's grace, all your ghee will be sold soon. My blessings are with you."

The shopkeeper did not return the money. Ultimately, the boy would have to come again to buy ghee. Who knew how many times in a day he would have to make the trip back and forth, and what frauds he would meet on the way. The shopkeeper gave Siyaram the best ghee in his shop. Siyaram was thinking in his heart, 'How kind this *sadhu* is. If he had not put in a word for me, why would the shopkeeper have given me the good ghee?'

When Siyaram took the ghee and started off again, the *sadhu* also went with him. On the way, he started talking sweetly to the boy.

"Child, my mother, too, had left me for her heavenly abode when I was three years old. Since then, whenever I see motherless children, my heart begins to break."

Siyaram asked him, "Did your father also marry a second time?"

The *sadhu* said, "Yes, child, otherwise why would I be a *sadhu* today? Earlier my father would not agree to marry. He used to love me a lot. Then I don't know why he changed his mind. He got married. I am a spiritual seeker, so I should not utter harsh words, but my stepmother was as harsh as she was beautiful. She would not give me anything to eat the entire day, and would beat me up if I cried. Father also turned his eyes away. He started hating the sight of me. Hearing me cry, he would start to beat me. In the end, one day, I left my house and struck out for myself."

The thought of running away from home had entered Siyaram's mind many times as well. Even now, the same thought was rising in his mind. With great enthusiasm, he said, "Where did you go when you left your house?"

The *sadhu* laughed and said, "That day all my troubles ended. The day I was freed of the ties of home and fear left my heart, from that day, my life improved. The entire day I sat under a bridge. In the evening, I met a great man. His name was Swami Paramanandji. He was a young *sadhu*. He took pity on me and took me under his care. With him I started travelling all over the country. He was a very good Yogi. He taught me Yoga as well. Now I am so adept that whenever I wish, I can see my mother; I can even talk to her!"

Siyaram looked at him with wide eyes and asked, "Hadn't your mother passed away?"

The *sadhu* said, "So what, child? Yogic knowledge has such power that you can call upon any deceased spirit you wish to."

Siyaram said, "If I learn yogic knowledge, will I also be able to see my mother?"

The *sadhu* said, "Of course! Practice makes everything possible. Yes, you need a competent teacher. Yoga can help you attain great powers, get as much wealth as you want in a second. Whatever the disease may be, you can prescribe the medicine for it."

Siyaram asked, "Where do you live?"

The *sadhu* said, "Child, I have no place anywhere. I roam all over the country. Well child, go now. I shall go to bathe and meditate."

Siyaram said, "Come, I will also go that way. I have not yet had my fill of your company."

The *sadhu* said, "No, child. You are getting late for school."

Siyaram asked, "When will I see you again?"

The *sadhu* said, "I will come again, anytime, child. Where is your house?"

Siyaram was pleased and said, "Will you come to my house? It is very near. It would be very kind of you."

Siyaram walked ahead, lengthening his strides. He was so happy as though he was carrying along a sack of gold. On reaching the house, he said, "Please come and sit for a while."

The *sadhu* said, "No, child. I will not sit. I will come again, tomorrow or day after. This is your house?"

Siyaram asked, "At what time will you come tomorrow?"

The *sadhu* said, "I cannot say for sure. I will come sometime."

The *sadhu* went on and just a little way ahead, he met another *sadhu*. His name was Hariharanand.

Paramanand asked, "Where all did you go? Did you find any quarry?"

Hariharanand said, "I roamed all over, but I did not find any quarry. When I did, it was an odd fellow, who started making fun of me."

Paramanand said, "I believe I have found one. If I trap him, I'll know."

Hariharanand said, "You just say so. Whoever comes along runs away after a few days!"

Paramanand said, "This time he won't run away, just you see. His mother has died. The father married again. His stepmother troubles him a lot. He is disenchanted with his home."

Hariharanand said, "Yes, if that is the case then he will certainly get trapped! You have laid it on thick, haven't you?"

Paramanand said, "Oh, very well! This is the best strategy. First we should find out beforehand, which houses in which locality have stepmothers in them. Then, we should only throw out lures in those houses."

* * *

22

Nirmala blurted out irately, "What took you so long?"

Siyaram mulishly said, "I slept somewhere on the street."

"I wouldn't have said this, but do you know what time it is? The clock struck ten long ago. The market is quite nearby," Nirmala said.

Siyaram retorted, "Not 'quite nearby'. It's right at your doorstep!"

"Can you ever avoid being rude? Why are you so cross? You act as if you had gone out for an errand of mine!"

Siyaram said, "Why do you have to mention irrelevant nonsense? It's not easy to trade, that, too, with the crooked *baniya.* One has to haggle for hours. A *Babaji* said a lot of things to him for me and only then did he give me ghee or else I would not have returned. I didn't stop anywhere for even a minute and headed straight for home."

Nirmala continued, "You went to get ghee and you're returning at eleven in the morning! Now when you go to fetch firewood, you will return only in the evening! Your father left without eating his meal. Why didn't you say earlier on that you would take so long? Will you get firewood now?"

Siyaram was unable to control himself now. He said in great irritation, "You may ask someone else to fetch the firewood. I am getting late for school."

"Won't you eat your meal?" said Nirmala.

"No, I won't."

"I am ready to cook. Yes, but I can't fetch firewood by myself," said Nirmala.

"Why don't you send Bhoongi?"

"Have you ever seen what she has brought?"

"Then I won't go at this hour to fetch your firewood," Siyaram asserted."Then don't blame me," said Nirmala.

Siyaram had not attended school for many days now. Running market errands had eaten into his study time – he had not even opened his school books for many days. What was the point in attending school when everyday resulted in rough reprimands or standing on the bench or wearing a dunce cap? He would leave home with books in his hands, but outside the city outskirts, he would sit under the shade of a tree or watch the passersby. He would return home at three in the afternoon. Today, he left home with the aim of sitting under the shade of a tree, but could not sit for long. His insides were burning. 'Yes, so now, even rotis were impossible to get! Could the food not be ready by ten? Given that *Babuji* had left, but did that mean that there weren't a few *paise* left for me?' mused Siyaram. 'Had my *Amma* been there, would she have let me go without eating and drinking something? I have nobody that I can call mine,' sighed Siyaram.

Siyaram was overwhelmed with wanting to meet *Babaji.* He thought, 'Where can I find him at this hour? Where should I go to look?' *Babaji's* gentle voice and optimistic consolations began to tug at Siyaram's heart. He grew terribly restless and said, "Why didn't I go with him? What is left for me at home?"

Today, he had changed his route and reached the ghee shop, instead of going home. He thought he might meet *Babaji* at the shop, but he was not there. After standing and waiting for a long time, he returned home.

He had just reached home and sat down, when Nirmala came to him and said, "Where did you go that you got so late? No meal was prepared in the morning. Is it going to be the same fast now also? Go and fetch some vegetables from the market."

Siyaram retorted, "I have returned after being hungry the whole day. You don't even serve me with a glass of water, and on top of that, you order me to go the market. I will not go to the market. I am nobody's servant. In fact, it's only roti that you serve me, what else? Such rotis I can get by working. If I have to perform labour, I will not work for you. You can go. You don't have to cook for me."

Nirmala was taken aback and wondered, 'What has happened to this boy today? On other days, he would quietly run errands. Why is he throwing tantrums today?' Even then, it did not occur to her to give him a little money for a meal.

Nirmala had become tightfisted over the course of time, and she said, "Doing housework is not termed 'labour'. Then, by the same argument, I can say I won't cook, or your *Babuji* can say he won't go to the court. What will happen then? If you don't want to go, then don't. I will ask Bhoongi. I never knew you disliked going to the market, otherwise, for a little extra money, I would have got those things from the market, and not sent you. From today, I won't ask you and I apologise."

Siyaram felt slightly embarrassed, but he still did not go to the market. He was preoccupied with thoughts about *Babaji*. He knew that the end of all his misery and seeing hope in his life lay in *Babaji's* blessings. Siyaram felt his unguided life would gain direction and focus under his tutelage. Siyaram became restless. He searched the entire market, but he could not find *Babaji* anywhere. Hungry and thirsty the whole day, the innocent young boy pressed his hands against his aching heart, and with hope and fear chiselled upon him, he searched and searched. He looked for *Babaji* all over in the shops, streets and temples. He wandered looking for that refuge and rest, without which his life was becoming unbearable. Once, he saw a saint standing in front of a temple. He appeared to be like *Babaji*. An exultant Siyaram joyously ran towards the saint. On approaching him, he stood near him, but it was some other saint. He grew disappointed and moved on.

As the evening progressed, the streets slowly became more and more deserted and silent. It was time to rest from a hard day's work. People had started laying out their bamboo cots or sacks on the streets, getting absorbed in sweet sleep, but Siyaram did not reach home. He was heartbroken because of that home, where, he felt, nobody loved him. He was a dependent, just because he had nowhere else to go. At this moment also, who was there to worry about him if he did not reach home?

'*Babuji* must have slept after his meals; *Ammaji* must be also preparing to retire to bed. Nobody would have even peeped into my room to see if I am there. *Buaji* must be worried. She will be waiting for me. Until I have reached, she won't even eat her meal,' and so he kept pondering.

As soon as Siyaram remembered Rukmini, he turned towards home. If nothing else, then at least, she would cuddle him in her lap and cry. She would keep a bucketful of water ready for him to wash his hands and face, when he returned from outside. Not all the children in the world rinse their mouths with milk, not all eat portions of gold; not all are so fortunate. There are many who do not sleep on a full stomach, but the one most distanced from home is the one bereft of motherly affection.

Siyaram suddenly caught a glimpse of Baba Paramanand as he was about to return home.

Siyaram rushed to him and held his hand. A surprised Paramanand asked, "Child, what are you doing here?"

Making an excuse, Siyaram said, "I'd come to meet a friend. How far is your place from here?"

"Child, we are leaving this place today on a visit to Haridwar."

Siyaram became morose. "Will you leave today itself?"

"Yes, child, I will meet you when I return."

In desperation, Siyaram asked, "Returning…?"

"I will return soon, my child"

Siyaram said in a suppressed tone, "I will come along with you."

"With me! Would your family allow you?"

"Nobody at home worries about me." He could not say anymore. His tearfilled eyes told his whole tale in a more poignant manner than his words ever could have.

Paramanand hugged Siyaram and said, "All right, child, if you so wish, you can join me. Enjoy the bliss of being in the company of saints and ascetics. If God desires it, all your wishes shall be fulfilled."

The bird hovering over a tiny seed eventually fell upon the seed. How will his life end, whether in a cage or under the butcher's knife – who knows what will happen?

* * *

23

Munshiji returned from the court at five in the evening and fell back on his bed. His aged body showed the effects of hunger. His mouth was dry. Nirmala understood that the day had gone without earning anything.

"Did you not get anything today?" she asked.

"I spent the entire day running from pillar to post, but in vain."

"What happened with the criminal case?"

"My client was sentenced."

"What about the case of the priest?"

"He received the court degree."

"But you were always confident that the case would be dissolved."

"Yes, I did say so and I still do. But who will think so much over it?"

"And what about the Seerwale case?"

"I lost that, too."

"Then you woke up seeing some unfortunate person's face."

Munshiji was not able to work at all. He hardly got any cases and the ones that came his way met a bad fate. Munshiji kept hiding his failures from Nirmala. The day when he did not make any money, he would borrow some and give it to her. He had borrowed money from nearly everyone he knew. He could not manage to borrow from anyone today.

Nirmala said, in a concerned tone, "If this is the condition of your income, then only God is our saviour. On top of that, the condition of your son is that it is difficult for him to go to the market. I feel like asking Bhoongi to do all the work. Your son returned home at eleven after buying only ghee. I gave up asking him to fetch firewood, but he didn't listen at all."

"So, you haven't cooked?" asked Munshiji.

"Because of such things, you lose your court cases. Has anyone cooked without firewood that I would have done the same?" said Nirmala.

"So, he left home without eating?" said Munshiji.

"What else was there in the house that I could have fed him with?"

Munshiji asked timidly and hesitantly, "Did you give him some money?"

Nirmala frowned and said, "Money grows on trees in this home, doesn't it?"

Munshiji remained silent. He waited for some time in the hope of some refreshments. When he found that Nirmala had not even sent for water, he went outside, disappointed. He grew increasingly restless thinking about Siyaram's condition. 'The whole day went by and he had not eaten anything. He must be in his room. If once, she had asked Bhoongi to fetch the firewood, what harm would have occurred? What was the point in being so economical that family members went hungry?' He opened his box and searched in case he might come across some money. He removed all the papers, searched each compartment, put his hands into the bottom of the box – but he could not find any. If Nirmala's box did not give forth money, then this box definitely stood little chance of producing any money. Call it luck or coincidence – when he shook the papers, a 25-*paisa* coin dropped out. Munshiji was so overjoyed that he jumped up. He had earned huge incomes before this, but he experienced true exultation on finding this small coin. Holding that coin in his hand, he called out for Siyaram with immense excitement. There was no response. Then he stepped into the room. There was no sign of Siyaram. 'Hasn't he returned from school?' he thought. He went right inside and asked Bhoongi. He came to know that he had not returned from school.

Munshiji asked Bhoongi, "Has he drunk any water?"

Bhoongi did not answer, wrinkled up her nose, turned her face away and left.

Munshiji walked slowly towards his room and sat down. He was deeply angry with Nirmala for the first time. However, in the very next moment, he felt wounded by the effect of his own anger. As he lay down on the floor in the dark room, he felt depressed about his son's condition and started cursing himself. He was also quite tired from the work of the entire day. In a little while, he fell asleep.

Bhoongi came by and called out, "*Babuji*, the meal is ready."

Munshiji woke up, started, and sat up. A lamp dimly lit the dark room. He asked, "What time is it, Bhoongi? I fell asleep."

Bhoongi said, "The clock at the police station has struck nine. Apart from that, I do not know."

"Has Siya Babu returned?"

"Had he returned, he would be at home and nowhere else."

Munshiji said, furiously, "I am simply asking you, is he here or not? And you are giving me all kinds of replies! Is he here or not?"

"I have not seen him. How can I lie to you?"

Munshiji once again lay down on the floor. "Let him come back. I will eat with him."

He lay for half an hour, fixing his eyes on the main door and waited. After that, he got up and went out. He walked for two furlongs towards his right. He returned and asked at the entrance, "Has Siya Babu returned?"

A voice was heard from inside: "Not yet."

Then Munshiji took the path towards his left and went up till the street corner. Siyaram was nowhere to be seen. Munshiji returned home and standing at the main door asked again, "Has Siya Babu come back?"

"Not as yet," came the answer from inside.

The police station clock struck ten.

Munshiji walked swiftly towards the Company Bagh. He thought, 'It's quite possible that Siya came here and went off to sleep, lying on the grass.' Munshiji searched each and every bench, every corner of the park; many people lay on the grass, but there was no sign of Siyaram. He called out 'Siyaram,' loudly but no voice answered back. It then struck Munshiji that there might be a school function The school was a little more than a mile away. He started walking towards the school, but returned midway. The markets were closed. He realised it was not possible for the school to hold a function this late. Even now, Munshiji was hopeful that Siyaram would have returned. He returned to the main door and asked again, "Has Siya Babu come back?" The doors were closed. Nobody answered. He called out louder this time.

Bhoongi opened the door and said, "He hasn't come back as yet."

Slowly Munshiji called Bhoongi closer and asked her tenderly, "You know everything that happens in this household. Tell me, what happened today?"

"*Babuji*, I wouldn't lie to you. The mistress will ask me to leave, what more? But this is no way to rear somebody else's son. Whenever any work arises, he is sent to the market. His whole day is spent running around in the market. He didn't fetch firewood today, so the stove wasn't lit. If anyone said anything about it, then she would sulk. When you are unable to look after him, who else would? Please come and eat your meal now. *Bahuji* has been waiting for a while."

"Tell her that I don't want to eat now."

Munshiji left for his room and took a deep breath. He was filled with compassion for his son. A prayer escaped his lips, "Oh Almighty! Isn't my punishment over yet? Do you wish to snatch the only support from this blind man?"

Nirmala came to the room and said, "Today, Siyaram hasn't returned as yet. I kept telling him I would cook, and that he should eat. But I don't know when he got up and left. God only knows where all he is wandering. He just does not listen. For how long should I wait for him? You can eat your meal. I will keep his food covered in the kitchen."

Munshiji glanced sternly at Nirmala and said, "What is the time right now?"

"Who knows? It should be ten."

"Not at all! It's midnight now."

"It's struck twelve? He has never been this late. For how long should one wait for him? He hasn't eaten since afternoon. I have never seen such a vagabond."

"He really troubles you, doesn't he?" said Munshiji.

"Just see, it's so late in the night and he doesn't care about coming home."

"Perhaps, it's his last mischief," said Munshiji.

"What are you saying? Where will he go? He must be lying at some friend's place."

"Maybe that's how it is. I hope to God it is like that."

"When he returns in the morning, do give him a dressingdown," said Nirmala.

"Yes, I will do so properly."

"Now, you should eat. It's very late."

"I will eat only after I have reprimanded him in the morning. If he doesn't turn up, where will you find such a faithful servant?"

Nirmala stiffened and said, "Do you think I chased him away?"

"No, who is saying that? Why would you be chasing him away? He used to work for you. Some ill must have befallen him."

Nirmala did not say anymore. She feared the matter would flare up. She went inside without saying that she was going to sleep. In a while, Bhoongi latched the inner door from inside. Could Munshiji fall asleep? Only one of his three boys had survived. If he, too, left – there would be nothing but darkness in Munshiji's life. Nobody would be left to take his name. Yes, the precious things that had slipped away from his life. Was it surprising that Munshiji's eyes were streaming with tears? In his unending repentance laden with regret and darkness, Siyaram was the sole glimmer of hope that could steady him. The moment this ray of hope disappeared, who knew what would happen to Munshiji? Nobody could ever visualise the depth and extent of his turmoil.

Many times, Munshiji's eyes closed, but believing he was hearing Siyaram's footsteps, he would start and sit up.

As soon as it was morning, Munshiji left to look for Siyaram. He was ashamed to ask anyone; how could he? He did not hope for any sympathy from others. Without saying it openly, everyone would think, 'Reap as you sow!' He roamed the whole day in the school compound, markets, orchards and parks. Only he knew how he summoned the energy when he had not eaten anything for two days.

At twelve at night, Munshiji returned home. A lantern was lit near the main door, and Nirmala stood there waiting for him. The minute she saw him, she said, "You never said anything and just left. Did you find out anything?"

Munshiji's eyes were burning with anger. "Get out of my way or something bad will happen. I am not in control of myself right now. It is all your doing. It is because of you that I am in this awful condition today. Was the condition of this house like this six years ago? You've devastated my well-established home. You've uprooted my lush garden. Only one stump remains. You will be satisfied only when you have wiped out its impression completely. I hadn't brought you to my home to destroy it, but to make our contented lives even happier. This is my repentance for just that. The boys who were treated carefully and gently, like tender leaves, you took them to be your servants, that too even when I'm alive. And I could see all of it and yet, I turned a blind eye to it! Go. Send some poison for me. That's it. That is all that remains to be done, so complete that, too."

Nirmala wept and said, "Of course, I know I am unfortunate or will I only know it when you tell me so? God knows why I was born into this world? But why do you believe that Siyaram won't return?"

As Munshiji walked towards his room, he said, "Don't make me angrier, go and celebrate your happiness. Your innermost desire has been fulfilled."

* * *

24

Nirmala wept the whole night. Such terrible accusations! She never had the courage to raise her voice even when she saw Jiyaram take her jewels with him. Why so? It was simply because she knew people would think that she was fulfilling her enmity by falsely implicating the young boy. Today, she was blamed even when she had remained silent then. Had she stopped Jiyaram, and overcome by shame, he would have run away, and then would the charge not have been firmly laid on him?

She wondered in what way she had mistreated Siyaram. In order to save some money, she would send Siyaram to the market to buy things. Was she saving cash for herself to buy expensive jewels with? With the ever declining income, she had no other way to save money, except by keeping a strict eye on every *paisa* spent. Nobody knows how unpredictable life can be; a youth's life could be unreliable, for the elderly, life could leave them without a place of their own. Knowing this, who could she have begged from for her daughter's marriage? She was not the only one responsible for her daughter. She was saving in order to ease her husband's difficulties. Why only her husband? Siyaram would be the head of the house after his father. Wouldn't the responsibility of his sister's marriage have fallen on him, too? Nirmala was cutting her cloth as small and fine as she could just so that it would help her husband and their son later. They would face great difficulty and a girl's marriage under such conditions was nothing less than grave distress. Even for such consideration, there was still only disgrace written in her fate.

It was afternoon, but even today, the kitchen stove was not lighted. Eating is also an important task in life, but nobody seemed to be conscious of it. Munshiji lay outside, still and almost lifeless; Nirmala was inside. The little girl wandered in the house, going in and out. There was no one to talk to her. Again and again, she would stand at the door of Siyaram's room and call out to him, "*Bhaiya.*" No one would answer.

In the evening, Munshiji came to Nirmala and asked for some money.

She said, "What will you do?"

Munshiji said, "Just respond to what I ask you."

She said, "You do not know? You're the one who brings money home."

"Do you have some money or not? If you do, give me some, otherwise give me a clear answer," said Munshiji.

Nirmala still did not answer him clearly. "If it's there, it will be in the house, nowhere else. I haven't sent it anywhere."

Munshiji went outside. He knew that Nirmala had some money; in fact, she really did have some. She did not say that she did not have money or that she would not give any, but it was clear from her speech that she did not intend to part with it.

At nine in the night, Munshiji went to Rukmini and said, "Sister, I am going out for a while. Ask Bhoongi to pack my bedding and put some clothes in the trunk and lock it."

Rukmini was cooking at that moment. She said, "*Bahu* must be in her room. Why don't you tell her? Where are you intending to go?"

"I am asking you. If I had to ask her, why would I ask you? Why are you cooking today?"

"Who else will cook? *Bahu* has a headache today. But tell me, where are you going at this hour? Why don't you go in the morning?"

"Three days have passed in just dilly-dallying. I will search all around, maybe I will find out something about Siyaram. Some people have been telling me that he was last seen talking to a saint. Maybe he misled him and lured him away."

"So, by when will you return?" enquired Rukmini.

"I can't say. It might take me a week or a month. Who can say with certainty?"

"What day is it today? Have you asked the priest whether you can go on a journey?"

Munshiji sat down for his meal. At this moment, Nirmala felt great compassion for him and her anger dissolved. She became calm again. She did not ask herself, but waking up her daughter and kissing her, she said, "Look, where is your *Babuji* going? Ask him!"

The little girl peeped from the door and asked in her characteristic baby-talk, "Where are you going, *Babuji*?"

"I am going very far, my daughter. I am going to search your brother."

Still standing at the door, she said, "I will also come with you."

"I have to travel far, child, I will bring gifts for you. Why don't you come here?"

The little girl smiled and hid behind the door. Then she poked her head through the door out for a second and said, "I will also come along."

In similar baby-talk, Munshiji said, "I won't take you along."

"Why won't you take me along?"

"You don't come near me at all," said Munshiji.

The girl minced towards her father and sat in his lap. Munshiji, for some time at least, forgot all his pain as he played with the little girl.

After his meal, Munshiji went out. Nirmala stood and watched. She wanted to say, 'Your going is useless,' but she could not say it. She mulled over giving him some money, but could not bring herself to do so.

In the end, she could not remain silent and said to Rukmini, "*Didiji*, will you please talk to him. Where is he going? He would not like me asking him, but I cannot stay silent. Without any address, where will he look for him? He will be troubled uselessly."

Rukmini looked at Nirmala compassionately and tenderly and left for her room.

Nirmala sat with her little girl in her lap, thinking, 'He might want to see his little girl or come to meet me before leaving.' However, Nirmala's wishes remained unfulfilled. Munshiji picked up his bedroll and sat in the *tonga*.

At this moment, Nirmala's heart wrenched as she instinctively felt that she would never meet him again. She became restless and reached the main door in order to stop him, but the *tonga* had gone by then.

* * *

25

Days kept passing by. A full month had passed but Munshiji did not return. He did not send any letter also. Nirmala was constantly preoccupied by the anxiety that if he did not return, what would happen? She was not worried about what Munshiji may have been going through, where all he would be wandering aimlessly or how his health was. She was only concerned about herself, and even more so, about her little daughter. How would the household be run? How would the Almighty reach her to the other shore? What would happen to the little girl? She had cut costs and saved some money, but everyday, it was dwindling. Every time she had to spend a *paisa* from this money, it would rankle as though somebody was extracting blood from her. Irritated, she would often rail against Munshiji. If the daughter cried for something, she would call her 'ill-fated' and get annoyed. Not just this, she felt that Rukmini's presence in the house was like a weight around her neck. When the heart aches and burns, even the language become fiery. Nirmala was a soft-spoken woman, but now she could be counted in the league of the loud and the sharp-tongued. Her speech would remain angry and unpleasantly sharp. Who knows what had happened to the gentleness in her speech? There was no trace of any sweetness in her emotions now. Bhoongi had been a servant in this house for a long time. She was patient and tolerant by nature, but even she could not bear the constant rudeness. One day, she, too, left the house. It came to the point that the little girl, who Nirmala loved more than her own life, too, became a victim of her angst. She was filled with hate when she now looked at the child. She would scold her furiously at every little thing, and sometimes, she would even hit her. Rukmini would make the weeping child sit on her lap and try to soothe her with caresses and kisses. This was the only shelter and solace for this poor orphan!

If there was anything that Nirmala liked now, it was her conversations with Sudha. She would seek opportunities for visiting her. She did not want to take her daughter with her now. Earlier, the daughter used to laugh and play at Sudha's place as she used to get enough food at home. Now wherever she was at Sudha's place, she would feel hungry. The little girl would keep saying she was hungry, despite Nirmala's efforts to silence her with glares and rounded fists. Sitting near Sudha, Nirmala felt that she, too, was a human being. As long as she was there, she would be free of her troubles, just as an alcoholic forgets about his troubles when intoxicated. If anyone who had seen her at home would see her at Sudha's place, they would fail to recognise her. The sharp and loud, rude and harsh Nirmala was soft and gentle with laughter, entertaining and sweetness itself. Her youthful persona, finding the road blocked in her own home, frolicked at Sudha's place. When she came here, she would be well dressed with her hair done up and for the moment, would confine her sad tale to her own mind. She would come here not to cry but to laugh.

However, this happiness was also not in Nirmala's destiny. Usually, Nirmala would visit Sudha's place either in the afternoon or evening. One day, she was so bored that she reached her place in the morning itself. Sudha had gone to the nearby pond to take her bath. Her husband, Doctor Sahib was getting dressed to go to hospital. The maid was busy with her work. Nirmala entered her friend's room and sat there in a relaxed mood. She thought Sudha was busy doing some household work and would join her soon. After sitting for two-three minutes, she took out an album from the almirah and seated herself leisurely on the bed. She untied her hair and lay on the bed and glanced through the album. In the midst of this, Doctor Sahib entered his wife's room to find his spectacles. Unhesitatingly he entered the room. Nirmala was facing the door, as she lay with her hair open on the bed. As soon as she saw Doctor Sahib, she was startled and frantically covered her head, got off the bed and stood up. Doctor Sahib, while going back, paused for a moment by the door *chik* and said, "I am sorry, Nirmala. Forgive me. I was not aware that you were here. I came here to search for my spectacles. I don't know where I have taken them off and left them. I thought they may be here."

Nirmala glanced around the bed and saw the spectacle case in a niche just behind it. She picked up the case, with bent head and straightened body, hesitantly stretched her hand out towards Doctor Sahib. Her mannerisms displayed her reserved persona. Doctor Sahib had seen Nirmala on a couple of previous occasions, but the emotions he felt at this moment had never entered his mind before. The fiery tempest locked in his heart for so many years burst into flames at the gust of this tiny breeze. He stretched out his hands to take the spectacle case and his hands trembled. He did not go out; he kept standing there, lost somewhere. Nirmala became fearful of the long, lonely pause and asked, "Has Sudha gone somewhere?"

Doctor Sahib, with his eyes cast downwards, replied, "Yes, she's gone to bathe."

He still did not go out. He just stood there. Nirmala asked again, "When will she be back?"

"She should be arriving," replied Doctor Sahib, still looking down.

Still, he did not go outside. There was profound conflict raging in his mind. It was not the binds of etiquette that held him back. It was a thin thread of fear, of cowardice, that kept his tongue in check. Then Nirmala said, "She must have started strolling around. I should go now."

The weak thread of fear also broke. Just as, a fleeing army is highly charged with unusual energy on seeing the riverbank, Doctor Sahib, too, mustered some courage. He lifted his eyes, looked at Nirmala and in a voice steeped with love, said, "No, Nirmala, she might be arriving soon. Don't leave now. For Sudha, you sit here everyday, today, stay for my sake. Tell me Nirmala, how long should I burn in this desire? I am speaking the truth, Nirmala… "

Nirmala did not hear anything more. She felt the earth spinning madly. Her life and breath were assailed by the attack of thousands of weapons. She wrenched a sheet from the clothesline and without saying a word, she left the room. Doctor Sahib was slightly irritated and his face looked weepy, but he just stood there. He did not have the courage to stop her or say anymore to her.

The moment Nirmala reached the main door, she saw Sudha getting off the *tonga*. When Sudha saw her, she got out of the *tonga* and went quickly towards her, intending to ask her something. Nirmala did not give her a chance and turned, keen as an arrow, and went away. Sudha stood for a while, astounded at what had happened. She could not understand what the matter was. She entered the house quickly to ask the maid what had happened. Sudha decided to find who the culprit was, and if the maid or any other servant had said anything objectionable, then she would dismiss him at once. She rushed towards her room. As she stepped in, she saw her husband sitting sullenly on the bed. She asked, "Did Nirmala come here?"

Doctor Sahib scratching his head said, "Yes, she had come here."

"Did the maid or any other servant say anything to her? She didn't even speak to me, just turned and left."

Doctor Sahib turned pale. He said, "I don't think anyone said anything to her here."

Sudha said, "No one said anything at all? Look, I am asking. God knows if I find out, I will dismiss the person at once."

Doctor Sahib was flustered and said, "I didn't hear anyone say anything to her. She must have missed seeing you at the main door."

Sudha said, "Really! She must not have seen me! I got off the *tonga* right in front of her. She did look towards me, but said nothing. Did she come to this room?"

The Doctor Sahib was getting quite fearful as if his life were deserting him. He hesitated a little and said, "Why wouldn't she have come?"

Sudha said, "Seeing you sitting here, she must have left. That's it. Some maid must have said something. They are of a low class. They don't know how to talk politely. Listen, Sundariya, come to my room, immediately!"

"Why are you calling the maid? She went straight to the door from here," said Doctor Sahib.

Sudha said, "Then you must have said something to her."

Doctor Sahib's heart started pounding. He said, "What would I have said? Am I such a village dolt?"

Sudha said, "You saw her coming, even then you kept sitting?"

"I wasn't in this room at all. I kept searching for my spectacles in the drawing room. When I didn't find them there, I thought they might be in this room. When I got here, I saw her sitting here. I wanted to leave the room, but she asked me if I needed something. I asked her to look around to see if my spectacles were anywhere. She saw my spectacles near the niche behind the bedstead. She handed them over to me. That's all the conversation we had."

"So, as soon as she gave you the spectacles, she left the room in panic? Why?" asked Sudha.

"She didn't leave in a panic. As she was about to leave, I told her to wait as you would be back anytime. If she didn't sit, what could I do?"

Sudha thought over something and said, "I can't understand it at all. I will go and ask her. Let's see what the matter was."

"So, go but is there a great hurry? The whole day lies ahead," said Doctor Sahib. Covering herself with her shawl, Sudha said, "I am in such great turmoil, and you say, why the hurry?"

Sudha strode towards Nirmala's house and reached within five minutes. She looked to find Nirmala lying on her cot, weeping, while her daughter stood beside her and said, "*Amma*, why are you crying?" Sudha seated the little girl in her lap and spoke to Nirmala, "Sister, tell me the truth, what is the matter? Did anyone say anything to you at my place? I have asked everyone but no one told me anything."

Wiping het tears, Nirmala said, "No one said anything, Sister, besides who would say anything to me there?"

Sudha said, "Then why didn't you speak to me and started crying the moment you reached home?"

"I am crying over my destiny, what else?" said Nirmala.

"If you won't tell me straight, then I will make you swear on me," said Sudha.

Nirmala said, "No swearing is required. No one said anything, why should I blame anyone falsely?"

Sudha said, "Swear on me!"

"You are being stubborn needlessly," said Nirmala.

"If you tell me, Nirmala, then I will believe that there was no real affection between us. It was only about verbal exchanges. I do not hide anything from you and you are considering me as a stranger. I had great faith in you. Now, I realise that no can be trusted to be really faithful to anyone at all times."

Sudha's eyes filled with tears. She put the little girl down and walked towards the door. Nirmala got up and held her hand. She wept as she said, "Sudha! I implore you. Don't ask me. You will hear something that will hurt you, and perhaps, then I won't be able to face you ever again. Had I not been destined to be so unfortunate, then would I have seen such days? Now my only prayer to God is that he takes me away from this world. God only knows what will happen in the future!"

A wise Sudha understood the message cloaked in these words. She understood that Doctor Sahib had somehow misbehaved with Nirmala. She was reminded of his faltering tone, avoidance of and hesitating in answering her questions, his guilt-ridden eyes and pale face. She shuddered from head to toe and without saying a thing, walked out of the house, like a tigress filled with rage. Nirmala tried to hold her back, but in vain. As she watched, Sudha walked out onto the street and then towards her home. Nirmala sat down on the ground and cried uncontrollably.

* * *

26

Nirmala kept lying on her cot the entire day. It appeared that there was no life in her body. She did not bathe; she did not get up to eat her food. In the evening, she caught a high fever that continued burning her body the whole night. The fever did not come down the next day, although it was slightly less than before. She kept lying on her cot, looking with innocent, clear eyes towards the main door There was complete emptiness all around, emptiness inside her and outside. There was no worry, no sorrow, and no memories; there was no energy and nothing stirred in her mind.

Suddenly, Rukmini came to her, holding the little girl in her arms. Nirmala asked, "Is she crying a lot?"

"She didn't even whimper. She lay quietly the whole night. Sudha sent some milk for her. She drank that."

"Didn't the lady deliver milk today?"

"She said she won't give milk unless she receives her earlier payments. How are you feeling now?" asked Rukmini.

"Nothing's wrong with me. Yesterday, I just had slight fever."

"Doctor Sahib is in a bad state," said Rukmini.

Nirmala asked worriedly, "What happened? I hope all's well."

"He is well enough that his corpse is to be lifted to be taken away. Some say he consumed poison, some say his heart stopped beating. God only knows what happened."

Nirmala took a slow, deep breath and in a choked voice, said, "Oh God! What will happen to Sudha? How will she live?"

Saying this, she burst out weeping and sobbed for a long time. Then, with great difficulty, she got up and prepared herself to visit Sudha. Her feet were trembling badly; she steadied herself against the wall, but her conscience was unwilling to stay back. 'God only knows what Sudha said to her husband after returning from here? I didn't even utter a thing. I wonder what she construed from my silences. What a sad end to a handsome, kind and cultured man!' Had Nirmala known the terrible repercussions of her anger, she would have gulped down the unpalatable and laughed it off.

Nirmala's heart was shattered when she thought that Doctor Sahib ended his life because of her callous attitude. She experienced such pain; it felt that spikes were twisting in her heart. She then left for Sudha's place.

The corpse had been taken away. There was absolute silence outside. Ladies had gathered in the house. Sudha sat on the floor, wailing. When she saw Nirmala, her cries grew into a shriek, then she hugged her and clung to her. They both cried for a long time.

When the crowd of ladies had dispersed and there was peace and quiet again, Nirmala asked Sudha, "Sister, what happened? What did you say to your husband?"

Sudha had answered this question so many times in her own head. The answer that had becalmed her was the same answer that she gave Nirmala. She said, "I couldn't have also remained quiet over this issue, Nirmala. Anger does arise over issues that cause anger."

"But I never said anything of the kind to you," said Nirmala.

"How would you have told me? You couldn't have said anything at all. But, he told me what had happened. At that point, I couldn't control myself. I said whatever came to my lips. When a sentiment or action enters the mind; consider that it has actually happened. When opportunity and deceit meet, then it is always fulfilled. By saying that it was all a jest, one cannot escape what one did. When such words are uttered in a solitary place, then it indicates bad intentions. I never said anything to you, Sister, but on many occasions, I had caught him staring at you. Then, I thought that perhaps I was imagining things. Now I know what was behind his peeping and peering. Had I been more worldly-wise, I would have never let you come home. At the very least, I would have prevented him from seeing you. Now I know what a man speaks and what a man thinks are two different things. What was destined by God happened. I don't consider being a widow any lower than being a married woman. A poor man is happier than that rich man whose wealth turns into a serpent ready to bite him.

It's easy to sleep on an empty-stomach, but eating poisonous food is far more difficult."

At that moment, Doctor Sinha's younger brother and Krishna entered. Chaos erupted in the house.

* * *

27

Another month passed by. Sudha left with her brother-in-law after the third day itself. Now Nirmala was left alone again. Earlier, she would laugh and smile and console herself. Now, all that was left to do was to cry. Her health, too, deteriorated everyday. As the rent was higher for the old house, she rented another that was cheaper. The house stood in a very narrow lane, where there was no sunshine, no fresh air. It was a small room with a tiny courtyard. The air smelt bad the whole day. Food was irregular because of the existent but lean financial conditions. Sometimes, fasting was resorted to – who would go to the market; there was no man in the house – no husband, no son; what was the need for women to eat everyday? If they ate once, then they could go without it for the next two days. However, fresh roti and *halwa* were made for the little girl. In these conditions, why would health not deteriorate? It was not just her worries, remorse, adverse situations, if there was one reason, then, one might have said something admonitory. This was a terrible assault on her mental, physical and spiritual selves. Moreover, Nirmala had vowed not to take any medication. What else could she do? Where was the scope for buying medicines from the paltry savings? Day-by-day, she turned frailer and weaker.

One day, Rukmini approached Nirmala, "*Bahu*, for how long will you weaken yourself like this? If there is will, then there is life and all is well. Come, I will take you to a doctor."

Nirmala said in a disinterested tone, "Whoever has to live to keep crying; it is better that such a person should die."

"Death won't come because you called him."

"Death comes uninvited; then why shouldn't he come if I called? It will take him a long time to arrive, Sister. The days I am living are passing heavily, like years, for me."

"Don't be disheartened, *Bahu*. What have you seen of the pleasant worldly comforts till now?"

"If this is the comfort of this life, then for all the days I have seen till now, I am replete and done with it. I speak the truth, Sister, I am bound by affection for this little girl, otherwise . . . God only knows what is written in this poor girl's destiny!"

Both women started crying. Ever since Nirmala has been ill and confined mainly to her bed, the slumbering compassion in Rukmini's heart had awakened. There was no trace of a grudge anymore. While working, if she heard Nirmala's voice, she would run to her. She would sit with her for hours, relating stories and the *Purans*. She would want to cook a meal that Nirmala would eat with interest. She would be deeply satisfied if she saw Nirmala smiling. She had the little girl in her arms most of the time, like a necklace worn with love. She slept when she slept, and woke when she awoke. The little girl had become the hope of her life, the basis on which her life stood.

After some time, Rukmini said, "*Bahu*, why do you lose hope? You'll regain your health very soon. If God wishes, you will be well very soon. Come along with me to the local doctor today. He is a good person."

"*Didiji*, I don't think any *vaid*'s or *hakim*'s medication will do me any good. Please don't worry about me. I will leave my little girl in your care. If she grows up, marry her into a good family. I could not do anything for her in this lifetime, except take the blame for bringing her into this world. Keep her unmarried or give her poison – whatever you do, but do not marry her to an unworthy man; this is all I implore you to do. I did not serve you in any way, and it will always make me sad. I was so unfortunate that I could not make anyone happy. Whoever my shadow fell upon, that person was destroyed. If *Swamiji* comes back home, please tell him this ill-fated woman asked his forgiveness for her crimes."

Rukmini, with tears in her eyes, said, "*Bahu*, you are not to blame for anything. I say this before God; I hold that there is no ill in your heart where I was concerned. Yes, but I always was deceitful towards you. I will regret this till my dying day."

Nirmala looked at Rukmini with desperation in her eyes and said, "This is not a matter that should be spoken of, but I cannot let it rest until I tell you. *Swamiji* has always looked at me with mistrust, but I have never, in my mind, neglected him in anyway. What was destined has already happened. Would I do something wrong and spoil my next life? I don't know what sins I committed in my past life, for which this was my repentance. In this life, if I planted thorns, then what would the condition be in my next?"

Saying so, Nirmala became breathless and lay down on her cot. She glanced at her daughter in a way that profoundly and eloquently reflected the entire sad tale of her life. Speech could not have been more effective.

Nirmala wept for three days. She would not speak to anyone, look at anyone or listen to anyone. She just kept weeping. Who could have guessed the extent of her agony?

On the fourth day, as evening approached, the long tale of suffering ended. At the time when all the animals and birds were returning to their homes, Nirmala's last birdlike life-breath escaped from the aim of hunters, the claws of predatory birds and the cruel beating by sharp winds and went to its abode.

People from the neighbourhood gathered. The corpse was brought outside. As people wondered about who would perform the last rites, an aged traveller arrived. He stood there, with a suitcase in his hand. It was Munshi Totaram.

* * *

Shatranj ke Khiladi

1

It was the time of Wajid Ali Shah's reign. The entire Lucknow city was preoccupied in enjoying every shade of pleasure: the upper class, the lower class, the rich and the poor. Some added their august presence to dance and song gatherings, while others derived pleasure from smoking opium. Happiness and pleasure emanating from comforting, sensual satisfaction were uppermost in every aspect of life. Pleasure thoroughly and constantly pervaded all of administration and governance, literature, the social set up, arts and the skills, business and occupations, food and drinks, and the general behaviour of all. Employees of the state pursued their selfish interests; poets were lost in detailing compositions of love and grief; artisans were captivated by their work of making *kalabattu* and embroidering *chikan;* perfumers were busy in distilling *itr* and making *surma*, toothpaste and facepacks. Only keen, intoxicating pleasure could be seen in everyone's eyes.

Apart from this, no one was conscious of what was happening in the world around them. Quail fights were in full swing, while the grounds were being prepared for the round of partridge fights that would follow. At some places, the fourfold *chausar* boards were laid out with the dice tumbling; many shouts of 'double six' could be heard. Elsewhere, serious battles of chess were taking place. From the ruler to the ruled–all were caught in the frenzy this popular fashion generated. It went to the extent that if the fakirs got some money, they would eat opium or drink liquor, rather than spend it on rotis.

Games of chess, playing cards, *ganjifa;* these sharpened the mind, enhanced the ability to think, and thus, solving knotty issues became a habit. These arguments were put forth strongly in their favour (the world is still not bereft of this category of people). That is why, if Mirza Sajjad Ali and Mir Roshan Ali spent most of their time honing their intelligence, then how could any intelligent person take any objection to it? In any case, what else would they do? They both had inherited estates and thus, did not worry about their livelihood or income. They just sat and indulged in pleasant gossip. Every morning, both the friends would partake of breakfast, spread out the chessboard, place their chessman and sit down to play. From then on, they remained blissfully unaware of time–when it was early afternoon, when it became late afternoon or when evening came by. Repeated calls of: "The food is ready!" would issue from the house. Their response: "We are coming. Lay out the tablecloth," would waft back, but no one went inside to eat. After quite a while had passed, the helpless cook would ultimately bring the food to the drawing room. Then, both friends would eat and play chess simultaneously.

There was no elderly person in Mirza Sajjad Ali's house, so all these games of chess were played in his drawing room in great comfort. However, the members of his family were neither happy with his behaviour nor with what was going on in their house. Besides what the family thought, even the neighbours and the servants of the house found great faults and passed comments such as these:

"It is an ill-fated game."

"It will ruin the household."

"God help that no one gets addicted to this game; that man is lost to God and the world, and is of no use whatsoever, neither belonging to his home or the outside world."

"It is a bad disease!"

Mirza's wife, the Begum, hated the game so intensely that she would look for opportunities to give her husband a tongue-lashing. She found such opportunities rarely and with great difficulty. While she was still asleep in the morning, the games would commence. Mirza would enter the inner rooms at night after she had gone to sleep. She could not say anything to him directly. So, she lashed out at the servants: "Does he ask for paan? Tell him to get it himself. He doesn't have the time to eat? Take the food and put it on his head! He can eat it or feed it to the dogs!"

However, she was not as greatly annoyed with her husband as she was with Mir Sahib. She had given him another name, 'Mir – the

Spoiler'. Perhaps, Mirza emphasised his innocence by ascribing all the blame squarely to Mir Sahib.

One day, Begum Sahiba's head started aching. She said to the maid, "Go and call Mirza Sahib here. He should get me medicine from a *hakim*. Run, be quick!"

When the maid delivered her message, Mirza said, "I will be there soon."

The maid relayed the message to Begum Sahiba, who was in a bad mood. How could she have been patient at all when she had a headache and her husband kept on playing chess? The Begum's face grew hot in anger and she told the maid, "Go and tell him that he must come now. Or else, she will go by herself to the *hakim*."

Mirza was in the midst of an interesting move; in another two moves, Mir Sahib would be defeated. Upon hearing his wife's message, he snapped in irritation, "Is she breathing her last? Can't she be a little patient?"

Mir Sahib said, "Wait, you may just as well go and listen to what she says. Women do possess delicate temperaments."

Mirza said knowingly, "O yes, why shouldn't I go now? In two moves, you are about to lose this game."

Mir Sahib said, "Oh you must not fool yourself with your victory! I have thought of such a move that your chessmen will stay put and you will be defeated. But, please go, why are you needlessly causing her grief?"

Mirza quipped, "I will only go after defeating you."

Mir Sahib said, "I will not play at all. Please go and hear her out."

Mirza said tiredly, "Oh, my friend, I will have to go to the *hakim*. It is not a headache. It is merely an excuse to trouble me."

Mir Sahib said, "Whatever it is, for her sake, it will have to be done."

Mirza, trying his luck, said, "All right, let's play one more move each."

Mir Sahib was determined, "No, not at all! Until you have heard what she says, I will not touch the pieces."

A helpless Mirza Sahib reluctantly went inside. When she saw him, Begum Sahiba softened her expression, but cried out as though in pain, "This good-for-nothing chess is so dear to you? If someone dies, you won't even think of getting up! God willing, no one should be like you!"

Mirza replied, "What could I do? Mir Sahib wouldn't agree to stop the game. I managed to extricate myself only with the greatest difficulty."

Begum said, "Does he think that everyone else also has time to waste just as he has? He has a family and children or has he put them all out of the way once and for all?"

Mirza said, "Mir Sahib is greatly addicted to chess. Whenever he comes I am forced to play with him."

Begum said, "Why don't you rebuke him?"

Mirza said, "We are of the same age but he is two rungs above me in status. I have to respect that."

Begum Sahiba said, "Then I will rebuke him. If he gets angry, let him. It does not concern me for, he is not responsible for our house! Hariya, go outside and pick up the chess pieces. Inform Mir Sahib that Mirzaji will not play now. He may be kind enough to take his leave."

Mirza said, "Ah, yes, go ahead and do something so untowardly! Do you wish to insult him? Wait, Hariya, where are you going?"

Begum Sahiba was annoyed. "Why don't you let him go? You will stop him only when he causes my end? All right, in that case, let us see whom do you stop, me or him?"

Saying this, Begum Sahiba angrily swept out of the room towards the drawing room. The helpless Mirza paled. He started entreating his wife, "For God's sake, I swear upon the holy Hussein. If you go there, it will be the death of me."

Begum did not listen to him and marched on till the door of the drawing room. Suddenly, she slowed down as though her feet hesitated, being tethered. She was abashed to approach another man directly, one who was not that well-known to her. She peeped inside; by pure coincidence the room was empty. Mir Sahib had moved a piece or two here and there and to establish his innocence, was strolling about outside. This was ample opportunity; there was no stopping her–Begum stepped into the room, upturned the chessboard, and flung some chessmen under the divan and some, outside. She shut the door and fastened the bolt. Mir Sahib was near the door; he saw the chessmen come flying out and understood that Begum Sahiba was in a foul temper. Quietly he took the path leading home.

Mirza said, "You have done the unthinkable."

Begum Sahiba said, "Now if Mir Sahib comes here, I will tell him to leave before he can even enter the house. If he spent his time lighting tapers before God, he would be a saint by now. You play chess and here, I will worry over domestic concerns! Are you going to *hakim* Sahib now or is there something else you need to do?"

Mirza left home, but instead of going to the *hakim*'s house, he went to Mir Sahib's house and narrated the entire tale. Mir Sahib said, "When I saw the pieces flying out of the door, I realised the state of events and ran immediately. She seems to be hot-tempered. But the way you have let her have the upper hand is not suitable at all. Why should she be bothered with what you do outside? She is responsible only for all household arrangements, so why do other matters concern her?"

Mirza said, "Anyway, tell me where will we sit to play now?"

Mir Sahib said, "There is no need to be downcast. We still have this huge house. We will sit and play here."

Mirza said, "But how will I make Begum Sahiba agree? When I used to play at home, she would be so angry. Now, if I sit here, then perhaps, she will just kill me."

Mir Sahib said, "Oh, let her say whatever she wants. When no heed is paid, she will be fine in a few days. Yes, but you must do this much–be a little strict from today."

* * *

2

For some unknown reason, Mir Sahib's wife thought it eminently suitable that Mir Sahib stayed away from the house. This was why she never criticised his chess playing; in fact, she would remind him of it if he ever got late in leaving the house. For these reasons, Mir Sahib mistakenly believed that his wife was exceedingly gentle, good-tempered and gifted with a sombre nature. However, when the chess sittings were conducted in her drawing room, the chessboard spread out throughout the day and night and Mir Sahib started spending the entire day at home; she was greatly troubled. Her independence and movements were severely hampered. Now, she was confined to the inner house the entire day. She longed to go out but never got the opportunity to venture out even till the front door.

Even the servants unhappily whispered and grumbled amongst themselves. Till the time Mir Sahib was not at home, they would lie around idle the entire day, swatting flies. No matter who came to the house or who left–they had no reason to be concerned. Now, at all times, they were at the beck and call of Mir Sahib. Sometimes paan was ordered, sometimes sweets were sent for. The *hukka* remained lit throughout like the flaming heart of a lover. They would repeatedly complain to Begum Sahiba: "Mistress, Sahib's chess has tied us up like a chain. Our feet have got sores from running to and fro the entire day. What sort of a game is this? Sit down to it in the morning and keep playing till the evening! An hour or so of playing is good enough for entertainment. Anyway, we have no complaints. We are Master's slaves and will do as he orders but this game is ill-fated Whoever plays it never prospers. Instead, it definitely summons some trouble to the house The destruction it causes spreads and it has been seen that one after the other, entire neighbourhoods are ruined. This very discussion rages in the neighbourhood. We are loyal to our Master and feel sad to hear him being spoken of badly so often. But what can we do?"

To this, the Begum Sahiba said, "I dislike it, too. But he just does not listen to anyone, so what can be done?"

There were a few old-fashioned conservative folks in the neighbourhood. They imagined various unhappy scenarios: "There is no sense of wellbeing now. When our elite are in such a state, then only God can take care of the masses. Chess will cause the end of this kingship. Its effects are harmful."

There was total chaos in the state. There was great trouble afoot; the populace was being looted in broad daylight. There was no one to listen to their pleas or complaints. The wealth of the countryside was forcefully drawn into Lucknow. There, it was spent mindlessly and freely upon prostitutes, pimps and varying pleasures. The debt owed to the English Company was rising day by day. The veneer of kingly rule was thinning–it was a poor coverlet, getting more drenched; sodden and heavier by the day. The lack of properly organised tax collection ensured that tax was not collected. The Resident gave repeated warnings but everyone here was so intoxicated with pleasure-seeking that nothing whatsoever had any effect. If a flea tickled their ears, it would have not stirred them.

In any case, it was several months now that chess was being played regularly at Mir Sahib's house. New problems were solved; new defences were put up; new formations of chessmen were made all the time. While playing, sometimes, there were tiffs; situations occurred wherein accusations were also levelled; but both friends would quickly reestablish amity. A few times, it so happened that the game would be stopped; an annoyed Mirza would sulk and leave for home. Mir Sahib would go inside to sulk. Along with a night of sleep, all the ill feelings would disappear, bringing back peace. The next morning, both friends would reach the drawing room, once again.

One day, as both friends sat and wallowed in the delights of chess quagmires, an officer of the royal army rode up to the door, asking for Mir Sahib. Mir Sahib was very frightened. What awful trouble had befallen upon him now? Why had this summon come? He could see his wellbeing ending. He quickly shut the door and said to the servant, "Tell him, he is not at home."

When he was told this, the rider asked, "Not home? Then where is he?"

The servant replied, "I do not know. What work do you have with him?"

The rider said, "Why will I tell you? They are calling for men for the *hazr*. Maybe some soldiers are needed for the army. Is he an estate owner or is he just having fun? If he has to go on a march, then he will know what the reality is!"

The servant said, "All right, I will inform him."

The rider pressed his point, "This is not a matter for you to merely pass onto him. I will be back tomorrow. I have been ordered to bring him along with me."

The rider left. Mir Sahib was trembling with fear. He said to Mirza, "Now Sir, what will happen?"

Mirza said, "This is a terrible nuisance. I hope I don't get drafted."

Mir Sahib said, "He has gone away saying he will be back again tomorrow,"

Mirza said, "It's a problem, what else? If we have to go on a march, we will be as good as dead."

Mir Sahib said, "That's it, there is only one option left. We should not meet at home. From tomorrow, we will play in one of the ruins along the River Gomti. No one will know we are there. The gentleman will come here and have to return empty-handed."

Mirza said, "By God's grace, you have thought of an excellent plan! Apart from this, there is no alternative."

Meanwhile, a little away from her house, Mir Sahib's wife met the rider and said, "You were excellent! Your story will send him far-off."

He replied, "I can make such fools dance by snapping my fingers! Their intelligence and courage has been totally sapped by chess. Now he will not stay at home even by mistake."

* * *

3

From the next day onwards, both friends would wake up very early and slip away in the pre-morning darkness that hid their faces. A small folded rug would be tucked under an arm and a box would be filled with paan. Then, they would go to a ruined mosque by the banks of the Gomti that had perhaps been commissioned by Nawab Asafuddaulah. On the way, they would buy tobacco, *chilam* and wine and reach the mosque. They would spread the rug, fill the *hukka* and sit down to play chess. Then they would lose all consciousness of the world and forget everything else. Words like the 'next game' and 'checkmate' amongst a few others were heard; apart from this nothing else was spoken. No yogi could have concentrated so well in his meditation. In the afternoon, when they felt hungry, they would go to a naan seller's shop to eat. There, they would smoke a *chilam* of *hukka* and fling themselves back into the hurly burly of their battleground. Sometimes, they would not even remember food; so absorbing was their game.

Meanwhile, the condition of the state had become truly frightening. The Company forces were advancing towards Lucknow. There was uproar in the city. The citizens were taking their families and retreating to the countryside. The two chess players were not bothered in the least. Instead, they feared that some government servant might spot them if they took the main road; they would be caught in vain; so, they crept home by the narrow alleys. They wanted to enjoy their many thousand-fold worth estates, freely, all by themselves.

One day, both friends were sitting in the ruined mosque and playing chess. Mirza's game was a little weak. Mir Sahib was checking him, again and again. At this time, the Company soldiers could be seen riding along in the distance. This was a company of English soldiers, who were going to establish their full authority over Lucknow.

Mir Sahib said, "The English Army is coming. God preserve us."

Mirza said, "Let them come. Save this round. I have checked you on this round."

Mir Sahib said, "We should watch for a while. Let's stand behind the wall!"

Mirza said, "You can watch, but, what's the hurry? Play the round first!"

Mir Sahib said, "They also have cannons. There must be about five thousand men. What kind of men they are! They have faces like red monkeys! One gets scared just looking at their faces."

Mirza said, a little impatiently, "Sir, don't delay matters. You may try fooling someone else with these excuses. This round!"

Mir Sahib, "You are a strange man. Here, the entire city is in trouble and you are bothered about this round! Are you aware that if the city is surrounded, then it will be difficult for us to reach home?"

Mirza said, "When the time to go home draws near, we will see – how about this round? That's it, this time there is certain defeat in this check."

The Army went by. It was ten o'clock. The next game was set out.

Mirza said, "What will we do about food today?"

Mir Sahib said, "Oh ho, today is *roza*. Are you feeling very hungry?"

Mirza replied, "No, God only knows what is happening in the city!"

Mir Sahib said, "Nothing must be happening in the city. People must have eaten and will be sleeping peacefully now. The Nawab Sahib must be in his pleasure-palace."

The two men sat down to play; soon it was three o'clock. Now Mirza's play was weak. The gong struck, announcing it was four o'clock and the Company Army could be heard returning. Nawab Wajid Ali Shah had been caught and he was being taken to some secret place. There was neither a stir in the city nor any violence. Not a drop of blood had been shed. Till that day, no ruler of an independent state would have been defeated so peacefully, without any bloodshed. This was not the non-violence that the Gods are pleased with. This was pure cowardice, the kind that makes the biggest cowards weep. The ruler of the vast state of Avadh was being taken along as a prisoner and Lucknow was sleeping, locked in the grip of frenzied pleasure. This was the height of political degradation.

Mirza said, "The Lord Nawab Sahib has been captured by these devils."

Mir Sahib said, "Must be so. Here, take this! Check!"

Mirza said, "Sir, just wait a little. Right now, I don't feel inclined to play. The poor Nawab Sahib must be weeping bloody tears."

Mir Sahib retorted, "He should be. Where will he get this luxury? What about this play!"

Mirza said, "One's entire life is not spent in the same manner! What a dreadful situation this is!"

Mir Sahib said, "Yes, that is true. Here, again, I moved. In the next move, its checkmate, you cannot save yourself."

Mirza said, "I swear by God, you are most pitiless. Seeing such a horrible tragedy, doesn't it make you sad? Poor, penniless, Wajid Ali Shah!"

Mir said, "First, save your own king then mourn over the Nawab Sahib. This is my move and . . . this, checkmate! Surrender!"

The Company Army passed in front of them, taking the Nawab with them. After their departure, the chessmen were rearranged for the next game. The sting of defeat hurts badly. Mir Sahib said, "Come, let us say a *marsiya* to mourn for Nawab Sahib."

However, Mirza's patriotism had vanished with the game he had just lost. He was getting impatient to avenge his defeat.

* * *

4

It was evening. The bats were shrieking in the ruined mosque. The black birds were flying to their nests, coming home to roost. However, the two players were playing doggedly just like two bloodthirsty warriors fighting each other. Mirza had lost three consecutive games; the fourth game was also not going well for him. He would vow, again and again, to win and then would play in a controlled manner. However, some move would miss the mark and spoil the game. Losing repeatedly stoked his feeling of revenge. On the other hand, Mir Sahib was delighted and sang *ghazals*, cracked a few jokes, as if he had found hidden treasure. Mirza, listening to him, would get annoyed, but would applaud him in order to hide his own embarrassment. As his game grew weaker, his patience also started deserting him. Now, he began to react angrily at everything: "Sir, don't keep changing your move. What is this? You play one move and then change it. Whatever you wish to play, play with a single move."

"Why have you kept your hand on that piece? Move your hand away from that piece. Until you've thought of your next move, don't touch any of the pieces. You are taking half an hour to play one move. This is not done. Whoever takes longer than five minutes to play a move–let it be understood that he has lost. Again you've changed your move! Quietly keep that piece back."

Mir Sahib's *vazir* was endangered. He said, "When had I made a move?"

Mirza said, "You have finished playing your move. Keep that piece back right there–in that house!"

Mir Sahib said, "Why should I keep it in that house? When had I even kept it down?"

Mirza said "You think that if you won't keep that piece down till doomsday, then no moves will be played? You saw your *vazir* beaten and you started cheating."

Mir Sahib retorted, "You are the one who cheats. Winning and losing are determined by fate, not by cheating."

Mirza quickly replied, "Then you have lost this game."

Mir Sahib persisted, "Why would I be losing?"

Mirza said, "Then keep that piece back in the house in which it was before."

Mir Sahib said, "Why should I keep it there? I won't."

Mirza said, "Why won't you keep it back? You will have to."

The clash escalated, with both of them resolutely standing by what they said. Neither one would bend in the slightest. Mirza said, "Had someone in your family played chess, then the proper rules would be known. They were grass-cutters; so, what kind of chess will you know how to play? One does not become part of the elite class just by inheriting an estate."

Mir Sahib said, "What? Your father must have cut grass. Chess is well-known to us as my family has been playing for several generations."

Mirza scoffed, "Oh, go on! Your ancestor's entire lifetime was spent working as a cook for Ghaziuddin Haider! Today, you claim to be part of the elite. It is no matter of jest to be an elite."

Mir Sahib said, "Why are you insulting your ancestors? They must have worked as cooks. We have always eaten at the king's table."

Mirza said, "Oh, come on, you grass-cutter! Don't exaggerate."

Mir Sahib said, "Hold your tongue or it will turn out badly. I am not habituated to hearing such talk. If someone so much as glares at me, I take his eyes out. Do you have the courage?"

Mirza said, "You want to see my courage? Then come on. Today, we will fight it out. That will decide matters one way or the other."

Mir Sahib said, "Who is scared of you?"

Both friends drew their swords from their waist belts. It was the age of supreme nobility; everyone had a sword, dagger, knife and so on, on their person. They were attracted to pleasure, but they were not cowards. Their patriotic sentiments had dwindled shamefully–why should one die for the king or the kingdom? However, there was no lack of bravery in personal matters. Both were wounded and fell down, and there they died, suffering greatly and slowly. The same people who did not shed a tear for their king, died in the defence of a chess piece, the *vazir*.

It was getting darker. The chessboard was laid out. Both the kings sat in their thrones; it seemed that they wept at the death of these two heroes.

All round, there was silence. In the ruined mosque, the broken arch lintels, tumbled walls and the mud-coated, dusty minarets observed the corpses and lamented.

***